Strange Relations

Stefan Jakubowski

To
Paula + Barry
Best Wishes
Stefan

Published by Zygmunt Stanley

ISBN 1905170203

A CIP catalogue record for this book is available from the British
Library.

www.stefanjakubowski.co.uk

Printed and bound in the UK
by Clays, St Ives Plc

Cover Design by Patricia Moffet
www.illustration.gb.net

For my wife Nia

Special thanks to Pat Moffett
and Rachel Loosmore

When the Earth came into existence it was a lonely place, nothing but rocks and the odd bubbling puddle. It was also a sad place; too sad for the Immortals upstairs. So it was deemed that life should be placed on the lonely spinning lump of rock.

Life to brighten it: plants, flowers, trees. Life to enliven it: insects, birds, aquatics, and mammals. But still something was missing. A vital essence; an ingredient. The world of Earth was a beautiful serene place, but.

Then someone thought it would be a good idea to introduce an idea he'd been toying with for some time; Man.

Well, you know the rest.

Or do you?

What if it was deemed that this mortal Man creature should be born into the world with an Immortal twin? A guardian angel, if you like, whose purpose was to help Man learn the lessons of life. Lessons of life that when learnt would eventually lead Man into the Immortal afterlife, the Light, Upstairs, when his time on Earth was done. And what if it was thought that Man would learn these lessons quickly and easily?

Well we all make mistakes. The powers that be had been somewhat short-sighted with their assumptions and had decided to allow Man almost limitless chances / lives to learn. Following? Good. But the mistake was not the obvious one of thinking Man would learn – *oh no* – it was in giving Man those *almost* limitless chances / lives.

What if someone were to actually reach their last chance? What if that someone then failed? And what if the angel had ideas of his own? What then?

The truth – no-one knows. But it wouldn't happen, couldn't happen, could it?

CHAPTER 1

The meeting was called to order by a tall gaunt-featured creature dressed in military garb; Captain World War One to be precise. He glanced down at the gathering standing before him (a misbegotten bunch of failures and nobodies as you'd ever be likely to see in any lifetime and, sadly, all linked irrevocably to him), sighed at the sight, coughed politely, then addressed them.

'We are gathered here today,' he started.

'Hey!' shouted a voice.

It was a voice known only too well to the gaunt-faced man on the podium. And one more often than not he tried to ignore.

'What's wit' the preaching? Yer not a priest no more so how's about cutting the baloney?' The voice was thick Irish/American New York Cop late 19th century.

'Chaplain,' corrected the man on the podium, his eyes boring into the heckler. He'd hoped to have heard less of the man since the downgrade, alas it had not been so. 'I am no longer a Chaplain. And may I remind you that as you are no longer a member of the *Four* you only speak to the *Podium* when spoken to.'

'Yeah – sure vicar, or whatever it is you's wants to call yerself. But jest get on with it, time's nearly up and me bags packed so it is.' This was of course meant figuratively, as the dead tend to travel light.

'Don't you take any notice of him, Chaplain, you're doing fine,' said a voice from beside the Chaplain, a voice that had tried but failed to go the course with elocution lessons and so still clung to its soft southern Irish beginnings.

'Er-hum, thank you, er, Laura,' said the Chaplain a little uneasy at having a female so close at hand, and not an unattractive one at that. He smiled weakly then turned his attention back to the crowd. 'Now if I may continue?' But before the Chaplain could, another voice interrupted. 'Orag uk ooag!' it said – no hint of an accent this time though.

'What now?' whispered the Chaplain under his breath as he craned his neck to get a better look at the author of this latest interruption and infringement of the rules, and then sighed, 'Oh dear,' when he saw who it was.

The Chaplain had absorbed most of the languages spoken since arriving in the afterlife and joining with his own particular gathering of past lives, but the oldest prehistoric tongues still sadly eluded him. And this one belonged to the oldest of them all, *Australopithecus robustus,* as far as he had been able to ascertain when talking to the others about her. Everyone called her Roberta for short.

'What did she say?' said the Chaplain, turning to Laura for help. He asked as quietly as possible. It wasn't quite quiet enough though.

'She said, "Get on wit' it, yer old fart!"' The Irish-American's remarks were met with raucous laughter from the rowdier elements within the gathering.

'She didn't,' reassured Laura, the look of disgust on her face barely disguising her own amusement at the remark. 'She says the others haven't arrived yet.'

'Haven't they?' said the Chaplain with genuine surprise. 'But they must be…it's nearly time.'

Confirming Roberta's observation that indeed two of the Four were missing, a sudden uncontrollable feeling that something was terribly wrong washed over the Chaplain, this feeling, because of the link between them, spread out to, and bewildered the gathering which started a muttering.

The Chaplain was aghast; this wasn't supposed to be happening, but he knew he had to be strong. He turned to Laura who was staring at the empty chairs where the other

4

two should have materialised by now and wondered why she too hadn't noticed they were missing. 'Please stay calm,' he whispered to her, pulling himself together. He turned back to face the gathering.

'Stay calm! There must be a logical explanation that I'm sure will soon be revealed to us.' He gestured dramatically upwards above the gathering's heads. 'It will soon be time for the Light!' Did he sound convincing? He wondered.

But the statement seemed to pacify the gathering and, for the moment, peace returned as they contented themselves with watching the space the Chaplain had motioned to. How long the moment would last, though, was anyone's guess but the peace couldn't last forever. Questions would soon be asked. Ones that the Chaplain knew he wouldn't be able to answer.

'Well?' asked Joe, the Irish-American, with uncanny timing.

'All in good time,' said the Chaplain keeping his eyes skywards.

Then suddenly there *was* light.

'See?' said a relieved Chaplain, hardly believing it himself.

But it wasn't the Light everyone was expecting and it took a moment or two before they realised it was also in the wrong place. This light was emanating from behind and not above, and standing in its glow was an elf.

Stepping from it, the elf, who looked extremely agitated, began to speak.

'There's a problem,' he said ignoring the crowd and looking up at the podium.

This was the signal for pandemonium, as everyone started to shout and question at once.

'Ord-er! Order plea-se!' pleaded the Chaplain. 'There may be a problem but there is still time. There is always time.' Again, at the mention of time, there came over the gathering, even the raucous element, a sudden uncanny calm, and quiet again held sway. 'Thank you friends, now let us hear what Geoff has to say.' All eyes turned to the elf.

Geoff, actually human but dressed as an elf, pointy ears and all – long story – was the newest and penultimate member of the gathering and Podium of Four and thus the latest in the long line of life's failures, passed through the murmuring crowd and clambered onto the podium beside Laura and the Chaplain. He whispered something in the Chaplain's ear, for a moment the Chaplain looked paler and gaunter than anyone would have thought possible, but the Chaplain rallied his spirits and turned once more to address the gathering.

'Ah-hmm,' he said, a feeling of discomfort forming beneath his collar, 'it would seem, dear friends, that the, er, Podium of Four is needed elsewhere for the moment due to, er, unforeseen circumstances. Which,' finger under the collar, 'I'm afraid, will cause a short delay in seeing the Light.' He then very quickly added, to head off any further outbreaks of pandemonium that might ensue, 'but the good news is there will still be time.'

With that swift but uninformative statement leaving half the gathering in a state of bewilderment, the other half in confusion, the Chaplain, Laura, and Geoff dematerialised from the podium, in what could only be described as a rather dull and disillusioned flash of light.

CHAPTER 2

Richard, Randy to his close friends, which was down to his best mate Tom "The Bastard" Hardy's perverse sense of humour, stared out through foggy and bloodshot eyes at the cold playing fields that beckoned. Then, with a deeply resigned breath, reluctantly left the relative warmth of the changing rooms and stepped onto the still slightly crisp frosty grass. He shivered as the cold air played about his bare knees, introducing itself to his body.

What the hell was he doing? he thought as he walked. If he had any sense he'd still be tucked up in bed nursing his hangover. But no, instead, here he was back again and doing his usual, now almost ritual, cursing about the effects of too much drink, the New Year, – God was it 2041 already? He'd be thirty-nine years old in March, – life in general and of course ruddy football played on a freezing cold New Year's Day morning.

As Richard approached the twenty or so figures that were waiting for him – twenty or so figures that, to Richard's mind, judged on their bulging stomachs, were nearly all in line for at least a mild cardiac arrest even before the game started – he looked at his watch. They wouldn't be pleased; he was nearly ten minutes late. He was right.

'Hoo-bloody-rah! look who's decided to turn up.' Yelled a disgruntled voice from amongst a score of grumbles as Richard reached the pitch on which he was to officiate.

The tentative smile on Richard's face at the greeting looked more like a grimace.

'Hope yer eyesight's better than yer timekeeping, Ref!' snarled another voice.

As Richard apologised for his tardiness he marvelled at how quickly his eyesight had been brought into question. It had to be an all time record; they hadn't even started the game yet. A hand shot out to greet him, not a friendly one though.

'John,' announced the owner of the hand gruffly. 'Valley Garage Nomads manager. I'll be lining for yer.'

Another hand shot out, just as friendly.

'Phil, Roach Garage Athletic, I'm their sub. I'll be doing the other side, until I'm needed on the pitch that is.'

Shaking the outstretched hand, Richard, making sure he didn't stare too hard at the mass of gut hanging out from under the sub's taut shirt, found himself wondering if calling themselves Athletic wasn't blatantly contravening a trades description act somewhere. Richard thanked them both and walked to the centre spot. Really he should have checked the nets, posts etc, for anything that could be deemed dangerous. But having given both teams the quick once over, Richard had decided that he'd already seen the most dangerous elements on the pitch.

'Come on, Ref, get a move on. I'm freezing me blooming knackers off here,' advised a young lad who had obviously not yet fully immersed himself in the rigours of heavy beer drinking and was thus still blubber-less and feeling the cold more than the others.

Richard put the whistle to his lips to blow for the start of the game but just as the air from his lips tickled the pea into action, a low lying nag of a thought, planted when he'd been greeted but held temporarily in check by more pressing matters, managed to find daylight. Richard felt himself, if that was at all possible, grow colder. The match was a bloody *local derby*, why hadn't anyone warned him? But of course Richard already knew the answer to that: he wouldn't have done it, that's why.

8

A little stunned and distracted by this minor revelation, Richard watched half-heartedly as a good impression of Tweedledum and Tweedledee rapidly ran out of steam chasing the first loose ball of the game off the pitch.

'Whose ball ref?' asked one of the Athletic players, seeing the ball going out of play as a good excuse to take one last drag on his cigarette before putting it out.

'Nomads!' said Richard with unsure certainty.

Off the pitch Tweedledee muttered something about Richard's parentage and threw the ball to the ground.

Damn, thought Richard who, going by the gestures of the "Assistant Ref" on that side, realised he'd probably made the wrong decision. Still, he was the referee and what he said went but, and this Richard felt was for his own safety, he felt he'd better forget his misgivings about being lumbered with this game for the moment and concentrate on the here and now. He could have it out later with the powers that be, but to do that he had to finish the match in one piece.

The throw was taken and Richard followed the play up the field towards the Athletics goal. As he ran, jogged rather slowly actually – there was no need for speed in this game – he tried to comfort himself with the thought that in ninety minutes his suffering would be over and he would be far away. But then of course he was forgetting half time, at least another ten minutes. Still, he had to keep positive, like a visit to the dentist, it would end.

But the thought did little to help his mood and as Richard glanced dispiritedly at the creatures surrounding him, watched as the Athletic player finished his cigarette and casually flicked it at the back of a passing Nomads player, he realised in that moment that there was also another very real obstacle in the way of him leaving on time; an obstacle as certain as the Pope being Catholic: *Injury time.*

As with a trip to the dentist there was always the chance of pain, and this was no idle check-up. Richard suddenly felt his heart sink into his boots.

*   *   *

Since taking up refereeing Richard had found that half the people on the pitch didn't know or care that there were rules while the other half thought that they knew them better than him. This usually went for some of the spectators too. Bearing this in mind, Richard was wondering into which category the fat number seven, who was squaring up to him with all the menace of an overweight Pitbull at the moment, would fall.

'What the hell was that Ref? He tried to kill me and you played on,' growled the player, who'd arrived in Richard's face with surprising ease, considering his alleged near death experience.

'I played advantage,' said Richard hoping to appease.

'What bloody advantage did I 'ave wiv me arse arse-ole deep in cold mud?' snapped fat number seven, spittle spattering from the corner of his mouth.

Richard, trying hard not to visualise the scene described, knew from bitter experience that the conversation with the fat number seven was now set to go down one of three possible avenues.

No 1: The player admits that he has made a mistake, apologises, shakes hands and goes happily on his merry way. This though, as myths and fantasies go, is up there with Nessie, the Goose that laid the Golden Egg and waking up to find it's all just a bad dream.

No 2: The player walks away cursing you, whilst also telling the world of your stupidity and incredible visual impairment. This was the usual, gratefully received, outcome, bearing in mind the rarity of No 1.

10

No 3: Quick head butt followed by dizziness and grass stains on back of kit. Now this option did occur and sometimes, on a rare occasion, the referee had been known to get in there first. All in all though pretty painful and messy, and the option Richard would rather pass on.

After what seemed a very long moment of tense and precarious balance between numbers two and three Richard was relieved to find option two finally coming out on top.

'What do you know anyway, yer four-eyed wanker?' gesticulated fat number seven, turning away.

Resisting the urge to book the player – why leave the proverbial frying pan etc? – Richard glanced at his watch. A minute to go until half-time and amazingly no injury time so far. Unless of course he counted the Nomad goalkeeper's puking fit just after kick off. A sudden idea materialised. Dare he, he thought, blow up early? What the hell if he did? If anyone queried his decision he could always bluff, besides he was desperate, to get off, and have a shot of the hair of the dog he had concealed in his shorts' back pocket. Richard made a decision, put the whistle to his lips, and blew.

To his relief no one questioned the early ending and so, like a naughty child who'd just achieved a rather underhand piece of mischief, he slunk away from the steaming bodies leaving the pitch and went to knock back a couple of stiff ones.

Thanks to the whisky, Richard had blown to start the second half in much better spirits. And at the moment it was still going well. Nil-nil, ten minutes to go, and an icicle's chance in hell of anyone scoring.

This half had gone much the same as the first, mainly a gaggle of unfit men milling around the centre circle and throw-ins that were mostly fouls. And foul, Richard had thought, was true in both senses of the word as each time

11

anyone raised an arm a penchant towards gluttony was revealed. Richard had vowed after the third such display that when the match ended he would investigate a healthier lifestyle for himself. He'd had a gutful of protruding bellies.

Six – five – four minutes to go. Richard's thoughts had now wandered to the long soak he was going to have when he got home. Sod the shower in the draughty shed laughingly called the changing rooms; it was to be boots off, trainers on, then straight to the car and home.

Three – two.

Richard could almost feel the hot water soaking away his woes.

One.

Then it happened, the unexpected, the last thing Richard wanted. The skinny lad, the one that had started the game complaining about his freezing knackers and had spent most of the game chatting with his girlfriend while jogging on one spot, suddenly had a domestic. Angrily turning his back on her he found the ball, which had bobbled away from yet another pointless midfield melee, at his feet.

Richard saw the look in the skinny lad's eyes as he regarded the alien object lying on the ground between his size tens. Damn, thought Richard, he's going to do something stupid. How right Richard was. The lad suddenly took off like the proverbial bat out of hell. Worse still he took the ball with him.

That was all Richard needed, some idiot scoring a goal in the last minute of the game. It had all looked so wonderful a minute ago, now it could all easily end in the arguments that a last minute goal in local derbies always caused. Richard hared after the lad who, it was now obvious, was the Athletic in the team name.

As the lad approached the eighteen metre box the thought of blowing early again came into Richard's mind. If he did it would save everyone, and him in particular, a lot of bother.

12

But he couldn't, he'd already done it once, his conscience wouldn't let him.

Thirty seconds left.

'Offside, Ref!' screamed the Nomad's manager, as he ran the line waving his flag like a manic whirling dervish.

If only, thought Richard, but the lad had started in his own half.

'Time, Ref!' shouted another voice from the small crowd of frozen supporters.

Twenty seconds to go. The skinny lad was bearing down on the Nomad's goalkeeper and was showing no signs of stopping, he was on a mission.

'Blow, Ref!'

Richard thought about it and put the whistle to his lips. He couldn't, could he? But it was a thought too late.

'OOH!' chorused voices from around the pitch.

Stopping in his tracks with only eighteen seconds left on his watch, Richard felt his boot languishing heart succeed in sinking through the bottom of them. The pukey Nomad's keeper, seeing the danger he was in, had done what keepers in his position wouldn't normally do – rugby tackled the skinny lad as he'd tried to skip round him. The pitch was suddenly in uproar.

'Penalty, Ref!' demanded someone.

'Send the wanker off!' advised another.

Horror of bloody horrors! Richard was stricken, his and all referees' worst nightmare had just happened.

'Nae way, Ref, time was up. Yer had yon tin whistle in yer mouth,' remonstrated the Nomad goalkeeper, in a broad Scottish accent, 'I saw yer do it that's why I stopped yon kiddie wink.'

Richard eyeballed the red-headed built-like-a-brick-shithouse Nomad's goalkeeper and weakly blew the whistle.

'Well, Ref, what is it?' asked one of the mob that had swiftly surrounded Richard.

'He's gone all white, the wanker.' It was noted.

It was something Richard was all too aware of, mainly because he knew what he was about to do. He reached into his top pocket and pulled out his red card. Rag to a bull some said later.

'You's 'ave got tae be blumin' kidding me,' said a female voice beside Richard as the card barely saw daylight. 'Me son does nae deserve that yer basturt!'

Doing his best to ignore the jeers and insults whilst hanging on desperately to his breakfast Richard attempted to push past the baying crowd to deliver the card and point to the penalty spot. But the Nomad keeper's mother hadn't quite finished with him.

'Up in Scotland the refs would nae have given it. Yer a stiff English twat, that's what yer are,' she mumbled angrily before turning to her younger son. 'Ere, give that tae yer ma Johnny.'

As Richard continued his attempted push through the crowd of baying players and supporters he was in no position to take in any one single threat. If he had he may well have ducked in time. But he hadn't and he didn't. A well-aimed cricket bat, a Christmas present for wee Johnny, wielded by the Nomad keeper's fiery mother with all the strength she could muster, hit Richard squarely on the back of his head.

Richard landed face down in the cold mud.

CHAPTER 3

Emergency minutes changed to tense waiting hours, which in turn slowly grew into worrying days. During this time Richard lay in intensive care, totally oblivious to the stream of visitors that came and went. But when the days gave way to weeks, the first excuses started to appear.

Relatives and friends with their own worries quietly made their guilty excuses to Richard's seemingly deaf ears; one by one making good their escapes. If *anything* should happen, *any* improvement was forthcoming, the hospital would contact them, they reassuringly whispered. It was all so sad, but they did have their own lives to lead. Until, as a month elapsed, Richard's last visitor came to make his excuses.

As Tom sat beside Richard's bed and looked at the quiet motionless body of his friend wired to various machines he became overcome with sadness and guilt, the latter an emotion he knew he need not feel; his excuse was truthful. He also knew that if Richard had been conscious he would have happily understood and told him not to be so stupid. It still didn't stop him from feeling guilty though.

They'd worked together for years, Richard a joiner, Tom an outside fixer, for a local joinery company. And before Richard's little "accident" the talk had been of looming redundancies. Now Tom had come to tell Richard that their worst fears had been realised and the company had gone into liquidation. Worse still was that the whole affair had been messy with little money, apart from what the government gave as redundancy, paid to the employees, and even that would be coming later rather than sooner. Tom came to the point. He'd been offered a contract in Dubai. It was short notice but unlike Richard he had a family to support.

As Tom got to his feet he wiped a small tear from his cheek and promised he'd try and visit around Christmas time, wherever he was, whatever Richard's condition. Tom wished his friend all the best and good luck and then, fighting back further tears, walked leaden-footed from the room.

It had been a sad farewell and as Tom stood waiting for the lift to arrive he was glad no one had seen his tears. The lift doors opened and Tom stepped in.

But Tom couldn't have been more wrong. The parting *had* been watched, and watched intently by silent observers who, even before Tom had turned to leave, had themselves already hurriedly left.

CHAPTER 4

Soon the Four met; three sat while the fourth paced back and forth like an expectant father of sextuplets who had just been informed that six had been a somewhat conservative estimate and that a representative from the Guinness Book of Records was on his way.

'What is it man? What *is* the problem?' asked the Chaplain, no longer able to contain his anxiety; even though *time* was on their side.

The fourth of the Four, a man called Sammy who'd started life with a silver spoon in his mouth and had hit heights as a renowned dancer cum singer, only to end his time on Earth in the gutter, stopped his toing and froing. Rubbing a grubby hand, which protruded from a frayed and tatty cuff, against a deeply furrowed brow the little tramp proceeded to tell what was worrying him so.

'It…it's worse than we thought,' he stammered.

'Worse than what?' asked Laura as Sammy the tramp started toing and froing again. 'We haven't been told the original problem yet.'

The tramp stopped and looked at Geoff who shifted nervously.

In life Geoff had always presumed himself to be the life and soul of the party. "Never even seen the inside of a kitchen at one," he told people. The truth was slightly gilded though: Geoff had never been to a party. He had tended to exist, in life, in his own little world where he could be what he wanted to be, when he wanted to, and not be bothered with the reality of things. Most of all though he had wanted to be a hero, but bad things worried him. Geoff had and still did run from bad things if he could.

It took a moment or two before Geoff got up his courage to explain. 'He hasn't done it,' he said at last. It was bad news: the worst.

'What!' exclaimed the Chaplain, plainly appalled at what he heard. He got to his feet swaying unsteadily. Laura went to his aid but the Chaplain waved her attentions away. 'Why, in all that's holy, not?' he demanded.

'H...he's had an accident,' explained Geoff who by now was feeling somehow responsible, even though he wasn't.

'When?'

'About a month ago. Their time.'

'That's terrible,' said Laura giving her attention back to the little tramp, 'but what could be worse than that?'

'Oh-oh,' exclaimed Sammy frantically ringing his hands. For a dead man he didn't look at all well.

'What?' said Laura slowly fearing the worst, even though she couldn't think, or didn't want to think, what *that* might be.

The little tramp rolled his eyes and flopped into a nearby chair. This was bad, there had always been a silver lining to everything for Sammy, although it had been a major downfall for him in life, but even he couldn't see one this time.

Geoff got to Sammy first and carefully tapped the little tramp's dirt stained face. 'I...I think he's fainted,' he said.

'Slap harder,' said the Chaplain.

A couple of slaps later Sammy was back in the land of the dead and looking like it.

'What do you know Sammy? Speak man!' demanded the Chaplain again. He was close to losing it and started to shake Sammy violently by the shoulders.

'Stop it! You're hurting him,' yelled Laura. It was a stupid thing to say of course, them all being dead, but that wasn't the point. Shoving the Chaplain aside she knelt before the shaken Sammy, her face level with his. 'What is it Sammy?' she asked gently, 'Tell me.'

Holding her in his gaze, a semblance of sanity poured back into Sammy's eyes as Laura spoke. 'He's dying,' he whispered.

'What did he say?' said the Chaplain, not sure if he'd heard correctly or whether to believe his ears if he had.

'He said he's dying,' Laura related, her voice now also in a whisper as if to protect herself from what she was saying. Laura's face, always the brightest and most cheerful of all the gathering, was now as drawn and as gaunt as the Chaplain's on a bad day.

'But he can't be he…he's our last chance. He can't!' As Geoff spoke his shoulders took on a life of their own. Soon his body was racked with huge tearless sobs.

'There must be something we can do. Isn't there?' said Laura looking to the Chaplain as she did her best to console Geoff. 'There's time, isn't there?'

But the Chaplain wasn't listening. He had slumped into a chair, his face blank and motionless. The lines that were usually etched across his face had disappeared leaving a glassy staring death mask.

'Tell me there is,' implored Laura as she left Geoff to stand helplessly before the Chaplain. Fear began to seep. There was no response, not the slightest of twitches; she began to shake him as he'd shaken Sammy.

'Speak to me. Tell me this isn't the end. Tell me – TELL ME!' Laura's voice rose to near breaking point as the manikin Chaplain stared straight ahead, ignoring her.

'It might not be.'

Spinning on her heels at the sudden intrusion of an alien voice, Laura was surprised and a little puzzled to find a face she recognised. It was Joe the Irish-American cop.

'Joe? What are you doing here?' she said calming down a little. She wiped a non-existent tear from her cheek (habits die harder than people). 'How did you get here?'

'You could say that I got in with a skeleton key,' answered Joe jokingly, his voice bringing a warmth with it that would have put the most nervous at instant ease.

'But your voice it's…'

'Different,' finished Joe.

'Yes.' Laura heard herself agree but wasn't sure if it was what she'd meant to say.

'Don't worry; I'm just borrowing Joe's form for a while.'

And strangely, even though the answer was cryptic, Laura found she wasn't worrying in the least. In fact she was feeling the best she'd felt in ages. Since she'd been alive in fact.

'What's happening to me?'

'You are within my aura, that's all,' replied Joe smiling at her. His smile was as warm and as calming as his voice.

'Who *are* you?'

Joe put a finger to his lips. 'No more questions, I've been sent to talk to you. To tell you, you must not worry, that there *is* still time. That there is always a chance.'

'But how? – he's dying!'

'Another question,' said Joe, his face ever so slightly darkening.

For a moment, a fleeting moment, Laura felt, inexplicably, afraid. But the feeling quickly vanished when Joe's smile returned.

'Sorry,' he said softly, 'I was teasing.'

Laura reddened, something she hadn't been able to do since the day she died.

'Now,' continued Joe in his soft way, 'down to business. As I was saying, there is still time. This isn't seen as yours or the mortals' fault. It was someone else's.' Joe's eyes flicked upwards as he spoke. 'Who shall not be named.' Joe smiled again, this time because of the bewildered look on Laura's face. 'Don't worry, even the best of us make mistakes.'

'Bu…' Laura quickly pulled herself up before another question passed her lips.

'No,' said Joe holding up an apologetic hand. 'Don't worry, I was rambling. You have a right to ask questions I suppose. But I'll only answer one, your question on how.' Joe paused, a serious look on his face. 'One of the Four has to go back with the mortal; he's no longer strong enough to go back alone. And it will be the Four's choice as to who goes.'

'But I...,' Laura started to protest.

'No more questions. I must go now.'

'But Joe...'

'What is it me darling?' asked an Irish-American voice.

Laura stepped back in surprise. Joe was plain old Joe again.

'And how the hell did I get here? I'm supposing it wasn't the doing of the little people.'

'You've got to go,' said Laura completely confused by what was happening.

'But I've only just arrived, haven't I? It'd be rude of me jest to leave like that, without a word of chatter to you or yonder sleeping beauties. Now wouldn't it be?'

Pushing Joe with all her might towards the door she hadn't noticed before, Laura gave a quick glance over her shoulder to see what he meant.

'Now come on girl, this is ol' Joe yer throwing out. Should yer be doing such a thing to an old friend?'

'Out!' said Laura, with one last heave that saw Joe disappear out through the door. It swung shut behind him and suddenly everything was very quiet. She had the feeling without knowing why, as she stood there amidst the quietness, that she needn't worry about him coming back anytime soon.

She now turned her attention to the sleeping beauties, as Joe had put it. The Chaplain was still sitting, his face rigid in his death mask. Laura tapped him lightly on a shoulder.

'What?' The Chaplain looked about him, bewildered. 'Laura? What's been going on? Have I been asleep?' The notion of sleep was an alien one, roughly one hundred and twenty-four years after he'd last succumbed to that particular pleasure.

'No…well I don't think so,' admitted Laura, who at this moment wasn't too sure of anything. 'We had a visitor.'

'What?' said the Chaplain, still slightly at sixes and sevens. 'Who?'

'Joe.'

'Joe? That blaggard, he knows he's no longer a Four. What did he want?' The Chaplain was slowly getting his wits together again.

'But it wasn't him.'

'What was that?' The Chaplain gave Laura a sharp look. 'Start making sense girl. What do you mean it wasn't him?'

'I'm sorry, it sounds silly, doesn't it? I mean it was Joe but it wasn't.' Laura was beginning to wonder herself now, it did sound silly, but she persevered. 'He had an aura.'

'An aura?' repeated the Chaplain, the look on his face changing from anger to one of apprehending awe.

'Yes,' said Laura, puzzled by the sudden change in the Chaplain.

'You know what this means, don't you?' said the Chaplain, rising from his chair.

Laura's face was blank. She had no idea what the Chaplain meant. Yet somewhere deep inside she had an intuition that, somehow, she did know.

'It means we were visited by someone from Upstairs!' The Chaplain's face, now excited, was split by an enormous smile. But as the enormity of his statement slowly sank in and his exuberance started to wane. 'Was he happy or angry?' he suddenly asked; his angst beginning to surface. The Chaplain scanned Laura's face for an answer. 'And more to the point, what did he want?'

Because of the Chaplain's behaviour Laura, started to worry again. Had she *really* spoken to someone from *Upstairs*? If so, why her? The Chaplain was the religious one. She felt as if the whole thing might overwhelm her, but as she roused Sammy and Geoff, from what did indeed seem to be a deep sleep, the feeling started to subside a little. And once they were wide awake Laura felt calm enough to tell them all what had taken place whilst they had slept.

'Wow!' said Geoff, thoroughly excited by the thought that someone had visited them from Upstairs. 'We must be important.'

'Only as the biggest failures of all time,' said the Chaplain grimly.

'We're not finished yet,' said Sammy, sensing that there might yet be a sniff of a silver lining in their situation, based on what Laura had told them. 'Who's going with him then?'

'I think you'll find that Laura meant that one of us should show him the way – a guide, so to speak.' As the eldest of the Four, the Chaplain felt he had better explain.

'No,' said Laura, trying her hardest not to undermine the authority the Chaplain thought he had, 'I believe Joe meant for one of us to actually go over to the other side.'

'Impossible!' blurted the Chaplain.

'Why?' said Geoff, 'thirty-nine years ago I'd have said it impossible for me to be sitting in a room talking to three ghosts. Let alone be one.'

'That was improbable, not impossible,' argued the Chaplain. 'What I mean is that it's impossible for a ghost to occupy a mortal's dead body, even if they do share the same soul.'

'But Richard isn't dead,' Laura pointed out as gently as possible.

The Chaplain fell quiet; it was all going way past his understanding.

23

CHAPTER 5

It was gone midnight when Richard received his unexpected visitors. A little disorientated by their arrival – they weren't expecting the sudden change in their surroundings – the Four gathered at the foot of Richard's bed.

'How did we get here?' said Geoff, staring wide-eyed around him.

'I think we've been here all the time,' answered Laura, recognising the room's door as the one she had only moments earlier pushed Joe out of. 'But don't ask me how.'

The others weren't about to, there was no point. Since their respective deaths their existence had been one long foggy road in which there were answers, but never to the questions that were asked. They doubted things were going to change now.

'What now?' asked Sammy looking down at the unconscious Richard. 'He don't look too good.'

'I think I know.' All eyes and ears turned to Laura. 'I think we have to wake him.'

'But won't that be dangerous? He could have a heart attack or something, waking up and seeing us peering down at him,' cautioned the Chaplain.

'He's dying anyway so I don't think that matters,' said Laura who then realized, from the look on Geoff's and Sammy's faces, just how callous she'd sounded. 'I didn't mean…sorry. I didn't mean it to sound like it came out.'

'It's all right, I think we all know what you meant,' the Chaplain reassured, conjuring up a smile despite his worry.

'But I also think you may be putting the cart before the horse, so to speak.'

'What do you mean?'

'I mean, shouldn't we decide who's going with him first and then wake him up? He's going to be confused enough as it is without having to sit through us debating about his future.'

The Chaplain was right of course; they had to make a decision.

'And I still say it should be me,' said Sammy as the discussion tumbled into its second hour. 'I was a dancer you know.'

'And what's that got to do with the price of beef?' pointed out Geoff, whose line of thinking was that, as he had been the last of the Four to cast off his mortal coil, it should be him that went; it was obvious. He'd be more in touch with the living world than the others.

'Beef? Dancing? What on earth are you two going on about?' spluttered the Chaplain who, of course, had other ideas. 'From what I can see and hear, it is patently obvious that *I* am the person most befitting to take on the task. You all seem to be forgetting why he has to go back, and the reason we are having to have this debate. Without that being achieved none of us will be seeing the Light. No, I think the situation calls for a man of my standing.'

'And what about me, you pompous ass?' said Laura, suddenly erupting. She had decided that enough was enough where the men were concerned. Since the so-called discussion had started she'd hardly been listened to, the men happy to view her as nothing more than peripheral to the argument.

'Typical men, the lot of yer.' Laura's elocution steadily falling by the wayside the angrier she became.

'But you're just a slip of a girl,' started the Chaplain, woefully putting a size ten in where any angel with an ounce of sense would fear to tread.

26

'Oh am I now?' stormed Laura; elocution lessons now history as fighting talk beckoned. 'And jest what the hell has that got to do wit' anything may I ask? Why if I wasn't a lady I'd…I'd…' Laura, arm raised menacingly, fought for self control. Her tough upbringing struggling with the way she had fought so hard to make herself. Eventually the latter efforts of her life managed to hold sway and Laura slowly lowered her arm.

'Sorry,' she said, her voice quiet but stressed. 'I don't know what came over me.'

'No,' said the Chaplain softly, 'it is I who should be apologising. I had no right to speak as I did. I'm sorry.'

Sammy and Geoff exchanged worried glances.

'Maybe we should draw straws?' suggested Geoff, attempting to pour oil on troubled waters.

'If we had some,' said Laura quietly.

All four became quiet. It was becoming obvious that it was turning out to be the same old story that possibly none of them was fit to go. The Chaplain had hinted at the reason Richard had to return to the land of the living, but hadn't actually said what it was. He didn't have to, they all knew full well what was needed. They knew why they were all still where they were, and bickering. It was down to sacrifice. Sacrifice without thinking about it – about the consequences of such an action. It was something that each of the Four and those before them had failed to achieve. The final Lesson to be learned before they could travel to the Light. And now it was down to Richard; the last of their line.

'I think it's time to wake him,' decided a sullen Laura, breaking the subdued silence that hung heavily in the air.

As Laura reached across to the unconscious Richard, the Chaplain gently put a restraining hand on her arm.

'We still haven't made a decision,' he reminded her.

'Do you think we're capable?' said Laura, looking the Chaplain in the eye. 'I think our fate lies with the living.'

The Chaplain removed his hand. Laura was right. Richard would have to make the choice.

'Is he coming round yet?' asked a very nervous but excited Geoff.

'I'm not sure.' Laura gently shook Richard again.

This time there was a slight murmur as Laura exerted a little more pressure.

'He's coming round, I heard him. Let me try.'

'Calm down, Geoff.'

'What's it like to feel again, Laura?'

'What?'

'You know – something warm.' The excitement building in Geoff was close to spilling over as he pressed against Laura in his eagerness to know, almost pushing her over.

Laura had reached across and touched Richard to wake him, without thinking. It had been the natural thing to do, if they'd all been alive that is. As such when realization of what she had done had sunk in; that she had touched a living person, a sort of euphoria had swept over them all.

'Calm down, Geoff!' It was almost an order, but Laura relented. 'Here, if you must, but be gentle.' Laura moved aside to let Geoff get close enough to touch Richard.

Gingerly, Geoff reached out a hand and touched Richard's face. It felt wonderful. Wonderful to Geoff to feel life again. His mind began to swim, to remember his own short life.

Not quite eighteen when he'd died, his memories were sadly few, but in the moment he'd touched Richard's warm flesh there were warm summer days, clubbing nights, and hot babes. It had to be him that went back, it just *had* to be. Then, as suddenly as they'd arrived, the memories were but memories themselves and Geoff was experiencing something else from his time on Earth: pain.

'Ow…Ow! Let go, yer hurting me. Ow!'

'When you tell me why an elf I don't know…what am I saying? What the hell do you think you're doing? And *who* the hell are you?'

There was a moment of mass panic around Richard's bed as his awakening turned out to be not quite what the Four had been expecting. Heart attack – maybe, serene meeting of minds – hopefully, but violence? Violence had been furthest from their minds.

'Well?' demanded Richard.

'Ow,' cried Geoff as Richard exerted more pressure on his thin wrist. 'Laura!'

'Laura – who's Laura?' demanded Richard, who, up until that moment, had been ignorant of the other's presence. This was partly due to the face-full of elf he was getting and partly to the lack of colour everyone had. Richard reinforced his demand by twisting harder but, to Geoff's relief, relented a little when a soft female voice spoke.

'I'm Laura,' said Laura, stepping forward. 'Please let go of my friend.'

Richard reluctantly relaxed his grip enough for Geoff to wriggle free, then scowled at Laura.

'We're sorry…' she started, but Richard was having none of it.

'Yeah – right. Sorry for what, I want to know and what the hell are you doing in my bedroom?' Richard then caught sight of the Chaplain and Sammy the tramp. 'And who the hell are they?'

'Please let me explain,' offered Laura as the situation threatened to spiral out of control. But again Richard wouldn't listen.

'Get out of my room and my house before I call the police and you have to tell your stories to them. And take the fancy dress party with you. Go on, get out!' Richard pointed to what would have been the door of his bedroom if he'd been in it. It was at this point that Richard had an inkling that things were maybe much worse than he'd first thought. 'Where's my bloody door gone?' he shouted. Panic boded – hysterics were surely not far behind.

'Please let me explain,' implored Laura grabbing Richard's arm as he started to get out of bed. He was beginning to notice the full extent of his surroundings. 'Listen to me. Things have happened, changed.'

Shaking himself free from Laura's grip and the confines of the bed, Richard advanced on the Chaplain who stood transfixed at the foot of the bed. 'What's going on?' he yelled into the Chaplain's face when he reached him.

'We are gathered here,' mumbled the Chaplain rather pathetically.

'*What?*'

'Don't mind him, he means well,' pleaded Laura catching up with Richard. She was frightened of what might happen next as she sensed the fear, bewilderment and anger building up within him.

But it was Laura that Richard wasn't taking a mind to. He grabbed the Chaplain by a lapel and raised his fist. 'I won't ask again,' threatened Richard.

Then, in what really was a flash, Joe was suddenly standing between Richard and the hapless Chaplain. 'What say we get back into bed, eh Richard?' suggested Joe gently, touching Richard on the face as he spoke.

Laura winced as he did it, expecting the worst. But to her and everyone else's surprise, Richard released the Chaplain and, smiling dumbly, clambered back into bed.

'Is he okay?' asked Laura, relieved but dumbfounded by Richard's reaction.

'I'm fine I believe. Just a little shaken,' replied the Chaplain, straightening his uniform.

'Not you, I meant Richard.'

'Oh!'

'He's fine as well,' reassured Joe.

'Are you from Upstairs?'

Joe turned to Geoff, raised a finger to his lips and smiled. 'Please gather round,' he said gesturing to the Four to come closer, 'I believe you may be in need of my help.'

'Thank you, your Worship,' said the Chaplain humbly, now recovered from his close call at the hands of Richard.

'You can call me Joe,' smiled Joe.

'You are from Upstairs aren't you?'

'Now Geoff, that's enough questions. Let Joe get on with what he wants to say.'

'Thank you Laura,' said Joe in a way that brought colour back to her cheeks again. 'And now I think we should get down to the business at hand.' Joe proceeded to talk at length to the Four, asking for ideas, coaxing them gently, towards a decision.

In the time space that the Four and Joe occupied this all took only a fleeting moment. In Richard's world three hours passed by, in which time he'd been checked over by a nurse who'd found nothing untoward, except a chill in the air. She'd checked the heating – nothing wrong with it, it was working fine; just one of those things, she'd decided. She had then busied herself with various duties, muttering about someone walking over her grave when she inadvertently walked through Joe, (who had absentmindedly noted she had years yet) then she'd left.

The decision was finally made; all the Four were to go, but only one of them actually with Richard. Richard was to choose; after all it was his body. The others were to go along as observers, to make sure he wasn't accidentally "helped" in his learning of the final Lesson by his bodily companion. The Four knew the final failing, the Lesson to be learnt, Richard didn't. And after all, none of them could call themselves experts in the field of sacrifice, could they? It would be no time for misguided advice or amateur meddling.

The Four now knew their impending fate, but, as for Joe, he was left wondering. How had they come to the decision they had? Maybe it was the fleeting interruption of the nurse that had distracted him? Maybe something yet to be revealed? Even he didn't know everything. Whatever it was, Joe wasn't completely happy with the outcome, but the decision had been made. All he had to do now was figure out a way of implementing it: his way.

CHAPTER 6

In the Shadow cast by the afterlife Geoff, Sammy, and the Chaplain stood and watched as Laura once more approached the deep sleeping Richard. If they'd been able to, they would have waited with bated breath.

'Second time lucky,' whispered Geoff, fingers crossed, as Laura sat beside the bed.

'Ssh!'

'Sorry.'

Laura reached across from where she sat, then hesitated. What if he became violent again? What if he doesn't want to help? The thoughts hung heavy as her hand hovered above Richard.

'What if you don't try?' The voice that entered Laura's head was calm and soothing, like a soft wave on a rocky shore.

Laura relaxed and in that moment knew that Joe, Upstairs Joe, would never be far away. She reached out fully now and touched Richard's face. His warm and wonderful, living, face. Richard stirred at her touch.

'Gently,' urged the voice in Laura's mind.

And gentle she was as she stroked Richard's brow, lightly brushing aside the hair that lay upon it. Richard stirred again, his eyes moving slightly beneath their closed lids.

'Richard,' whispered Laura in the softest of voices.

Richard's eyelids flickered for a moment then opened. His eyes were calm with no sign of fear or anger to cloud them. He spoke. 'Hello,' he said, his voice steady.

'Hello,' said Laura smiling down at him.

In the Shadow three figures tightly held hands.

'Who are you?' asked Richard hesitantly, his senses not yet fully alert.

For a moment Laura did not answer, could not, she was awe-struck, in danger of being overcome by the enormity of the moment. Richard shifted his weight and twisted himself onto an elbow so he could get a better look at his visitor. Laura could only stare back.

'And,' said Richard shifting his gaze to take in his surroundings, 'where am I?'

Laura at last found her tongue. 'Hospital,' she answered warily, 'you had an accident.'

Struggling a little, mainly due to bed stiffness, Richard pulled himself into a sitting position and stared at Laura with some semblance of recognition.

'And you are? – No, don't tell me. Your face, seems familiar.' Richard's forehead creased as he sought to remember. 'No – it's gone,' he finally had to admit.

'Laura.'

'Laura? I think I remember that name, but...' Richard shook his head in defeat, he just couldn't recall where or when. But there was something else, although the name and the face of the young woman sitting beside him were both familiar in some way; they weren't knitting together as he felt they should. The memories, if that's what they were, were disjointed. One, he felt, belonged somewhere in his past, the other to a dream.

'I visited before – earlier,' said Laura trying to help but hesitant about whether she should. Even though Laura felt that Joe was near, she was still wary about how things might yet turn out, how Richard would react when his memory did return.

As she spoke, Richard was searching his mind for something to latch onto. Some island of thought amidst the sea of doubt and bewilderment that he could use as solid ground. He looked at Laura again, studying her; then something, the smallest of sparks, smouldered into life somewhere in the depths of his mind.

'I remember something, but I'm sure it was a dream. It's vague but I believe you were in it.' Richard's face took on a different look. One that Laura wasn't sure about. 'It was strange. There were creatures in it, drab grey creatures.' Richard stopped talking and looked even deeper into Laura's face.

Laura shrank back under Richard's close scrutiny.

'And you were with them, but you were also grey.' Richard was now struggling with the words he was saying, as if what they were leading to might choke him. Richard suddenly felt he had to back away. Something about this young woman sitting beside him was unsettling. No, that wasn't the word. She was scary, she just wasn't right somehow.

'Richard?'

'I think you should go now. I need to see the nurse.'

Now it registered, the look on Richard's face, it was fear. Frightened by this, Laura felt a wave of panic wash over her; she stole a glance in the direction of her friends and what she saw frightened her even more.

In the corner, huddled together in the Shadow, her friends stood watching; but they now were as Richard had described them. Drab, colourless and gaunt. Like characters from the silent movies she'd so loved as a child, but these were different, these were what bad dreams were made of. They scared her; the others were scaring her. Sweet Geoff and his ridiculous costume, Sammy the hapless tramp and harmless old Chaplain were scaring *her*.

Shocked by what she was seeing, Laura stood up, sending the chair she was sitting on clattering backwards. What was happening to them? She clasped a hand to her mouth to stifle a scream that was building and gasped as it touched – it was warm – she was warm. She was breathing. Laura stretched her arms out before her and stared at them. They had colour; but didn't they always? Laura, her head beginning to swim, staggered forward and gripped the bed's headboard tightly to stop herself from falling.

On the bed, Richard's search for the call button was cut short by concern for his young visitor's sudden distress.

'You okay?' he asked, reaching out to her, the fear he had been feeling somewhat diminishing. Richard looked at the small frightened girl beside his bed and wondered how he could have been afraid of someone so obviously vulnerable. It was, after all, just a dream, wasn't it? And this girl was real, as real as he was. Richard's fear now completely evaporated, leaving in its wake a feeling of foolishness.

'Laura,' he said, gently touching her arm, 'I...' Richard faltered, trying to find the words he wanted to say. 'It looks as if you've seen a ghost,' he eventually attempted to joke.

And that was just it. As Richard spoke, Laura realized that it was exactly what she was doing. What *she was,* in essence. Something, like dying, to know but not think about. She stared at the three ghosts huddled in the Shadow. They weren't to be feared but to be pitied. They were afraid, perhaps more than she was. Then, as these thoughts went through her mind, an overwhelming feeling of peace began to envelop her and in that instant she knew that her destiny, all of their destinies, rested with her. Laura pulled herself together and turned to Richard.

'Do you trust me?' she asked, bluntly.

It was unexpected and a strange question but inexplicably Richard found that he felt he could. He nodded.

'Then I've something to tell you.'

From depth of the Shadow the other three watched as events unfolded.

'What's she stopping for?' whispered Sammy, who was still holding out for a silver lining, even after everything that had happened.

'I think she's frightened.'

'Of what?'

'That he'll go Roberta again I expect.' It was Geoff's idea of a joke. Roberta – ape, ape – Roberta. But the others didn't get it, and ignored him.

'She's moving again,' observed the Chaplain with a tingle of anticipation.

'She's going to touch him,' said Sammy, hardly able to bear it.

'Touching his face,' said Geoff almost dreamily as he recalled his own warm encounter.

'Is he awake yet?'

'You can see for yourself, can't you?'

But Sammy couldn't, his eyes were tightly shut.

'Oh for goodness sake, open your eyes, man,' said the Chaplain, rolling his own skyward.

Cautiously Sammy did, just in time to see Richard's eyes flicker open. Quickly closing them again, Sammy reached for the other's hands. He found no resistance and gripped tightly.

'He's speaking to her,' said Geoff, intent on giving a running commentary.

'Sssh!' said the Chaplain, straining his ears, 'I can't hear what he's saying.'

'It's going wrong again. I can feel it,' groaned Sammy from beneath his clamped eyelids.

'He's panicking!' continued Geoff's commentary.

'What do we do?' said Sammy feeling his silver lining under threat again.

'Stay calm. Look, Laura's looking our way.'

They all looked and found themselves immersed in inexplicable feelings of pain and despair.

'Why's she looking at us like that? What's happening?' said Sammy, now wishing he had not re-opened his eyes.

But the other two were equally at a loss.

'I don't know,' said the Chaplain, perturbed.

'I don't like it, she – she seems different,' whined Geoff as Laura's eyes bore into them.

Then it dawned on the Chaplain that Laura *was* different. Indeed as different as ever she could be. As different as life and death – literally. He spoke, deliberately.

'I believe Laura is alive.'

Geoff and Sammy stared and gripped each other's hands all the tighter as they noticed for the first time the colour, Laura's colour. She stood holding her arms out in front of her and then, linked as they always were, always would be, they felt her sadness and pity, and understood.

The feelings remained only for a few moments longer then, the pain, sadness, pity and despair disappeared, leaving behind a serene calmness for each in the Shadow to bathe in. The Chaplain, Sammy and Geoff were no longer afraid.

CHAPTER 7

Richard gazed intently at the girl as she picked up the chair and sat back down beside him. He guessed that she was somewhere in her early twenties but, and he couldn't think why he did, he felt she was a lot older.

Her face was gently lined, mostly laughter lines that spoke of wisdom rather than age. She had a happy face, a complete lack of sternness to its elfin shape which was encased, like a portrait Richard thought, by soft brown curls that rested gently on petite shoulders. Richard felt he knew her somehow, yet didn't. Maybe he was feeling the first throes of love? No that was stupid, it was something else he felt. But what?

'Are you ready yet?' Richard asked as Laura sat down.

'Sorry? Oh…yes.' Laura glanced once more in the direction of the Shadow. They were still there, and why shouldn't they be? But now they looked less apprehensive, more eager. She returned her attention to Richard who now had a look as expectant as that of her friends. 'Do you believe in ghosts?' she said, not batting an eyelid.

As this was not what he had expected her to say, (though what it was that he had been expecting, he didn't know) Richard found it an impossible task not to smile.

'Ghosts?' he said, trying to stop the smile turning into laughter because of her look of seriousness.

'Yes,' replied Laura, her jaw jutting out. She was finding it hard again just as she thought she was coming to terms with the situation. To make things worse she had an impulse to cry and act all girlie; which wasn't her at all.

39

It was going wrong again. He was laughing at her. But she had to control her newly found emotions, the baggage that came with living. Inside, Laura was in turmoil, she began to feel stupid. Her cheeks were going red, and she wished he wouldn't look at her that way. How she'd forgotten what it is to be alive! It was ghastly, it was painful, it was so damned wonderful. Tears began to fill her eyes.

Richard's smile disappeared. He hadn't meant to upset her. What he had been half expecting, or hoping for, was for Tom the "bastard" to come bursting through the door with a resounding "got yer!" He now knew it wouldn't happen.

'Do *you*?' he asked, reaching towards a tissue box on the bedside cabinet.

Blinking tears from her eyes, Laura looked at the Shadow. 'Yes,' she said taking the tissue Richard had offered. It was all she could say for the moment.

'She's not going to do it,' gulped Geoff, pushing a knuckle into his mouth and biting on it.

'She will – she must.'

'Look at her eyes!' exclaimed Sammy, in wonder and awe. 'She's crying.'

They looked on in astonishment. It had been a long time since any of them had seen tears, real wet tears.

'Why is she doing that?' mumbled Geoff between knuckles.

It was a question that didn't need answering. They all already knew why, they all felt Laura's feelings, although it did lose a little in translation. The gulf between life and death was both narrow and wide, the transition between the two a fine sliver, a fingertip away, but, emotionally, separated by a chasm as wide as any that could be imagined.

The three fell quiet again within their cocooning Shadow. They watched and waited. They had trust in Laura to come through, but what she was attempting was only the tip of the iceberg. Richard's reaction was the unknown quantity, the hidden bulk beneath their sea of hope. Only he could sink or save them.

Richard waited until he felt sure Laura had recovered before saying anything else. He decided to humour the girl for the time being. He had had a feeling that there was something about the girl; that somehow there was a connection between the two of them; a feeling that worried him. He would listen to whatever she had to say however stupid it sounded; after all he wasn't going anywhere. And if it turned out that she was just some nutter who wandered in from another ward, then so be it. He could wait, he doubted that it would be long before she was missed. But if she wasn't a nutter and no white coated heavies paid a visit? Well, Richard didn't want to think about that scenario. No, much better to think of her as a nutter that would go away sooner or later.

'Are you okay?' asked Richard, handing Laura another tissue, his voice, despite his misgivings, genuinely sympathetic.

'Yes, thank you,' sniffed Laura, pressing the fresh tissue against her nose. She blew into it. 'It's just a shock that's all.'

'Is it?' said Richard, incomprehension showing on his face.

'I'm sorry,' said Laura sniffing and now smiling a little at Richard's bemused look, 'I'm rambling.'

'No problem, it happens to the best of us,' smiled Richard, reassuringly.

'It's just that I've got something very important to tell you and…and I'm finding it difficult.'

'Steady girl,' whispered a voice from the Shadow which only its occupants could hear.

'It's about you and me and,' Laura hesitated for a moment but steeled herself, 'and the dream you said you had.'

Richard had the distinct feeling he wasn't going to like where this was leading, but he continued to play along. 'The

41

greyish one with you in it?' he said. He *was* playing along, *wasn't* he?

'Yes,' said Laura nodding. Laura stared deep into Richard's eyes – it was now or never. 'But it wasn't a dream. It was real.'

Go to yellow alert, thought Richard, his fears seemingly well-founded, when's Napoleon coming to tea?

'I'm a ghost. We all are.'

'Good morning Napoleon!' said Richard, inadvertently speaking aloud.

'Sorry?'

Embarrassed by his faux pas, Richard tried to cover his tracks by urging Laura to go on with her story. He stole a quick glance towards the door – any moment now would be good.

Not having actually caught what Richard had said, Laura continued. 'And we need your help.'

Not mine darling. This time Richard's thoughts stayed firmly where they should. He took another look towards the door.

'Richard?'

'Eh – sorry.'

'Am I scaring you?'

She was and she wasn't. 'What? No, of course not. You carry on.' It was the "wasn't" that was worrying Richard most.

'We need you to get us into the Light,' said Laura, now getting down to the nitty-gritty. 'Without it none of us will be able to go and thousands of years of trying will be wasted.' Laura continued urgently. 'I know we are but one, and only the smallest cog, and that it is your life we're talking about, but it is only you that can do it – so please,' implored Laura, her dark brown eyes searching Richard's.

The blank look on Richard's face said it all. He just didn't have the faintest idea what she was going on about.

'She's blown it,' wavered a voice in the Shadow.

42

'Maybe not.'

'What do you mean?'

'I'm going to talk to him, before it's too late.'

'You can't, not like this.'

'It has to be done.' And with that the Chaplain stepped from the Shadow to the foot of Richard's bed.

'Hello,' said the Chaplain politely, 'I don't know if you remember me, I'm Black, Chaplain Black.'

There was no scream, just an awful silence. Behind the Chaplain, in the Shadow, Sammy turned away, his silver lining shredded, while Geoff stared in open-mouthed horror. Laura, mortified was rooted to the ground, and Richard had gone into whatever world it was that coma patients existed in.

'What the hell did you do that for?' snapped Laura angrily, regaining her wits. 'Look what you've done. I was just beginning to get through to him.' Laura squared up to the Chaplain.

'I think not Laura. He was slipping away, I had to do something.'

Things were starting to turn nasty; then Sammy and Geoff stepped from the Shadow.

'It's no-one's fault,' said Geoff. 'No-one's to blame. None of us has ever done anything like this before.'

'He's right, none of you are to blame.' Joe had once more made a timely appearance, his voice, calm and reassuring. 'It's the human condition that is stopping you. It seems Richard will never be able to accept who you are and what you are saying.'

'Then we are doomed,' said the Chaplain, his face suddenly dark and ancient.

'I didn't say that,' said Joe, moving between the Chaplain and Laura and placing a hand on each of their shoulders.

'Then what *do* we do?' asked Laura, her face a mask of puzzlement as it searched Joe's.

'You will try again, but this time you will talk to Richard's inner self.'

'His inner self?'

'His Spirit if you like.'

'Will that help?'

'You shall soon see, Just have a little faith and patience, that's all I ask.' Then as suddenly as he'd appeared, Joe was gone again.

'Now what?' said Sammy, whose glimpses of silver linings were coming and going as quickly as Joe was. He was finding it hard to keep up.

For the moment they were at a loss to know what to think and what to do next. Even with Joe's reassurance the Four couldn't help but feel back at square one again. However the moment of doubt was just that, a moment.

'I believe you were on the verge of asking me something?' said a voice from the bed. Richard, or at least his Spirit, was sitting up. Behind him his physical self was out to the world, sleeping like a baby.

'Richard!' exclaimed Laura, taken aback.

'Of course. You were maybe expecting someone else?' Richard raised an eyebrow and waggled an imaginary cigar in front of his face, Groucho Marx style. It seemed Richard's inner self had a sense of humour.

'No…well…it's…can you see *everyone*?' Laura stammered.

'Yes.'

'And you're not afraid?' asked Laura, almost afraid to.

'I've seen the light, so to speak,' answered Richard smiling, the imaginary cigar still waggling. 'Been put on a level playing field, or field of play as us refs like to say – TA-RA – if you know what I mean?'

'Ask him what he knows' whispered the Chaplain.

'Ask him what he means' said Sammy.

'Hello – I am here you know,' said Richard, feigning annoyance.

44

'Oh – ahem – sorry,' said the Chaplain, avoiding Richard's wounded look.

'And the answer to your question is nothing; squat-diddly so to speak, except I'm here as you see me.' Richard, feeling the Chaplain had suffered enough under his stare, now gave his attention to the rest of the worried faces that were eyeing him nervously. 'The powers that be deemed my Spirit stronger than the flesh and I quote "more able to accept you" but that is as far as they would go. Though be warned – they told me to say that – my reaction when I awake as a whole maybe quite different to what it is now.' Richard sat back, watching the Four's reaction.

'But you will remember?'

'Yes, but not all things; how I "Spirit Boy" got here for instance. And as I said, it will all be a tad harder to come to terms with when I properly awake. The old boy's not as out-going as I am.' Richard thumbed at his sleeping self as he spoke. 'Now, shall someone begin?'

Where did one start with so fantastic a tale as the Four had to tell? The answer? Simple – at the beginning of course.

It had started – them – the meaning – the beginning – such a long time ago. Roberta had been the first of the line. She was given Lessons to learn – choices to make. They had been simple but, for her, as for many others, at the time, some proved elusive. There was no blame though – after all, she was only "human".

So the failed lessons were passed on once Roberta's life ended and her spirit passed into the afterlife. Her time on Earth was over but the Soul that was her remained, entwined with the next spirit whose job it now was to learn the old lessons not yet learned and to learn new ones of its own. The lessons were still simple but not easy – they were never meant to be.

So it continued. One spirit after another passing into the afterlife but the Soul ever present, an umbilical cord linking the line of spirits as one, for that is what they were. Once the Lessons were learned, the spirits, encased as one in their joint Soul, could pass into the Light from the afterlife, one long line of the Strangest Relations together at last: as one forever. And then the process could begin all over again, a chance for a new Soul and Spirit to look for the Light.

But now enter the *But*. Normally, and this is using the word on the very edges of its meaning, it would take only a few lives / spirits to understand the choices they had to make and thus learn the Lessons. Sometimes, and this was very rare, it took only a couple of lifetimes to achieve; though this was usually more down to luck than judgement. But a right choice is a right choice in the scheme of things and therefore would never be ignored. And as humans did eventually in time learn their Lessons, however many fingers they burnt trying, it was decided that a limit would be made as to how many lives / spirits / chances a soul could have. This was a decision made by Upstairs to tidy any undue and unforeseen loose ends. The limit was thus set, using the rule of thumb as to the human condition and ability, at just under, somewhere near, infinity, but not quite. All in all an impossible and unreachable amount of chances were allowed. And thus you now have it, the *But*, an impossible amount of chances that was in very real danger of actually being reached.

The sad fact of the matter was that Richard was the last chance at the end of a very long line of pitiful failures. There would be no-one after him to take the reins. No more chances to learn lessons or make choices. Failure for Richard was the be-all and end-all for all of them. At that moment, as Richard listened, there was one Lesson, one choice, still outstanding. If Richard didn't make it then there would be no Light. And if that happened no one, including Upstairs, knew or dared to think of the consequences that it might bring.

With her story ending at the present time, the Four waited uneasily for Richard's reaction.

For a long while Richard just sat and said nothing, pondering on what he'd been told. Even in his spirit state it was a lot to take in. Eventually he felt ready to speak.

'And so I'm to learn the last lesson in life and then everything will be okay?' he said, his face etched with the effort of understanding.

'Yes,' replied Laura, exchanging hopeful glances with the others. It seemed that Richard, or at least his spirit, was taking things a little more calmly.

'And you are all here to help me?'

'Yes.'

'Well that seems easy enough.' A ripple of relief spread momentarily among the Four at Richard's words. 'Once you tell me what the lesson is I can't honestly see a problem.'

The ripple was all too brief. Laura looked at the others who smiled weakly back at her.

'But we can't,' said Laura despondently, trying very hard to hide the dismay within her. 'I thought you understood. You've got to work that out for yourself.'

'But why are you all here if I've got to decide for myself what the lesson is?' puzzled Richard.

Again Laura looked at the others. Things were definitely not going as well as she'd first hoped. 'We've come to help,' she tried to explain.

This did not help Richard one little bit. First they were there to help, then they couldn't, and then they were again. What was going on? It was beginning to get a little too much to understand, even for Richard's spirit.

'Then pray tell what it is exactly that you are going to help me with?' he said exasperated.

It was then that it dawned on Laura that they had forgotten one vital element of the story she had told. It was no wonder Richard was puzzled. No wonder it had seemed so easy at first. So intent on telling the story of their line, they had forgotten the most important part of it, why they, the Four, were there. Taking a deep breath, both metaphorically and physically, Laura elaborated.

Now the others realised their mistake as well. Fingers were rapidly crossed, eyes found other places to look as Laura's words echoed around the room. Sammy turned away completely, hands covering his ears.

'I'm *dying!*' exclaimed Richard, his eyes widening with the enormity of what Laura had just told him. 'What do you mean, dying?' Hardly able to take it in, he pointed to himself lying on the bed. 'Look at me. Does that look like someone who's dying?'

Four solemn reluctant heads nodded as one.

'But?' Richard tried to protest, but the words he wanted failed him, sticking in his throat.

'Please calm down, Richard,' begged Laura, 'everyone's dying from the moment they're born.' A terrible thought and perhaps not the best argument in the circumstances but it was Laura's way of attempting to placate him.

As it was, for the moment, it looked like it was working. Richard began to see a light at the end of this particularly dark tunnel. He'd obviously jumped the gun. It was just Laura's way of explaining things. Richard started to relax a little; just in time for Laura's next bombshell.

'You have got over a *month* to go.' Laura thought that she was helping. A month of life to her at that moment was, well, a lifetime in itself.

'A month!' yelled Richard, as panic started setting in. 'What the hell do you mean, a month?'

'It's plenty of time for what you've got to do,' continued Laura, completely missing Richard's point – on life, his life.

Richard's face dropped. 'But we've – I've – I've got things to do. There are places to visit, people to meet,' he said desperately. 'I want to meet the Pope.' Richard threw that in for good measure just in case it made a difference but he knew, the spirit being what it is, that there really was no way out. 'I can't die now, I'm...I'm...' Richard struggled for words, ending quietly with 'too young'. He sagged forward onto the bed, his head in his hands.

As Laura watched she felt glad Richard's spirit was taking it so well.

'What's happening?' whispered Sammy from his refuge behind the Chaplain. 'Has she told him?'

'Not everything,' replied Geoff, only his whisper wasn't what you would call discreet.

Richard's head slowly disengaged itself from his hands. 'What does he mean "not everything"?' he said, deliberately, looking hard at Laura.

Laura stared icily at Geoff.

'Well?' said Richard, his eyes narrowing.

'I was coming to that when you went off on one,' she snapped, her anger at Geoff focussing on Richard, for an instant.

'Well, pardon me for getting upset at my impending doom. *Bad* Richard!' Richard slapped his own outstretched hand. 'How *dare* you get upset over such a *trivial* thing?' He slapped his hand again.

'It won't help, you know.' It was the Chaplain, feeling that his knowledge of life was now called for.

'What do you know?' glared Richard.

'Only that what is, is.' The Chaplain's voice was both calm and detached – as if he was looking at something else far off in the distance. 'The wheels turn and we only have so much time. You are lucky indeed.'

'Lucky? You call this bloody *lucky*?' Richard's face burned with rage. How dare this jumped up, stuffed-shirted, busybody Captain of the God-squad tell *him* how lucky he was?

'Lucky to know how long you have.'

Inside Richard, inside his Spirit, a nerve was touched and the storm began to ebb. Richard, in his heart, knew that all his procrastinations would come to nothing; could come to nothing. The Chaplain was right in his way, fate had dealt him

49

a card and now he had to play it. Richard resignedly slumped forward onto the bed once more.

'May I continue?' asked the Chaplain.

Richard, his head in his hands again, nodded.

'What Laura had been about to tell you is that you are too weak, or at least your body is, to return on your own. One of us has to go with you.'

Richard raised his head slightly so that one eye was looking at Laura. 'Move in, he means?'

'Yes,' replied Laura.

'My house?'

'No,' Laura hesitated, 'your body.'

The expected rant never came; Richard was too far gone for that. Without taking his eye off Laura, he spoke slowly and deliberately, he had to. He had to hear himself say it, otherwise he would think it was all in his mind.

'One – of – *you*,' Richard paused to look at the Four, 'has – to – get – *into* – my – body – *with* – me?'

A mutual nod.

'Who?' Richard couldn't believe he was actually asking.

'That is for you to decide,' explained the Chaplain.

Lifting his head from his hands completely, Richard switched his gaze in turn to each of the Four.

'Do I have to?' asked Richard, his throat excessively dry.

'Yes, I'm afraid so,' said Laura – she almost gasped the words, yet suddenly she felt like laughing, the relief that they were getting somewhere nearly too much to bear.

Sitting upright, Richard pushed his hands through his hair. At last he felt he was seeing the full picture. He didn't particularly like what he saw, but he was seeing it all the same.

'I've got a month…'

'About a month,' interrupted Laura.

'About a month and in that time I've to learn this final lesson with one of you inside me? But whoever it is mustn't help me?'

'Yes.'

'And I'm our last chance?'

'Yes.'

'And, let me get this straight, if I fail then it's blammo-goodnight Irene for all of us and none of us gets to see the great Upstairs or wherever it is they keep the Light?'

'Yes,' said the Chaplain although he wasn't sure where Irene fitted into the equation.

'And we'd be the first ones ever not to have made it?'

'Yes.'

The yes's were now coming a little too frequently for Richard's liking but he still had questions to ask.

'And nobody from Upstairs knows what will happen then?'

'Yes…No…I mean…we don't think so.'

'Then why the hell did Upstairs put a limit on the bloody thing?'

'We believe,' stepped in Sammy, 'that they didn't expect that any soul could be so stupid as to actually reach it.'

'So who's to blame? This Roberta?'

'You, technically,' said the Chaplain.

'Me!'

'Well yes and no,' said Laura quickly.

'What?'

'Us, I suppose,' said Sammy.

'So we're all to blame?'

'Sort of,' finished Geoff.

There followed a few moments of silence in which the Four exchanged uneasy glances; no one was sure what to do next.

'Can I think about all this for a moment?' asked Richard, as he tried to come to terms with all that had been said. All of a sudden he was feeling very old and very, very tired.

The Four readily agreed, it wasn't only Richard that felt the need for a time out. They silently waited and watched as Richard started the task of digesting all that he'd been told.

51

'In private.'

Apologies, then Richard watched as the Four wandered to the foot of the bed, and then wondered as three of them disappeared as if into thin air. But he said nothing; he had enough on his plate and that was weird enough for the moment. He decided to forget what he was seeing.

Richard lay back on the bed and changed his train of thought in order to try to remember his last fully conscious day on Earth. To his surprise, he found little success, with nearly all of that day remaining foggy. He remembered how cold it had been, little things, but he had no recollection of the incident that had steered him towards his present situation. With that train of thought being of the short and sweet nature, Richard turned his attention back to more present problems. He glanced at Laura, the only one of the Four still visible; she seemed to be talking to herself. Was he really related to her? To the others? It all seemed too fantastic, too unbelievable, but here he was disentangled from his own living body. Richard stared up at the white ceiling, a low burning lamp sunk into it, and tried to merge the reality he knew with what passed now as reality.

For what seemed like ages, Richard pondered on his fate and, to a certain extent, the fate of the others. He now, quite calmly, came to a decision. What choice did he really have? Richard sat up and called to them.

Sammy, Geoff and the Chaplain joined Laura beside the bed, each of them looking as apprehensive as the other.

'I've made a decision,' announced Richard.

'You're going to help us,' said Laura, hardly able to contain herself.

'I think that goes without saying, doesn't it?' said Richard, a little annoyed that Laura should be considering any other possibility, even though he didn't seem to have a choice. He had actually been at the point of announcing who he thought should go back with him to the land of the living. But, before he could say what he was actually going to say, Joe made yet another unscheduled visit. This one, though, was not to be a popular visit and didn't produce the calming effect his appearances usually achieved.

'Not necessarily,' Joe announced.

'What do you mean?' asked Richard, intrigued by this latest development, but at the same time a little perturbed by what the repercussions might be – especially as he'd finally managed more or less to come terms with everything and had been on the verge of making a decision.

'Yes, what do you mean?' agreed the Chaplain in a disgruntled voice, thus heralding a small leaning towards dissent amongst the troops.

'Richard does have a choice.'

'What do you mean, he has a choice?' asked Laura, facing Joe. 'I thought you said Richard was too weak to go back on his own?'

'It now seems that that isn't strictly true,' explained Joe to an increasingly dismayed audience.

'Do tell,' prompted Richard, feeling the need once more to remind people that he was still there.

'What it means is that Richard now has a choice. He can go back on his own and enjoy the last of his days as he sees fit, however long that may be.'

'You don't know?' queried Richard, still trying to verify that he did still exist.

'Or go as was discussed, taking one of you with him. In which case of course his last moments on Earth won't be his own but shared.'

Richard was sure Joe had given him a strange look as he finished speaking, but then again everything was strange, he shrugged it off.

'What do you think is best?' asked Sammy, trying not to think what all this might be doing to his silver lining.

'As I said, it is Richard's choice, but I must make it clear that if Richard chooses to go on his own he will be very weak and may not have enough strength to reach the end of his allotted time. And if that happens he may not accomplish the learning of the final Lesson.'

No pressure there then, thought Richard, who had resigned himself to the fact that for the moment he didn't seem to exist.

'But even if he does decide to take one of you back with him that is still no guarantee that the final Lesson will be learnt. Now I must go, but I will be back when Richard has made his decision.'

'So the choice is?' asked Richard, wanting the whole thing clarified to a much simpler level, one which he could understand. But the question fell on deaf ears, or rather, ears that were no longer there. Joe had already gone; leaving four expectant faces staring down at Richard. Richard stared back. What was he to do? It seemed that he was damned if he did and damned if he didn't.

'Can you give me a moment?' he said.

CHAPTER 8

Having retreated into the Shadow to await Richard's decision, three of the Four – Laura having discovered earlier, much to her chagrin, that she could no longer enter as technically she was not dead, for the moment anyway – huddled together to discuss their dilemma.

'What do you think he'll do?' whispered Geoff.

'I fail to see that he has a choice,' replied the Chaplain in the self-deluding manner that could be his trademark on occasions.

'It's rude you know,' complained Laura in what she thought was the general direction of the Shadow, 'having a meeting of the Four without me.' She couldn't actually see it anymore as the gap between life and death was widening the longer she remained a living being.

'Laura's talking to the wall,' observed Sammy.

'And that is precisely why I think the decision as to who should go should be down to us. It is painfully obvious that in her state she is no longer able to contribute objectively to our debate,' spouted the Chaplain.

'What state's that then?' asked Geoff, trying hard to understand just what the Chaplain was going on about.

'Why the *living* state of course,' said the Chaplain throwing his hands into the air. 'You cannot possibly expect anyone living to make a rational decision. No, it is up to us.'

'Richard's making one,' Sammy pointed out. He was of a mind that Richard should be included in all the decisions, especially as Upstairs had said so.

'Yes – yes of course, I know that. But I'm talking about the more important decision of who goes with him.'

'So you think he'll take one of us?'

'Hey guys come on out, we need to talk.'

'She's still talking to the wall.'

'Ignore her and, as to your question Sammy, yes I do think Richard will see sense and allow one of us to accompany him.'

'I wouldn't,' admitted Geoff coyly.

'You wouldn't?'

'No, I wouldn't. I wouldn't want to share my last moments on Earth with a total stranger, even if they *are* me – related – oh, you know what I mean.'

'Chaplain! Come out now!'

'Nor me,' agreed Sammy reluctantly.

'But that's selfish.'

'Would you then?' asked Sammy.

'Well of course I would. There would be no hesitation in my mind for a moment in offering myself to help others.'

'Your nose is growing.'

'What?'

'I think what Geoff means is that he doesn't believe you.'

'Preposterous,' said the Chaplain looking aghast.

'There you are. Talk to me.'

'She's talking to the other wall now.'

A little flustered by the allegations, the Chaplain decided that it was time Laura was brought into the conversation, time to get an unbiased opinion on matters. He also knew that she rarely knew when he was lying. Not that he ever lied of course.

'Laura!'

Laura spun round to find the Chaplain and the others standing on the far side of the bed.

'Where the hell have you three been?' she snapped, eyes glaring.

'Now, now Laura,' soothed the Chaplain smiling and holding up an appeasing hand; much as the Christians may have done to the lions in the Coliseum.

'Don't you "now, now" me, you pompous ass!' snarled Laura.

'Well really,' protested the Chaplain, trying to ignore the sniggers emanating from behind him.

'Hey – steady on there.' Richard had been quietly watching Laura's antics in the room since the departure of the others into the Shadow, pretending he hadn't noticed as she had wandered from one wall to the other. He smiled at her. 'I hope this fight isn't over me?'

Laura blushed a little as she found herself the centre of attraction. 'It wasn't,' she said 'It's just that everything's so important and they seem intent on playing silly beggars.' Laura looked daggers at the other three.

'Weren't,' said the Chaplain before he could stop himself.

'Were.'

'Stop it this instant!' Joe was back, no soothing tone this time. 'It's no wonder you've taken so long to learn the lessons,' he said angrily, 'your future, or maybe lack of it, hangs in the balance and you act like squabbling children.' Laura started to say something but Joe stayed her words with a wave of his hand. 'I believe Richard has something to tell us – maybe a mature conclusion to our dilemma.' Joe stared hard at the Chaplain as he spoke, before turning to the bed and Richard. 'Richard?'

Richard coughed nervously, as he prepared to deliver his decision. Four sets of hopeful eyes bore down on him, four sets of eyes which, however much they denied it to themselves, were desperate to taste life again. No matter how brief it was to be. They were also desperate for the chance to start the long awaited journey into the Light, at last.

'Right,' said Richard a little nervously, 'after several minutes of hard and difficult thought, and the toss of a coin.'

'A coin?' interrupted Joe, slightly perplexed.

'Only joking,' smiled Richard thinking that maybe joking wasn't the way to go judging by the look on Joe's face. 'I've decided' – he thought of doing a pretend drum-roll but thought better of it – 'to let one of you come back with me.' There – he'd said it now; though he was sure he would be sorry for it somewhere down the line.

'Hurrah for Richard!' shouted Sammy letting his emotions get the better of him. He felt as if he could almost touch his elusive silver lining.

'But,' added Richard, dampening Sammy's enthusiasm for the moment, 'I'm undecided as to who that will be.' The room fell ominously quiet. 'Joe, can I ask you something? Private like.'

'Of course,' said Joe ushering the Four away, his voice back to its soothing self again.

Richard waited until he felt the others were well out of earshot before continuing. 'I get the idea of someone coming back with me, but what's to stop them from tipping the wink, so to speak?' he whispered.

'Ah – well, that's a good question and one that has been discussed.'

'And?' said Richard giving Laura a quick sideways glance. Obviously something else she had forgotten to tell him.

'The decision was made that all of the Four would go with you to keep an eye on each other.'

'What! All *four* in me?' Richard was panic stricken by the idea.

'No – no,' smiled Joe, 'just one "in you", as you say, the others will be found suitable vessels when the time arises.'

'What do you mean suitable vessels?' Richard wasn't sure he liked the sound of that.

Neither did the Four as the sound of the conversation between Joe and Richard seeped across the room to them. It was true that it was something that they had decided upon between them, but they hadn't really thought about how it would be achieved.

'Yes Joe, what do you mean?' asked Laura, bravely leading the way.

'There really is no need to worry,' said Joe cutting her off at the pass, with a calm smile and calm words, 'all will be revealed after Richard has made *his* choice as to who goes back with him. Richard?'

All eyes were back on Richard.

'Right, fair enough,' said Richard, not entirely sure that he believed Joe – he didn't know why – something in his voice, 'I've decided that before I decide I should like to know everyone a little bit better.'

Looks were exchanged.

'What do you mean?' asked the Chaplain, finding his voice.

'What I mean is that before I decide who's going to share my last moments with me, I would like to know each of you a little bit better. And, if you like, listen to each of you state your case as to why it should be you.'

'A wise decision Richard,' praised Joe. 'You can't just be taking anyone with you.' Joe glanced momentarily in the direction of the Chaplain, who swiftly gave his shoes a once over. 'I feel sure that your future is now in good hands. Good luck Richard.' With that wish still hanging in the air, Joe was gone again, leaving Richard and the Four to their own devices.

'So, who's first?'

The Four started to put forward their respective cases as to why they should be chosen to accompany Richard, Geoff going first. Richard had in fact already narrowed the list to three. The Chaplain would not be going. The reason was size. Richard at about one metre eighty tall and reasonably lean, just couldn't envisage how a man of nearly two metres, who had obviously been a great lover of puddings when alive, could possibly fit inside him. Of course he knew the Chaplain would be in spirit form and that that would make a difference, but all the same it didn't seem right somehow. No, a decision was made; the list was now shorter by one.

'And I can teach you to dance,' finished Sammy.

Sammy was the last to put his case and, tempting as the offer sounded, Richard decided to resist. The list was shortened again.

Richard was not so shallow as to sweep someone aside just on the strength of one sentence. He'd taken full account of everything that Sammy had had to say – his silver spoon in the mouth upbringing, his talented mid-years, and his eventual sad demise. In Richard's eyes Sammy was much the same as the Chaplain in many respects, an alright guy, a little misunderstood maybe, but all in all a nice enough chap underneath it all. And, as with the Chaplain, in the end, it was something more personal to Richard that had finally brought him to his conclusion. In Sammy's case it was his smell. No one else seemed to notice, maybe they'd been together too long, maybe dead people no longer possessed a sense of smell, but Richard did, and could, and no way was he having it in *his* body. Richard had made a vow as he had listened to Sammy's story, that on his last day on Earth he would make sure that he showered and shaved. The thought of spending eternity, however it was to be, smelling like a drain just didn't appeal.

Then there were two.

Each story told had been interesting in its own way, but in truth none of the Four between them had managed to put forward a good enough reason why any of them should be the one to go.

Richard found himself reflecting on the Chaplain's story even though he'd already decided against him. It had included a brief history of his new found relatives: his before lives. It seemed that the whole line going back to Roberta had been full of people, or spirits, loaded with good intentions, with the *odd* exception. Here and there a black sheep had appeared to make things worse for others. Old Tobias the highwayman was a good example. A good man at heart, Tobias was always courteous to his victims and never killed anyone; he was also willing to donate some of his ill-gotten gains to the poor. A man of perhaps slightly tarnished ideals, but Tobias had a fault that let him and everyone else down: Tobias just couldn't resist "tampering" with the men in the coaches he robbed.

As Richard baulked at the thought of old Tobias and his doings – he was only twenty the day he was hung, – he thought of the saying beloved of old people when given the chance; "The Road To Hell Is Paved With Good Intentions." Maybe they were right? Maybe it was his family motto and he and the others were destined never to reach that elusive Light.

He couldn't let himself dwell on it though; he had a decision to make, however flimsy a chance he thought they had. Time to give some more thought to Geoff's and Laura's efforts.

First up had been Geoff, the youngest of the Four; born 10th March 1984 – died 9th March 2002. Richard had noted that they had the same birthday, they all did. Whoever the Upstairs were, they certainly worked quickly when replace-ments were needed.

Geoff, five feet nine inches tall – Geoff had died before the catastrophe of total metrification – spiky black hair, skinny, – would fit nicely – and not really an elf – bonus – he just had had the misfortune of dying while pretending to be one. He had wanted to be an actor; an actor who would take any job as long as it included dressing in fantasy costumes. Richard suspected that Geoff was a closet wannabe hero, also a little on the effeminate side, not that he would hold that against him – each to his own as the French say. Richard quickly played Geoff's story, which was sadly on the short side, him dying so young, through his mind.

61

Geoff had been working outside the local multiplex cinema promoting the latest blockbuster starring elves. This accounted for Geoff's attire of green hose and pointy ears, which, sadly for him, he had taken into the afterlife with him.

As Geoff pranced out front with an advertising placard draped around his neck, an old lady in the queue waiting to enter had the misfortune to be mugged. Geoff, being Geoff – his own words – immediately leapt into action to give chase. But upon leaping into action, Geoff's placard snagged his tights – he still has the ladder which he shows with pride – sending him sprawling into a head-on collision with a coach load of day-tripping children dressed as boy wizards. Geoff had recalled with warmth that as he lay dying he heard cheering; cheering for Geoff the Elf, Geoff the H*hero*. Consequently Geoff had died happy, but sadly ignorant of children's cruel instincts.

The story finished and Richard found himself with more questions than answers. Though, he had to admit, Geoff's reason for being the one to go back did make some sense.

But there was still Laura's story to mull over. Laura was another who had been beckoned by the bright lights of stage and screen. Only for Laura, things had not worked out so well. She had got no further than a waitressing job in a seedy hole and, of course, her elocution lessons.

Her life in London, living in a tiny cramped flat near Paddington, with others in the same boat, was a far cry from her roots in the lush countryside of Eire. She never forgot her home and tried to visit as often as her meagre wages would allow. But while there was love and generosity in her Spirit – she never went back empty-handed – there was also a dark side. She could be greedy and rash, and resentful of good advice from her well-meaningfamily.

It was Laura's last day on Earth and when she was approached by a sly seedy wretch claiming to be a producer, (of *what* Laura never thought to ask), she paid no heed to warnings to avoid such men.

As Laura had spoken of her last moments, tears had welled up and fallen from her eyes. Tears, Richard had thought, of shame and regret.

Even when this so-called "producer" introduced her to a tatty and battered motorbike the alarm bells that should have been ringing didn't. She was blinded by the lights of distant stardom. All producers were slightly eccentric, weren't they? she told herself. This might be her chance. Taking firm hold of the hand that was held out to her, Laura, grubby apron still wrapped around her, meekly went to meet her intended destiny with the infamous "casting couch".

The road was wet and the motorbikes tyres were bald. The "producer" couldn't stop in time and bike, "producer" and Laura skidded into a line of waiting traffic. Laura, at only twenty-four, lay beneath a bus, her hopes, her dreams, her life, all dashed.

When Laura, still crying, had turned away Richard had at first felt sorry for her. But the pity he felt for her gradually changed, certain misgivings found their way into his thoughts, misgivings about her state of mind. Had she learned any lessons? Could he trust her not to interfere for her own ends? Richard wondered and although he felt time was running short and that he was almost certain who he would choose, he found himself running through each of their stories again.

CHAPTER 9

When Richard woke from his coma, causing much amazement and hushed talk amongst the hospital staff in the process, he had just completed his fifth week in hospital. He was still very weak, very much in need of bed rest, his fractured skull not quite healed, but well on the way to recovery.

The way he had healed was the cause of more quiet whispering. Richard's skull hadn't just been cracked in one single place; the x-rays taken on admittance had shown a mosaic of fractures in serious danger of turning into a hole the size of the end of a cricket bat. At the time, and this was only discussed as an option, it was felt that if Richard survived his injuries a plate of some description would be needed; no plate was ever ordered. And now all that was left of the mess that had been the back of Richard's head was a faint, rapidly healing, hairline fracture. A "miracle" some were calling it. "Sloppy admin" said the more sceptical.

Now, two weeks from that day when Richard woke with a miracle stuck to the back of his head, he was ready to go home. Richard asked for his miracle to be treated as low key and that no one was to be notified of his leaving. He would tell the people that mattered most in his own time, and as far as Richard was concerned, that meant Tom. Come Christmas, Richard's shopping trip for cards was going to prove a very short trip indeed; or so he figured. The hospital hierarchy, the worrying whiff of a possible law suit lingering under their noses long enough, readily agreed. Goodbyes and grateful thank-yous were said and then Richard left in a taxi.

The journey home was short but seemed like an eternity. Richard grabbed his belongings as they arrived and climbed from the cab. He was glad to be out of the hospital. Glad to be opening his gate. And glad to be walking up the small concrete path to his small terraced house. In a nutshell, Richard was glad to be home. The first thing he was going to do was have that long soak he'd promised himself on that fateful day seven long weeks ago. And then, once he was relaxed and had a stiff drink in his hand, he was going to telephone the local Football Association and tell them that from that moment he was retiring from the game. No more freeze-yer-balls-off mornings for him, he was hanging up his whistle for good.

Waiting for Richard, as he'd stepped through the doorway and into his hall, had been a small drift of envelopes, some white but mostly brown, mixed with the usual flotilla of junk mail. He'd swept them disdainfully aside with his foot into a pile for later sorting and most probably binning. They could wait, Richard was in no hurry or mood to do anything but what was uppermost on his mind.

The stairs had been taken two at a time. Bag thrown on the bed followed by the clothes he was wearing. Dressing gown wrapped round him, Richard went on a mission to the drinks cabinet – bottom of the spare room wardrobe – and straight to the whisky. The doctors had told him to go easy on the alcohol until his medication was exhausted, but one little drink wouldn't hurt, would it? A small one to celebrate his homecoming, and, as Richard saw it, the start of a new life.

Richard took the not so small drink to the bathroom and then downstairs to the lounge while he waited for the bath to fill. There he lifted his glass in toast, something he often did when alone, to Freddie his most loyal, trusted and uncomplicated companion and, his best friend after Tom.

'Salute!' Richard raised the glass to his lips. But the glass didn't reach them as he suddenly hurried across the lounge to the sideboard.

Freddie, to Richard's horror, was lying belly up in his tank. Putting his glass down, Richard reached for a dust covered envelope that lay propped against the late Freddie's home, it was addressed to Laura. What the hell? Richard opened it.

It read:

> Dear Laura,
> Thanks for doing this. Sorry I couldn't talk to you in person but my flight's been brought forward, hence the garbled message on your answer machine.
> I've left Freddie's feeding instructions under his food (can't go wrong).
> Oh, and keep an eye on his water. Don't want the little fella swimming in a sea of green, do we?
> See you in December (I hope)
> Love Tom.
>> xxx
> P.S. Keep us up to date on Randy. Phone when I can! Bye!

Laura, thought Richard as he crumpled the note, why the hell did Tom leave Freddie in the hands of that scatty bitch? She's got a brain the size of a pea, and that, more often than not, rattles aimlessly in her thick skull. A grim-faced Richard threw the note onto the top of the sideboard and fished Freddie tail first from his tank. Richard stared at his late companion who stared back at him through grey lifeless eyes.

'Never mind mate,' said Richard, giving Freddie a little shake, 'once I've had my bath I'll take you into the garden and put you with the others.' Richard had a small place set aside in the back garden beside the rockery that he used as a goldfish cemetery. Since the demise of the first Freddie –

sadly there had been a long line of them since – who had simmered to death when inadvertently left overnight on the lounge heater, Richard had always kept at the ready an empty kitchen size matchbox should the need again arise.

Richard plopped Freddie back into the water and watched as the lifeless fish skimmed in an arc through the greenish hue and bobbed back to the surface again.

'Bitch!' said Richard as he reclaimed his glass.

The steam was heavy in the air and rivulets of condensation were trickling down the bathroom mirror as Richard tentatively placed a big toe into the hot foamy water of his promised bath. Heaven, pure heaven, thought Richard as his body eagerly followed his toe into the depths of the hot green frothy liquid. He stretched out and almost purred with the delight of it. This is what life is all about, deemed Richard as the water tickled under his chin, a hot steamy bath, a good book – Apomas by someone called Stanley – and a large glass of unmolested expensive single malt.

As Richard lay in his bath he tried to fill his mind with simple uncomplicated things, things that didn't have anything to do with the past or the future; he just wanted to savour the moment before he had to deal with life again. But, try as he might, he just couldn't seem to relax like he wanted, something was bugging him, nagging at his subconscious, so he refilled his glass, dropped the book, and turned his mind to poor old Freddie.

He would pop down to the pet shop as soon as he could and get another Freddie, it was the least he could do, it was what he always did, when a Freddie passed on. It was his way of remembering the first Freddie and each since, stupid he knew, but it was a constant in his life and everyone needed a constant, or that's what he told himself, and at the moment he felt the need for a constant more than at any other time. Richard took another swig from his glass, wondered if Tesco sold goldfish, and then laughed to himself – save time if they did, he could order one over the net. Then his mind drifted to other things, to Laura, her of the pea brain.

'Blast that stupid woman!' he said, surprising himself. He hadn't meant to say it out loud.

Blast that woman for spoiling his homecoming, his *dreary* little homecoming. Drinking and melancholy invariably became bed-mates for Richard. Blast her for killing Freddie! As he tried to think of something apt to curse her with he took another healthy swig from his glass.

'Bloody Laura the Lackadaisical,' blurted Richard as another gulp of brown nectar disappeared down his throat. Richard started to enjoy himself. 'Laura the Loser!' This was better than solo I-spy, he mused as he tried to think up further insults. 'Laura the Limp!' Richard laughed out loud at this one and the connotations it brought to mind. Worse if she was a bloke. 'Maybe she is?' he laughed out loud, remembering her lack of chest. Richard decided to toast Laura's chest and took another swig.

It was a good game, as some old game show host used to say, and it was getting things out of his system. The assault, his redundancy – which he hadn't given that much thought to – and his lousy friends and family.

'To Laura the…,' Richard struggled a moment before, 'waitress!' came out. As it did something deep in Richard's subconscious stirred, but for the moment stayed where it was, brooding and waiting. Richard looked at his glass. 'Where the bloody hell did that come from?' he asked, looking into its emptiness. 'I must have had more than I thought.'

Reaching over the edge of the bath, Richard grasped the bottle standing beside it and studied it, its shape, its colour, its contents – should he?

'What the hell?' He decided and poured himself another.

Besides, the Laura game was getting boring now and he was tired, it had been a long hard life so far. Sipping at the replenished glass, the whisky *was* going down well, Richard suddenly felt very tired. It may have been the long life, the day, or maybe the hot bath mixed with too much drink and his medication, or a mixture of the lot. But whatever the reason Richard began to drift into sleep, a sleep that would be far from restful.

Shapes came and went, drifting indeterminately through Richard's subconscious. At first they were blurred, unfamiliar, but gradually they became clearer.

Nurses from the hospital, Freddie, and then it was as if his life was running before him, but so fast he could hardly keep pace. It slowed and Tom came and sat beside him, he looked grim but didn't speak, and then there was Laura. She drifted closer and seemed more real somehow; it was as if he could reach out and touch her. She came closer and now it was if she was mocking him.

The bitch! Richard reached out towards her but his hand recoiled as if an electric shock had coursed up his arm. The mocking creature had changed, suddenly, from Laura the fish killer to someone else, someone he felt he should know, another Laura; a Laura that wasn't mocking but reaching out to him. But it was wrong, Richard tried to move away, he didn't want contact, he didn't want her, something was *wrong* about her, he had to get away.

Tepid water splashed from the bath onto the book Richard hadn't got around to reading as he came to with a sudden start. Feeling uncomfortable and disorientated, Richard slowly got to his feet and stepped unsteadily from the bath. The dream was still with him, he could still see the girl reaching out to him in his mind's eye, he shivered, he was sure he knew her. But from where he wasn't certain.

Shivering, Richard grabbed his robe from the back of the door and put it on. He could almost remember something, something that nagged at him, something he felt he should remember, but was being kept back from him. Maybe he *didn't want* to remember?

Richard picked the bottle and empty glass from the floor, he couldn't recall finishing it, and poured himself another drink. Wrapping white and wrinkled fingers tightly around the glass – just how long had he been asleep? – he knocked it back in one. He then remembered Freddie, too late to bury him now, he'd have to do it in the morning.

Without unplugging the bath Richard dragged himself, to the bedroom. The clock on the bedside cabinet read eight o'clock, it wasn't that late after all, Richard had forgotten the time of year, nights still drawing in early. But it was still too late for poor old Freddie; he was too tired even after his impromptu nap in the bath. Richard threw back the duvet and climbed into bed. Within seconds he was asleep again, but this time he slipped into deep fitful sleep.

CHAPTER 10

Richard shot bolt upright in bed, his eyes wild and rolling and his forehead beaded with sweat. Facing him at the foot of the bed was a deep dark shadow that the moonlight pouring in through the window was powerless to explore. Richard opened his mouth and tried to speak but it was as if he'd forgotten how.

Just visible inside this shadow were three grey and dreary figures watching Richard intently, studying him, seemingly waiting for something to happen. After a while one of the figures spoke. 'Well?' it asked, the question plain and simple.

Richard's mouth twisted in response giving his face a look of pain. It continued trying to form words, answer the question, but the movement felt alien. Richard's mouth stopped its struggle and fell open, saliva collecting on his bottom lip.

'Well, that's a great start,' observed one of the figures. As he watched the saliva begin to accept gravity.

'We knew it was going to be difficult. Joe said…'

'Joe said – Joe said!' snapped Geoff before the Chaplain could finish. 'What does Joe really know?' Geoff was still smarting and angry at Joe's last minute intervention which stopped him from going back with Richard into the land of the living. 'I was chosen not her. I should have gone.'

'Joe gave his reasons,' said the Chaplain, attempting to placate him, 'It was nothing personal.'

'Yeah Geoff, calm down, we're all in this together. It didn't really matter who went as long as one of us did,' said Sammy, a lack of conviction in his voice.

'You wouldn't be saying that if you'd been chosen.'

Sammy decided with a shrug of his shoulders that the point wasn't worth arguing about, mainly because he knew it was true, and turned his attention back to Richard who was trying to speak again and giving a passable impression of a sea lion waiting to be fed in the process.

'I'm sure Laura will do her best,' said the Chaplain, completely missing Geoff's point.

'Even if she is a girl,' chipped in Sammy pointlessly but under his breath. Grief, he thought, that sounded bitter. But the others hadn't heard; he was glad, he didn't mean it. 'Well, what happens now?'

'We wait I suppose.'

'For what?'

'Laura to make contact.'

'Maybe it'd help if we threw her a fish,' suggested Sammy.

'What?'

'Never mind.'

'Its going wrong isn't it?' said Geoff, his mind at last on the present, as he watched Richard's facial antics with some concern.

'Of course not, things take time to get used to, that's all.' But even the Chaplain wasn't as confident as he tried to make out. He was sure Joe knew best but, and there was always a but, even the best laid plans? A sudden noise echoed around the room and brought the Chaplain back from his doubts. 'What!' he exclaimed.

'Whaa!' echoed the sound again.

'The lady speaks, I think,' pointed out Sammy helpfully, noticing the Chaplains momentary lapse.

'Whaa-a?' said Richard.

The three stepped from the Shadow as Richard's mouth struggled with its task.

'Easy Laura, take your time. There's no hurry.'

Richard took a deep breath and tried again.

'Wha…wha…at hap…pened?' asked Laura as at last she gained some semblance of control over Richard's lips and vocal chords.

'You nearly drowned him, that's what!' snarled an unhappy Geoff.

'Geoff!' snapped the Chaplain then, speaking softly, 'Are you all right Laura?'

Richard slowly and shakily nodded his head.

'We were worried for a moment there,' said Sammy walking around the bed. He was suddenly feeling very sorry for her and for the way he'd been thinking. 'You sure you're okay?' he asked putting a reassuring hand on Richard's shoulder. Sammy had to admit, for a girl, Laura was one tough cookie.

The Chaplain joined Sammy, in his concern and by Richard's side, leaving Geoff to sulk on his own at the foot of the bed. 'How are you feeling?' he asked as he sat on the bed beside Richard, his voice echoing his emotion.

Turning, his head twisting awkwardly like a puppet whose strings had tangled, Richard faced the Chaplain. Richard didn't look well; it was as if he'd aged ten years overnight. He opened his mouth and Laura spoke again, her voice sounding terribly forced and distant. 'D…id I rea…ly near…ly dro…wn h…im?' she asked.

They tried not to show it but both Sammy and the Chaplain were shocked by Richard's haggard appearance and Laura's pitiful voice.

'Of course not,' reassured the Chaplain smiling. 'He was in a bathtub not a swimming pool. Although it did look at one time as if he was having a particularly bad dream.'

Richard's body, under Laura's disjointed direction, did its best to reciprocate the Chaplain's smile. The result was rather lop-sided but under the circumstances no one felt the need to mention it. Richard turned awkwardly again and came to rest in a more comfortable position. Laura's voice, like the voice of a distant ventriloquist, tumbled again from Richard's mouth.

'I-think-I'm-okay-b-but…' she had a worried look across Richards face, 'I don't thin-k he knows I'm here or…or rememb-ers.' Laura's voice was sounding a little better, as if some internal pressure had been lifted. But though it had been less of a struggle to speak, what she'd said hadn't been good news. She now looked at the Chaplain and Sammy through fearful eyes that for the moment were more Laura than Richard.

It took a few seconds for what Laura had said to sink in before anyone responded.

'But that can't be,' mumbled Sammy, the first to regain his wits. His face now showing the fears he'd been trying to conceal. 'Joe said…'

'*Joe said.*'

'Shut up Geoff!' said the Chaplain angrily. It had always taken, in death as well as in life, a lot to try his patience but Geoff was now pushing it to its limit.

'Stop it all of you!'

The three stopped their bickering instantly at the sound of Laura's now clear but distraught voice. Tears were running down Richard's face.

'It's not about you, any one of you; it's about all of us together.' Richard's tear stained face stared up at them. 'Not you Geoff, not you Sammy, or you Chaplain. Arguing won't help any of us.' Laura's voice trailed off into uncontrollable sobs.

'We're sorry,' said the Chaplain weakly.

'Are you?' sobbed Laura.

'Yes,' agreed Geoff looking at the others for some sort of guidance. 'We are.'

Using Richard's hands as best she could, Laura started to wipe away the tears from his eyes. 'Then act like it,' she sniffed, 'We've got to work together and try to work out why things aren't as Joe said they were going to be.'

Head slightly bowed, Geoff moved from the foot of the bed and sat beside Richard's feet. He felt bad, maybe worse than the others, but he felt it was wrong that Joe should have overruled Richard when he'd chosen him. He supposed there must be a reason for it, though he couldn't think of one, but who was he to question? Joe was from Upstairs and he was just a spirit in a mortal's soul, a Soul that was shared by everyone in this little bedroom and more besides. Perhaps it was time for him to grow up and take a hand in his future? All their futures.

'It could be his medication,' said Geoff, standing up to be counted, at last.

'His medication?' repeated Laura, Richard's face looking puzzled.

'They could be acting as an inhibitor or something like.' Geoff's revelation was met by four blank faces, one of which was hidden somewhere in Richard's psyche. 'His medicine could be blocking out Laura and his memory of us.' He tried to explain.

'You know, I think you could be right.' Richard's face suddenly brightened up as something clicked inside Laura. A part she wanted to audition for was that of a pharmacist so she'd got herself a little education down at the local library.

'He is?' said the Chaplain looking doubtfully at Geoff.

Geoff was suddenly feeling very pleased with himself.

'It would explain why just as I think I'm getting close to the surface I'm met with a sudden POW!' explained Laura causing the Chaplain to jump. 'It's as if a fog suddenly comes from nowhere and envelopes me, almost smothering me.'

'And now?'

'It's still there but not so strong. It feels patchy as if it's coming in drifts.' Laura shrugged Richard's shoulders, it was the only way she could explain it.

'But do you think you'll be able to contact him anyway?'

Richard looked at Sammy with what could have been Laura's own eyes. 'I don't know,' she admitted.

77

'Then we have to do something about this medicine,' said the Chaplain getting to his feet with purpose. 'Any ideas?' He looked in Geoff's direction.

'Throw them down the toilet?' suggested Geoff feebly knowing full well that in their current state they could only touch things in the living world. The dead being able to move things was only a figment of the imaginations of clairvoyants. He looked meaningfully at Richard.

They all looked at Richard.

'I can't do it,' said a horrified Laura as she realised what they meant.

'There's no one else,' grimaced Geoff.

'But how? I can hardly move his hands and head. How am I going to get him out of bed, let alone be able to get him to throw his medicine down the toilet?'

'You'll just have to try.'

'How?' said Laura, exasperation setting in.

'While he's asleep?' suggested Sammy.

'That's it,' agreed the Chaplain, 'you'll have to do it while he's sleeping.'

'BUT HOW?' screamed Laura throwing up Richard's hands in what should have been a show of exasperation but instead came across as a peculiar impression of a man with jelly arms.

The Chaplain continued unfazed. 'With practice of course, like now while he's asleep, you'll have to practise.'

Richard's head sagged forward a little as Laura tired with the effort of keeping it up and listening to the Chaplain drone on. 'And if he wakes while I'm doing it?' she whispered. It was a good question and got their attention.

'Er…well,' stammered the Chaplain looking to the others for support. 'I don't…er…know. Geoff?'

For a moment Geoff looked like a rabbit caught in headlights but he managed to rally. 'Maybe he'll think that he's sleepwalking.'

'In bed?'

'Sleepmoving?'

'I used to sleepwalk,' said Sammy with a far away look in his eye. 'Why, I even sleepdanced a couple of times.'

'Did you hurt yourself?' asked Geoff, quick to wriggle out from under the spotlight.

'Nah – well, maybe a couple of times,' admitted Sammy, lost in nostalgic memories.

'That's amazing,' said the Chaplain suitably impressed. 'I mean the dancing of course, not the hurting.'

And so it would have gone on, this Sammy appreciation and ignore everything you don't want to cope with club, if Laura hadn't interrupted. She was way past exasperation now. 'Excuse me!' she said. 'And if I cause Richard to have an accident, then what?' She got their attention back.

The others pulled themselves together under Richard's glare that Laura had partly managed to master.

'You'll have to take it easy I suppose,' said Geoff, not really helping.

Richard's face turned into what Laura hoped looked like a disdainful stare. 'He's only got two weeks to live, or have you all forgotten?'

'We'd better leave you to it then,' said Sammy without much thinking what he was saying.

It wasn't what Laura had expected to hear, considering all their futures hung in the balance. 'Is that it then?' she stormed. 'You're all just going to leave me now and skulk back into the Shadow. Is that all you pitiful bastards can come up with?'

'What else *can* we do?' replied the Chaplain meekly.

Of course he was right; deep down Laura knew there was nothing else they could do. They all knew it. Laura was on her own, figuratively speaking, for the time being.

'Will you be close by?' Laura's voice had changed, sounding small, very feminine and very vulnerable, which was almost comic considering where the voice was coming from. The others didn't laugh though; they were feeling just as vulnerable as Laura was.

'You know we will,' said the Chaplain softly, 'we always have been.'

With that the Chaplain, Sammy and Geoff turned and slowly went back into the Shadow which then disappeared from the living world. As they went Laura knew in her heart that they would be close, but knowing this wasn't enough to stop the tears from coming again.

CHAPTER 11

Laura lay staring up at the ceiling wondering what to do next. Her first attempt at tablet discarding had ended in a disastrous bout of cramp for Richard who'd stomped angrily around the bedroom cursing under his breath.

That had been over an hour ago and Laura was now contemplating her next move, whatever that was going to be. She was also mulling over why Joe had failed to let her in on a certain little secret, a little detail she felt sure she should have been privy to. She'd found that she was able to feel everything, at least up to now, that Richard felt, which at the moment meant that her own calf was still smarting somewhere in Richard's. Worse, she couldn't do anything to help ease it herself. Laura decided to try and take her mind off it.

The ceiling was covered in cracked ice polystyrene tiles, which should long since have been extinct in Richard's era, they looked yellowish. Did Richard smoke? God, she hoped not, the thought of dirty filthy smoke filling her lungs just didn't appeal.

Moving Richard's eyes away from the ceiling, Laura let them fall on the window. There weren't any nets up, just a couple of curtains that Laura couldn't quite make out the colour of in the gloom. Each fixed back to the wall with a tieback. Richard seemed quite domesticated. Laura smiled inwardly, her mother would have quite liked the idea of her bringing someone like Richard back home to Ireland with her, bless her. For a moment Laura's mind started to wander back home but, she couldn't, she couldn't afford the luxury of succumbing to such thoughts. There would be time for such things later, maybe, for the moment though there were more important things at hand.

Laura waited another half hour or so, she guessed this as the clock on the bedside table was turned away from her, before her next attempt. Her leg was feeling a little better so she was going to take a chance. Laura gently raised Richard's head from the pillow, a murmur, she quickly replaced it. Richard turned on his side and gave out a half snort, half snore. Laura found to her annoyance, that she was now facing the bedroom door. She'd quite liked the window view, Richard's robe hung from a peg on the back of it; she thought it looked quite drab; a throwback to some other era perhaps.

Now what did she do? Try again now or wait for she didn't know how long? A complete snore this time and Richard turned more onto his face. Laura groaned inside, she hated men that snored, and tried to concentrate on her task. It was then that she realised fate may have given her a helping hand of sorts. Half of Richard's right leg was hanging tantalisingly over the side of the bed, she could feel it. A *half* chance? No, more than that, something else had happened. Like a forty watt bulb changed for a hundred, it came to her. She'd been going about everything all the wrong way. Why try to will Richard's body to react, as she had been doing, when you were actually sitting in the driver's seat?

Closing her eyes, and Richard's, Laura attempted to shut everything except Richard's body from her mind. She then let her mind roam free. Immediately a multitude of feelings and senses, the like of which she could barely remember, washed over her. Richard's big toe on his right foot twitched, and then his whole right foot moved ever so slightly. She could do this, she knew she could. It was just a matter of sort of wearing Richard; wearing him like a coat – or a new skin. Laura shuddered a little at the thought then concentrated harder, this was it.

*   *   *

'What do you reckon then?' asked Sammy as he and the others stepped back into their own realm of being.

'About what?' replied the Chaplain distractedly. His mind was on other things.

'Laura of course, do you think she can pull it off?'

'We can only pray.'

Sammy stopped in his tracks and turned to Geoff who was lagging slightly behind. 'What does he mean pray? That's a dumb thing to say.'

'I don't know,' shrugged Geoff, watching the Chaplain striding purposefully ahead. 'I guess he means just that.'

'We've got to pray?'

'Why not, it won't do any harm to try and there's nothing else we can do, is there?'

Frowning, the little tramp thought about this for a moment. No he supposed it wouldn't hurt but could he remember how to? It had been a very long time since he'd asked anyone for anything, against his religion so to speak, let alone someone's God. Did he say someone's? Surely he meant his God? Sammy quickly shook himself clear of that particular train of thought, religion and all that jazz. 'Do you think it'll work?' he asked anyway.

'Your guess, Sammy,' said Geoff picking his pace up after the Chaplain who was in danger of leaving them behind.

Sammy stood for a few more moments weighing things up. Would it work? Could there possibly – 'Nah,' he decided out loud. 'Hey Geoff, wait up.'

The Chaplain had been preoccupied with other things when Sammy had asked his question. As the eldest of the Four it was his job to keep the rest informed as to how things were proceeding. And at the moment, as he paused before the door of the Grand Waiting room where the others would be eagerly awaiting news, he didn't know how to.

All the past lives of Richard, his, their connections, were in there waiting for answers to questions that he wasn't sure, no, *knew* he couldn't provide. The Chaplain placed a hand on the door, took a deep breath of nothing and, old habits, he thought, pushed the door open.

Slowly but surely all of Richard's leg, under Laura's guidance, had moved out from under the confines of the duvet and into thin air. And there it now hovered defying gravity, his toes just inches from the carpet and, as Laura saw it, success. There was however one small snag, how did she complete the move without doing some sort of injury to Richard?

Holding her nerve, Laura twisted Richard's body slightly until – yes – a toe was touching the floor. The eagle had landed – a giant step for womankind – Eureka! Only now she was positioned with Richard's face stuck firmly in his pillow. What now, Houston?

Laura twisted again until all of Richard's foot was on *terra firma*. But another problem, his left arm was trapped beneath him / her. Damn! Laura started to rock Richard's body back and forth very gently, her plan to shift Richard's weight onto his right side hoping that the momentum would somehow give her a chance to dislodge the arm beneath.

It had seemed a good idea at the time but a better one would have seen her taking the other bedside cabinet into account. Richard's left arm was free but he was now firmly face down on his pillow and wedged tight against the cabinet. Then something else happened, something odd that Laura found trouble putting her finger on. What the hell was it? Then the penny dropped. Too long dead and fifty odd years of not needing to breathe was the problem, she concluded. But now that had all suddenly changed and a face deep into a pillow didn't bode well for the continuation of that particular need of the living. Richard, she, was suffocating.

Frantically Laura tried to swing Richard off the bed, the time for caution, was out of the window. He'd just have to wake up and to hell with the consequences; a confused and bewildered man was better than a dead one, she knew that for a fact, and besides she wasn't feeling all that bright herself.

Richard's body moved again but it was nowhere near enough, Laura didn't possess the strength yet to move him in one go, and was getting weaker by the second with the effort. What the hell did she do? And then as if by magic, just as panic had got half a foot in the doorway, that old one hundred watt popped back into being and Laura knew what she had to do. She had to let go, let Richard's own inbuilt defence mechanisms take control. Laura did just that and moments later Richard rolled coughing and spluttering to the floor.

A sea of faces stared up at the Chaplain as he prepared to address them. He felt nervous, which was strange, he couldn't remember the last time he had felt that way. The Chaplain thought back, it was when he was alive he was sure; it was when he was in the trenches.

The Chaplain was having a touch of déjà-vu. The faces that were looking up at him had the same haunted look on them as he'd seen many times during the Great War. They held the look of people going into the unknown, of people going over the top. The Chaplain quickly whispered a little prayer and then began to speak.

Putting the beaker down, the water had felt cool against his sore throat, Richard looked closer at the reflection staring back at him from the bathroom mirror. Had he looked that old before the hospital jaunt? Richard touched his face, it seemed swollen. Maybe, or maybe it was due to the choking fit he'd just experienced. And that was something, what the hell happened there? If it wasn't for the fact that he was alone and certain he'd locked the house up tight he'd have sworn somebody had tried to smother him. The face in the mirror stared back; it wasn't giving any clues. Shivering a little, though not from any cold, his house was always warm, something he prided himself on, Richard left the mirror behind and went back to the bedroom. Outside, the night was reluctantly relinquishing its hold to the start of another day.

Sitting on the bed Richard surveyed the mess his choking fit had produced. The bedside cabinet laid on its side, its single drawer broken, contents strewn across the carpet. Deciding that he was too tired to start any clean-up operations right then but also deciding that he wasn't tired enough to want to sleep any longer, maybe he'd slept himself out over the last few weeks, Richard decided to get up. Kicking aside a sock from his path Richard's mind turned to the idea of breakfast. Maybe that's what he needed, a good old fashioned high cholesterol breakfast, something you couldn't get for love nor money back in the hospital; something solid to get him back on his feet again. His stomach suddenly rumbled with unadulterated anticipation at the thought of it.

And not too far away, a relieved someone was eagerly agreeing.

It had come as a bit of a shock to Laura when she discovered that she was still connected to Richard, in the physical sense, while he was conscious. The feeling as she felt Richard's movement was both frightening and exciting to her. Frightening as doing anything taboo is – exciting as in everything that was happening, especially the aroma, again something that had existed until now as a distant memory, of bacon and sausages happily frying in the pan.

Joe had said that the only thing linked would be their minds, apart from that is when Richard was asleep, she could then be in a position of control over the sleeping body, something Joe had vehemently advised her against actually doing. Laura hoped he would understand that last night had been an emergency.

Laura watched with mounting anticipation as Richard busied himself about the small kitchen. Things were slowly coming back to her, things long forgotten since her passing away. How could she have possibly forgotten the simple pleasure in taking a cup of tea? But forget she had and how she now marvelled at its refreshing taste, instantly bringing with it memories of other times, other places and then people. But Laura was awake to the fact that she dare not dwell on such things, the past was the past, she was there for the future.

After a while Laura found she wanted to go further than tastes and smells. But she hesitated, she knew she couldn't. She wanted to touch things, the softness of wool, the coolness of cotton. She knew she shouldn't. Of course she'd felt what Richard had felt, the seat he was sitting on, the cup which held the tea. Felt the food in his mouth and the soreness as the crispy bacon, (Laura felt he should have taken it out of the pan sooner,) had scratched its way down Richard's throat. But Laura wanted more, much more. She wanted to feel things for herself, not just the things Richard chose to touch. She had a sudden and dangerous urge to touch everything. An urge she was finding harder and harder to control.

And that's how Richard found himself, for no apparent reason, rubbing a clean cotton tea-towel against his face.

CHAPTER 12

Nothing the Chaplain could say would appease the unhappy crowd milling listlessly below him as he stood on the Podium of Four. How he'd ever likened the brave men of the Great War with this rabble standing before him he couldn't understand.

'Wot's 'appening?' shouted Lillian, a rather large, dubious looking woman, at the top of her voice. Lillian, Lil' to her "friends", had met her end during the Great Fire of London, though not at the hands of the fire. Mister – "nuffin I could of dun" – Lillian had enjoyed a long, happy, and very peaceful life after his beloved had so sadly, yet conveniently, "perished in the flames".

'Oi! I said, wot's 'appening?'

The Chaplain was trying hard to ignore the woman. He'd seen her many times around the place but had only stopped and chatted the once when he'd been introduced as a new death and his memory still burned with the embarrassment of it. He, under the mistaken belief that Lillian had held the admirable position of working in the nursing profession when alive, had asked her quite innocently if she'd enjoyed her job. It turned out that "Lady of the Lamp" held an entirely different meaning where Lillian was concerned. The Chaplain had hurriedly scurried to some dark corner or other with Lillian and Joe's laughter, (it was the Joe from Downstairs who'd made the introductions,) ringing in his ears. Yes, once had been quite more than enough.

'Cum on Rev'rant wot's 'appening?' she yelled again in her nearly cockney accent.

The Chaplain, now getting a little hot under the collar, decided he had no recourse but to answer the annoying woman's questions. 'As I've said,' he rallied, trying not to look directly at her, 'All will be well. I assure you, now-.'

'Yeah, cum on Rev'rand, tell the boys what's "appening" why dun't yer.'

The mimicking voice cutting through the Chaplain's assurances was one he instantly recognized as Joe's. Typical of him to stick his oar in when one had his back to the wall, thought the Chaplain, getting as uncharitable as it was possible for him to get. Since Joe's demotion from the Four, when Geoff arrived, he was always trying to throw what authority he thought he had about. Once a cop, always a cop and a New York one at that, not that the Chaplain had anything against New York cops of course, or cops in general, but they tended to be louder in his book than other policemen, as he preferred to call them. Sometimes he wondered how their mutual Soul had achieved such diverse diversity.

'Please be patient,' said the Chaplain, again not looking directly at his verbal assailant. 'We have plenty of time.'

'Would yer look at him, butter wouldn't melt in 'is mouth so it wouldn't,' retaliated Joe winding up the surrounding audience as he did. 'But it's nothing but blarney so it is, isn't it Rev'rand? Yer nothing but an old gobshite!'

The Chaplain, his collar near to melting point, turned to Sammy and Geoff, who were standing just behind him, for a bit of support but as soon as he looked at them he knew he was on his own. Geoff had adopted the caught in a car's headlights look and Sammy – well, Sammy looked as if he was asleep.

'Sammy?' said the Chaplain, concern managing to find a way through his troubled mind.

But before he was able to get an answer, Joe, who'd managed to push his way through the crowd, started to clamber up on to the Podium.

'Now Joe,' protested the Chaplain, feeling things were gradually pushing him out of his depth. Laura had always been the only one able to pacify Joe when he went off on one. 'I'm afraid I must protest and ask you to leave the Podium immediately.'

'And why in the world would'ya be wanting me to do that Reverend?' said Joe, winking vigorously. 'I thought you of all people would be pleased to see me?' Joe gave another wink then proceeded to talk to the crowd in an incredibly false Irish accent.

When he'd finished, the whole room lay under a veil of tranquillity. Joe turned to the Chaplain who'd nearly fallen from the Podium with shock when it had clicked that a switch had taken place. 'I don't think we'll be having any more problems from them.' Another wink. 'And thank you.' Joe spoke this in almost a whisper, seemingly directing his words towards Sammy but in a way so as no one would notice.

The Chaplain, still a little stunned, thanked Joe in return but then found he hadn't the foggiest idea why. He knew he'd heard Joe speaking to the crowd but for the life of him he couldn't remember a single word of what had been said. And now he came to think about it, he couldn't remember what the problem had been, if indeed there had been one.

'Now I must go,' said Joe raising his arms in a prophetic gesture, 'as the time for you all to join Laura in the living world is nearly upon us. But before that time comes,' a look of concern crossed Joe's face, 'I think it would be wise of you to visit Richard as soon as possible whilst still in your current condition.'

Sammy, now alert but a little perplexed, Geoff and the Chaplain looked at each other; they knew they had to join Laura sometime, but now, so soon, had time gone so quickly? Surely they were supposed to go nearer to Richard's death, to his choice? But things were becoming confused, of course they had to be with Richard when Laura makes contact, but surely – surely they weren't ready – were they?

'When?' started the Chaplain but his voice fell on empty space, Joe was already gone, his New York vessel clambering bewildered from the podium.

'What do we do now?' worried Geoff as his mind wandered into the unknown which was his immediate future.

'And what did he mean when he said it would be wise to see Richard A.S.A.P?' queried a puzzled Sammy.

But the Chaplain was as much in the dark as they were and could only shrug his shoulders. In his mind though, he couldn't help but worry that something was wrong and that that something was to do with Laura.

CHAPTER 13

Richard threw the tea-towel to the floor and stared at it as though it had more than the usual two heads you would normally associate with something not quite right. Why the hell had he just held the tea-towel to his face like that for no apparent reason? Was he going mad? Richard calmed a little when it was obvious the tea-towel wasn't going to get up and move by itself and began to rationalize. Maybe it was a backlash from his injury, a nerve re-aligning or something? Richard gingerly plucked the tea-towel from the floor and threw it into the washing machine. Maybe the bloody thing was haunted? He quickly slammed the door shut after it. Or maybe he was more tired than he realised?

Reason set in and Richard settled for tiredness as the culprit for the tea-towels shenanigans. He was just exhausted after all that he had been through over the last few weeks and had simply done it without thinking. That was all it was. Richard decided to have a lie down and take a couple of the pills the hospital had supplied him with. Half an hour later Richard was back on his bed and totally dead to the world.

What had she done? Laura was horrified as she resurfaced. She'd just grabbed at the tea-towel without thinking. No — that was a lie and she knew it. She had been thinking and only too well. Laura had w*anted* and Laura had g*ot*. She had been selfish with no thought as to how Richard might react. And look where selfishness had got her last time, skidding on her backside across wet tarmac and into the side of a bus, that's where. Although in her defence, as far as this instance of selfishness was concerned, she hadn't really expected anything to happen, she was, well almost, as surprised as Richard when it had. Her mind turned to Joe and again she hoped he'd understand. In the meantime Laura determined to pull herself together and be more guarded against other weak moments, but she had the horrible feeling that that was not going to be easy.

Laura stared up at the ceiling and tried not to think, she'd decided that it was bad for her. Drat! she thought, as she realised she was doing just that. But things would be all right, wouldn't they? And the others would be back that night as arranged, when Richard was in his deepest sleep and the pills he was taking were at their weakest, this was a general consensus, based only on their conclusion about the pills' effect being right. Laura hoped they were, if Richard was to catch a glimpse of them before she'd had a chance to contact his mind she didn't dare think what might happen. What about the tea-towel though? Damn! She was doing it again, thinking.

Time passed by and Laura was still trying to blank her mind. But not only was she still thinking but now she had the urge to pull the curtains back that Richard had drawn, so she could see the day.

'Blank-blank-blank,' she told herself as loudly as she could in her mind. At least she assumed she was saying it in her mind. But she wasn't sure; she thought she'd better check. Laura slowly opened Richards's eyes to see, she'd closed them to help her avoid seeing the curtains, it didn't answer her question though, but at least she could be thankful that Richard was still asleep and in the same position.

Laura gently turned Richard's head to face the bedside cabinet that was still standing; he'd placed the pills he was taking on top of it. Maybe she could do it now, throw the pills away – problem solved and the way would be open for contact. But he wasn't in a deep sleep, what if he was to wake as she was tipping them down the toilet?

'Oh stop thinking!' Laura went suddenly quiet, that was her wasn't it? Of course it was, who else could it be? Laura lay perfectly still and did the opposite. What she had to do of course was to think. Think as much as she could, firstly, it would, hopefully, keep her sane, secondly, while she was thinking she wasn't doing anything physical. She found herself checking again to make sure Richard was still in the same position, he was and Laura relaxed. She could feel his breathing, his lungs gently inhaling then exhaling, feel it in her own lungs so long devoid of such a necessity. Laura started to count her blessings and relaxed further but in the back of her mind she knew it wouldn't last, this small oasis of tranquillity, soon her thoughts would turn to action again, bringing back that particular anguish. Laura knew she needed the others; she wasn't strong enough on her own, but could she hold on? She hoped she could.

While it was deemed unusual for "ghosts" to be abroad in broad daylight it wasn't impossible, though on the whole it was frowned on and not advised by the Upstairs. The dead after all were meant to walk the night. Why? No one really knew the reason, it was just written that way. So across the room, unbeknown to Laura in her struggle, Sammy, Geoff and the Chaplain were looking on with slight apprehension.

'Are you sure it's safe to be here?' worried Geoff, nervously glancing at the daylight beyond the curtains.

'As long as we stay in the Shadow, I believe,' replied the Chaplain uncertainly.

'She looks okay to me,' observed Sammy, looking at Richard while at the same time wondering if his statement was as stupid as it sounded.

'That is to be seen, we shall find out soon enough tonight. In the meantime I think we should take turns to watch her,' suggested the Chaplain, his voice a lot calmer than he was.

'But we can't see her,' said Geoff.

'Richard then.'

'But then what, if anything happens? We won't be able to do anything,' pointed out Sammy.

'Let us hope nothing happens then, shall we?' replied the Chaplain dryly.

'Why can't we see her again?' asked Geoff, now absorbed in the fact that he couldn't, and needing the point clarified once more.

'Because she's inside Richard,' answered the Chaplain, refusing to condemn Geoff as being as stupid as he sometimes was.

'Oh – right,' said Geoff, realizing that he may have given away just how stupid he could be.

'Where are the others going?' asked Sammy after a few seconds of silence and hard thinking on his part.

'Others who?' said the Chaplain, still a tad irritated by Geoff's stupid question.

'The others who aren't watching Laura.'

'Nowhere, everyone stays together.'

'But you said…'

'It was a figure of speech,' said the exasperated Chaplain. Couldn't they see that there were more important matters afoot? 'Now let's settle down and wait, and give the stupid questions a rest.'

And after Geoff had thought of another stupid question, but had then thought better of asking it, that's exactly what they did.

The day wore on and at about mid-day Richard roused himself, got up, and left the room. The three watched from the Shadow. Everything appeared fine so far. Moments later Richard reappeared but only to pick up his pills, and that was the last they saw of him until later that night. It had been decided that it was best not to leave the safety of the Shadow and follow.

Just after the clock in the bedroom declared the witching hour Richard returned. He looked refreshed – well, fresher –

and happier than they'd ever seen him, which they were happy to take as a sign that nothing untoward had happened whilst he'd been out of their sight. The three relaxed a little and were beginning to think that perhaps Joe's portent of trouble may have been wrong.

'He looks okay,' said Geoff straining to see what Richard had in his hand.

'Yes, but complacency killed the cat,' stated Sammy seriously, tapping the side of his nose with a finger.

'Curiosity,' corrected the Chaplain.

'Not the one I'm thinking of,' said Sammy indignantly.

'What happened?' asked Geoff giving up on his scrutiny of Richard's right hand.

'Never mind,' said the Chaplain cutting the conversation off at the pass before it could start down the road to tedium. 'I think we should be concentrating on Laura and Richard. He's beginning to look a little tired, hopefully he'll fall asleep soon and we will be able contact Laura and see if she can throw any light on what Joe was saying.'

Richard meanwhile had crept under his duvet and was now sitting propped up, with the help of his pillows, against the headboard.

'He doesn't look all that sleepy,' said a miffed Sammy, now intent on contradicting for the sake of it after having his tale cut short.

'What's he reading?' asked Geoff, turning his attention back to what Richard had been carrying and turning his back on the small cold war brewing behind him.

'Does it matter?' snapped the Chaplain, narrowing his eyes at Sammy.

'It's just that I don't recognize, it that's all.'

'That's because you've been dead these past thirty nine years man!'

'I only asked,' said Geoff, visibly shrinking under the Chaplain's sudden onslaught.

'He was only asking,' backed up Sammy, coming to Geoff's defence.

'Good grief! What is wrong with you both?' But even as the Chaplain growled his words it dawned on him that there was nothing wrong with either of them, it was him. He was the one with the problem.

The problem was that he was worried. He'd been worried since the day he'd been told of Richard's accident. He was worried that all that he held sacred would be lost, from his stiff upper lip to his beliefs; that he was helpless to do anything about it. But this wasn't the way to go on. What was he doing? Saying? This self pity. Where was his faith?

Awash with sudden guilt, the Chaplain looked at Geoff and for the first time realised just how young he was; how young he'd been at the time of his death. And the tramp, he was now seeing that Sammy was dealing with things in his own way. He was just being himself, that's all; the best way he could in the circumstances. The Chaplain opened his mouth to speak and for the first time in his life, or death for that matter, he found he was about to admit to being worried – no, not worried – afraid. 'I'm sorry,' he said holding his head in his hands. 'I don't know what came over me.'

Sammy went to speak but the Chaplain stopped him.

'No, that's a lie,' he said, looking Sammy in the eyes, 'I do know.'

'That's okay, you don't have to say anything,' said Sammy, instantly understanding. Sammy wasn't just a pretty face and empathy could easily have been his middle name.

'But I do, Sammy, that's the point. I do.' As the Chaplain spoke, a small wonder of impossibility happened, a small grey globule slipped from the corner of his eye and slid slowly down his cheek. 'I'm frightened, Sammy and worse still I'm taking it out on you two dear friends.'

Geoff felt himself welling up inside and turned away as Sammy put a comforting hand on the Chaplain's arm.

'As we keep saying, we're all in this together. We've just got to remember, that's all,' said the little tramp, trying to be reassuring.

The Chaplain sniffed, which didn't actually achieve anything, and nodded. 'Thank you Sammy, you are a good friend.'

'No, I'm not, I'm more than that. I'm another part of you, of Geoff,' Sammy pointed to Richard on the bed, 'of him. We're all the same.'

Sammy's little speech had a direct effect on the Chaplain. 'You're right,' he said, brightening up considerably.

'I know I am,' smiled Sammy.

'Although,' said the Chaplain quietly, a frown forming, 'there is just one little thing that still concerns me.'

'Spill,' said Sammy with an accent from his younger happier days.

'It's what Joe said.'

'You mean joining Laura quicker than expected?'

'I mean the how?'

As if awakening from deep sleep Laura's eyes gently flickered open. For a moment she wasn't sure where she was. She lay still and stared straight ahead for a moment or two. Then she remembered the fog, not a real one, but one that had invaded her mind. Laura tried to think. The fog had appeared a while after Richard had gone back to bed, while she was trying hard to combat the urges she'd been having. It then came back to her, she remembered how she'd been thinking that the fog was something to do with the pills Richard had taken, the extra one he'd taken, and how once realising this she had welcomed it and the peace it was bringing.

Everything felt all right. Laura slowly moved her eyes to the right, the bedside lamp was on. What time was it? Was it night already? Laura decided that it must be; she'd been in the fog for what seemed ages. What Laura hadn't decided though was whether Richard was awake.

It was obvious that he'd been moving around the house since her drug induced stupor, the lamp being on was proof, also the magazine that he was holding in his hands. Laura tried a peek down at it. It was lying open at its centre, a picture covering both pages, but she couldn't quite make out what it was a picture of. Laura, the fog gone but having left a mark, finally slumped back with the effort. Or had Richard?

The sudden thought that she may have moved Richard again without thinking filled her with trepidation. Laura lay perfectly still and waited; as she did, a new fear gripped her. What if Richard was at that very moment trying to move and found that he couldn't? Who was lying still, her or Richard, or both in an immovable tug of war?

This was stupid, she had to pull herself together, she was getting paranoid. Laura calmed, she could feel herself lying still, could feel Richard, his blood flowing through his veins, the steady breathing that would have told her that Richard was asleep. She had to relax and get a grip. Detach herself or she would find herself no more than a quaking obsessive jelly.

Laura took a slow deep breath, at least it felt like one, and concentrated. It was working; she could feel herself taking control of her body and mind. She could now feel that Richard was asleep. He must have dropped off whilst sitting up in bed reading the magazine she had been unable to make out. As gently as she could, she moved her – Richard's – head until she could see the clock's face. It was half past three; the others should have been here by now. Carefully moving Richard's head back to the forward position she looked towards the foot of the bed.

The shadows were darker tonight, there was no moon to cast its eerie light into hidden corners, but they were ordinary shadows that she was seeing.

Laura, now confident that Richard was out for the count, shifted on the bed, pushing him into a more comfortable position. The crick in the neck that he was well on the way to getting was also affecting her. There was a slight worrying click as Laura twisted Richard's neck but at least the ache eased. She shivered. A sudden coldness had come on the room sending goose pimples across her and Richard's shoulders. At the foot of the bed the shadows were getting even darker, denser, gaining substance. The others were here.

Sammy stepped first from the Shadow, his dirty face one broad grin. Following close behind came Geoff, he too looked like the cat that had got the cream.

'What are you two so happy about?' asked Laura suspiciously. They were so buoyant they could have raised the Titanic.

'Nothing really,' said Sammy, perching himself on the edge of the bed.

'There must be something,' said Laura, curiosity getting hold.

'They are just happy to be…,' the Chaplain paused as he stepped from the Shadow's depths. 'Just happy to be,' he finished. 'And you Laura, *how* are you?'

Laura instantly thought the question sounded strange. Something in the way the Chaplain had asked it, the way he was standing, lips pursed, hands clasped together in a way that only clerics and money lenders could achieve. But she answered anyway.

'Good, good,' gushed the Chaplain looking altogether the pious gatherer of the flock.

'What's going on?' Laura hadn't liked the question and she definitely didn't like the way they were all looking at her. 'Have I got two heads or something?' At this point she thought she had better check just in case she had somehow drifted from Richard's mortal coil without realising. She hadn't, so, using her female senses, deduced that they were up to something.

'There is nothing going on,' assured the Chaplain, who was as good a liar as he was a sinner.

'Bollocks!' Laura narrowed Richard's eyes.

'Now Laura,' a note of panic was in the Chaplain's voice as, for the first time, the idea occurred to him that maybe Laura wasn't the soft touch he thought she was.

'Don't "Now Laura" me. You know you can't lie to save your own life, Chaplain.' As the Chaplain tried hard to contain a greyish blush, Laura turned her attention to what she regarded as the weakest link in this little chain of intriguing deceit. 'Well Geoff, what's up?'

Geoff glanced nervously at the other two for help but none was forthcoming, he was on his own.

'Well!' demanded Laura.

'Joe said,' said Geoff, who'd obviously decided why put one foot in it when you can put two.

'What?' snapped Laura, glaring at the fast wilting Geoff who gave one last imploring look at the others for help.

Sammy shrugged hopelessly; he knew when the game was up. And the Chaplain, well, he felt he'd done enough damage already.

'Joe said…' stammered Geoff nervously.

'Joe said?' demanded an increasingly irate Laura.

'He said we had to visit you and…'

'And what?'

'And…I mean…as soon as possible.'

'You said "And",' said Laura now smelling the rotten odour of conspiracy.

'I meant as,' said Geoff weakly.

Glaring furiously Laura turned the full force of her gaze from Geoff to the Chaplain and then on to Sammy.

Wincing under the force of it, Sammy felt he had to say something, whatever the consequences, after all Joe hadn't said not to tell Laura anything. As a matter of fact Joe hadn't really said an awful lot. 'He's telling the truth Laura,' he finally blurted.

'And are you?' came the acid reply.

Sammy all of a sudden felt terribly guilty without quite knowing why. 'Yes – but.'

102

There's always a but, thought Laura.

'Joe said it differently,' Sammy tried to explain, 'he made it sound sort of urgent.'

'Urgent?' questioned Laura, her glare intensifying.

This was it, thought Sammy, in for a penny, in for a pound as they say. 'As though there was a problem with you.' There he'd said it, but he found he was lacking that certain warm glow he'd associated with the act of confession.

For a very long moment Laura just stared at Sammy. But any hopes he or the others had concerning an amicable ending to proceedings were dashed as Laura exploded.

'What the hell do you mean a problem with me?' she seethed. 'What sort of a bloody statement is that?'

Horrified, Sammy looked to the Chaplain; he'd never known Laura so angry before. The Chaplain stepped forward aiming to remove the *thorn from the foot* and calm Laura down but this only succeeded in making Laura all the more angry. She didn't need pacifying by some overbearing dog-collar.

'Get out!' she screamed, giving scant regard to where she was or who she was in. 'Get out – get out!'

'But Richard?' said the Chaplain still trying to placate.

'Sod Richard,' snarled Laura, her face, or rather Richard's, a scowling mask of anger. 'And sod you!' With that Laura threw a pillow at the beseeching chaplain.

Thinking that now was as good a time as any to leave, the three scurried back to the safety of the Shadow. Outside Laura had left the bed and was now shouting, facing the Shadow and its occupants.

'Maybe we should go,' suggested a mortified Geoff.

They all agreed and, as it had arrived, so the Shadow left, leaving the fury of Laura behind.

CHAPTER 14

The Chaplain, Sammy, and Geoff stepped from the Shadow, glad to be back on their own side.

'Well that went well – not,' said Geoff stating the blatantly obvious and confusing the Chaplain with his late twentieth early twenty-first century description of a non-event in the process.

'He means it didn't go well,' interpreted Sammy, noticing the Chaplain's slightly perplexed expression.

'Then why doesn't he say so?' said the Chaplain.

'That's the younger generation for you,' sighed Sammy with fake resignation.

'Older,' corrected the Chaplain, 'technically we're the younger generation.'

'Whatever,' said Sammy dismissively, not wanting to get into some one-sided argument about nothing. A field he felt the Chaplain was an expert in.

'She was well pissed,' continued Geoff to himself as much as to anyone.

The Chaplain didn't ask but assumed that as Laura didn't look inebriated, Geoff had to be referring in some way to her current state of mind.

'She was, wasn't she?' agreed Sammy who was always one of the first to introduce himself to new arrivals, he liked to keep himself up to date as much as possible on fads and fashions in the living world. In life Sammy had always regarded himself as a bit of a swinger. A word which he soon found, when talking to Geoff, was not now used in quite the same context.

'I take it Joe was right then, there is something amiss with Laura.'

'Hallelujah, Chaplain!' said Sammy smiling, 'I think we all agree on that one, but what do we do about it?'

The Chaplain suspected a touch of sarcasm in Sammy's voice but decided to ignore it.

'Maybe Joe will tell us,' said Geoff hopefully.

'Well, I don't know about that,' replied the Chaplain, looking at Geoff thoughtfully. 'I have the feeling that we won't be seeing Joe for some time. Don't you think so Sammy?' The Chaplain shot Sammy a slightly puzzled glance, which he returned.

'Yeah, I know what you mean Chaplain,' agreed Sammy, his answer double-edged. 'Don't you feel that Geoff?' he asked, frowning.

'I don't know what I feel,' Geoff admitted, shrugging his shoulders. 'I just wish Joe would tell us what to do and tell us who we're supposed to be sharing with on the other side. I don't like this waiting about.'

'You mean which form we will be taking,' corrected the Chaplain, who instantly began to regret his words when he saw the furrows on Geoff's worried brow deepen.

'What do you mean?' Geoff had gone a lighter shade of grey as he fought to understand what he was hearing.

'What I meant was…was that…' The Chaplain was struggling. He'd opened his mouth without thinking when it should have been clear that, for some unknown reason, Joe, or whoever pulled his strings, Upstairs, had decided to keep Geoff in the dark about certain things. And looking at Geoff the Chaplain now realised that compared to Sammy and himself, with their singular fears, Geoff was harbouring a whole armada of unanswered ones that hadn't needed adding to. 'That.' finished the Chaplain, hoping that that would be just that.

'What he means,' broke in Sammy, who, for a fleeting moment, in the Chaplain's eyes, appeared to be wearing shining armour, 'is what form the Transition will take.' It was flimsy and sounded so even to Sammy's ears. 'Didn't you Chaplain?'

'Er – yes,' agreed the Chaplain grateful for Sammy's intervention, 'that is exactly what I meant.'

For a moment or two Geoff looked uncertain as he thought over what Sammy and the Chaplain had said. 'You mean male or female?' Geoff said at last, a slight uncertainty to his voice, although he did sound a little brighter.

The others who'd been waiting with a mixture of apprehension and puzzlement hadn't a clue where Geoff's conclusion had come from, but, any port in a storm.

'That's exactly what I meant,' said the Chaplain lying through his teeth and praying at the same time that he sounded sincere. He would, he vowed, pray later for forgiveness for his indiscretions.

'And it doesn't matter whether it's male *or* female?' enquired Geoff, with more than a slight emphasis on female, which the others thought it better to ignore. There was no point in rocking the boat now that it was happily bobbing beside the quay.

'I doubt so,' said the Chaplain more than happy to play along now that it looked like he'd got away with his slip.

'And now that that little misunderstanding looks to have been resolved,' said Sammy nipping in quickly before the Chaplain got carried away, 'how about one of us goes back and checks to see if Laura's managed to calm down a bit?'

'Well, I don't think…' started the Chaplain, before a winking Sammy stopped him.

'But it would be a good idea just to check.' Sammy nodded his head in Geoff's direction. 'Don't you think Chaplain?'

'What? Oh…I see,' said the Chaplain, but not that clearly.

'How about it Geoff? Fancy popping back discreetly to see how Laura's doing?'

'Sorry?' said Geoff, who, for the moment, seemed to be somewhere else.

'Would you pop back and have a look in on how Laura's doing?' repeated Sammy.

'Yeah okay,' agreed Geoff vaguely as visions of females of all shapes and sizes paraded before him in the little world he was occupying, 'no problem. I'll see you in a while.' He turned to go.

'Don't let her know you're there,' reminded Sammy.

'I won't,' Geoff called back as he entered the Shadow.

A few seconds later, when Sammy was sure Geoff had gone, he turned and faced the Chaplain with a bemused look on his face. 'He doesn't know, does he?'

'It would seem not,' agreed the Chaplain grimly.

'But why? It doesn't make any sense, why shouldn't he know what's going to happen to us? What do you think Joe's playing at?'

'I have no idea,' said the Chaplain, frowning. 'But it could have something to do with why he chose Laura rather than Geoff to join Richard.'

'Do you think he's too young or something? I mean being both young in age and in his time with us.'

'Like I said, I have no idea. It could be for any reason.'

'It's going to be a bit of a shock for him.'

'I believe it will,' agreed the Chaplain nodding. 'I just hope it won't be too much of one, we may need him on the other side, especially with the way Laura is playing up at the moment.'

There was a moment or two of reflection before either of them spoke again, their minds travelling different yet parallel paths. Thoughts of the present and of all that had happened since their respective arrivals in the afterlife came to their minds. The feeling of being shrouded, almost suffocated, in the mysteries that it held. And how, when questions had formed in their minds at the very beginning about the how and why's of their new existence, other questions had too

108

quickly followed behind, urgently fighting for understanding themselves, jostling for a place, uncontrollably knocking those before from their minds, before they'd had a chance to glean an answer. And how the more you had struggled to fight the flow, the more you'd got weighed down until all that was left was the feeling that things were best left alone; then and now.

Sammy broke the silence with the question that had been last on his mind. 'Do you think one of us would have been better going in Laura's place?' he said; the feeling of an unreachable itch irritating somewhere inside.

'It is too late now although I am still of the belief that Joe does know best,' said the Chaplain retrieving a little of his faith. 'And as someone once said, "That which the heart does not know the heart does not grieve over," or something like that. My memory isn't what it used to be.'

'I suppose you're right,' conceded Sammy, 'but I can't help but feel sorry for Geoff going into the unknown like he is. When do you think they will happen?'

'The Transitions?'

'What else?'

'Anytime I suppose.'

'Which do you want?'

'I know the one I don't?' replied the Chaplain, grimacing at the thought.

While the others were pondering their respective fates back in the afterlife, Laura was climbing back into bed. She rearranged the pillows, took a quick glance at the cover of the magazine Richard had been reading – SOLAR POWER-THE NEXT GENERATION –, discarded it then laid down to once again study the polystyrene ice flow on Richard's bedroom ceiling.

Laura was in a dilemma. She could be asking herself why she had flown into such a rage with the others, doing a little soul-searching maybe, but there was no need to because Laura

109

already knew the answers, the reasons for why she'd acted the way she had. She gathered they knew, or at least Joe did, she was sure, about her shortcomings. That's why she'd blown a convenient fuse.

She stared hard at the ceiling. Joe had explained as simply as possible how simple everything would be, so why the problems? And it was no good blaming Richard's medication, for her they were just a convenient excuse. Problems there were, things were not easy, and these things were getting out of control; *she* was getting out of control. She wanted to touch, to see things, to breathe deeply of the early morning air. And though she knew, if she was patient, she could do all of these through Richard, it wasn't enough. Laura wanted the choice, she wanted to do these things when she felt she wanted to, not have to wait.

A decision lay before her like a fork in the road but Laura knew that it wasn't going to be that straightforward. Whichever path she decided upon would throw up numerous other forks and barriers. Would any of them ultimately lead to the finish point she and the others so dearly wanted? To the Light and whatever lay beyond? The pressure was building. Turning Richard's head, she looked at the small plastic tub sitting on the bedside cabinet that held his pills. Laura stretched out a hand and took the tub of tablets from the cabinet. Flipping its lid she looked inside. The fork in the road had suddenly become a crossroads.

CHAPTER 15

Problems, choices, decisions were not the exclusive domain of the mortal being. Even as Laura struggled with hers, there sat, in a place far removed from any reality perceived by the living – or dead – world, a lone solitary figure, a figure that was something to all mortal men and women yet existed in many different guises in their mortal minds and visions.

The sitting figure appeared still; yet a watchful eye would swear that a continuous myriad of wondrous changes were taking place within a blinking of that eye. Wings, the colour of the whitest of doves, shimmering for a measurement of time, barely existing, replaced by the weight of a world. An old face, a serene face adored, the face of some nameless creature to be feared in the darkest of places, then that of another to be held in wondrous awe. The figure wore, carried, all of these, was all of these and more and yet as immortal and as wondrous as the figure was, it was troubled, troubled by things that the merest mortal would cast aside as trifles not to be bothered with. But then they didn't know what this creature knew and as such this was the figure's lot. He was the beginning, the catalyst, the end. He was Joe; he wasn't.

Joe sat and wondered how he had let things come to this. He stared out at the endless nothingness that surrounded him, wondering. Why was he so troubled by this Soul? Because all that is, and would be, rested with it; it would be the first one ever, contrary to mortal beliefs, not to reach the sanctity of the Light.

He rose and as he did so the shimmerings sped and changed until they were but an intangible blur, and in that moment he was Joe and yet not so. Joe stood and the

111

shimmerings suddenly stopped their manifestations and he was as the Four saw him, just a man. Reaching his arms out fully above him he gave voice, though as no mortal being could or ever would.

'And what will become of *me* if I fail?' he beseeched, the sound of his voice echoing as a hundred thunderclaps at once amongst the endless nothingness about him. Cracking and whipping as it sought something on which it could conduct its awesome power.

But, like Laura, there was no need for his questions as the answers were already within him, had always been within. Pulsing, pushing with a ghastly force that could, would if unleashed, lay waste to mountains and civilisations at no more than a whim, a power that needed only the merest of cracks to pour forth with its rabid lust for a new and terrible existence. Joe held his breast and pushed back on the ceaseless movement within. He held until the force relented and ebbed and when at last it did, he fell weeping with the effort and relief to his knees. But even as the sweet relief filled his body he knew the beast within lay but a mortal man's skin away, and that another failure could see it win through and burst forth. And then what?

Joe slowly got to his feet, his body bruised and battered, as this other futile question surfaced, yet another he had the answer to. But now as he stood there, ragged as he was, he knew that it was long past the time for the final passing, for all his bold statements to the contrary, and he knew that Destiny was eager and looking over his shoulder, waiting for the choice to be made.

But it wasn't Joe's to make, that belonged to the poor Soul whose last spirit was encased in its last mortal coil. The Spirit belonging to the mortal called Richard had to make it and it was the hardest one of all, for in it lay the Destiny that would shape the future of all things.

CHAPTER 16

'Do you think we should call him back yet?' asked Sammy who sat cross-legged and staring intently at a gaping hole in the sole of his right boot. He was wondering how long it had been there.

'I don't see that it matters one way or the other,' came an almost but not quite despondent reply.

Just how long it was that they had been waiting for the supposedly imminent transition to the other side was anyone's guess and it was beginning to take its toll.

'I think we should.'

'Go ahead then.'

'But what if he starts asking questions again?' said Sammy, prising himself away from the hole and squinting up at the Chaplain. He was squinting because he could, no other reason.

'Then don't – look, haven't you anything else to do?'

Sammy found himself thinking this over for a moment or two before answering. 'I can't remember,' he said.

'What do you mean you can't remember? What sort of answer is that?'

'I just can't,' said Sammy rising, his face looking puzzled leaning towards worried. 'I can't seem to remember anything past us sending Geoff back to Laura.'

'Rubbish!' said the Chaplain giving the idea short shrift. He knew how Sammy could be.

'But I tell you I can't!' A small amount of panic working its way into Sammy's voice was just enough to make the Chaplain sit up and take notice.

'Are you sure you're not pulling my leg?'

'You try,' said Sammy, furrows etched across his brow.

Still not entirely convinced that Sammy was telling the truth, but impelled just enough by the tone of his voice, the Chaplain tried.

'Well?' asked Sammy, hardly giving the Chaplain a chance to think.

'Sssh!' said the Chaplain, eyes closed. 'I'm concentrating.'

'Well?' repeated Sammy just as impatiently. But this time he didn't need the Chaplain to answer, he knew by the look on his face. 'You can't, can you?'

'I can recall going to see Laura, but,' the Chaplain's voice sounded slightly uneven as he spoke, 'even that is not totally clear.'

'What's it mean?' Sammy and distraught were fast becoming joined at the hip.

The Chaplain looked pensive as he answered. 'I'm not completely sure, but at a very hazardous guess I would say that it has started.'

'What's started?' Sammy moved closer to the Chaplain, looking uneasily around him as he did.

'The Transition.' The Chaplain's voice had evened out again but was now teetering towards excitement. 'I believe the journey may have started.'

'What?…How?' Sammy thought about it. 'Minds first?' he said, looking bewildered.

'It's the only answer,' said the Chaplain, his voice firming with growing conviction.

It was only a guess but Sammy did calm down a little, though there was still an element of alarm in his voice as he spoke. 'Maybe we should get Geoff back,' he said. Strength in numbers, he was thinking.

'It might be for the best,' agreed the Chaplain.

The Shadow arrived back bringing with it a rather shaken Geoff. The Chaplain and Sammy helped him from it.

'Good grief man, what on earth is wrong?' asked the Chaplain, pretty certain he already knew the answer. He was wrong.

'It – it's Richard,' Geoff managed to utter, dashing the Chaplain's theory. Geoff covered his face with his hands as despair threatened to overcome him.

'What's wrong with him?' said Sammy, a horrible feeling rising in his gut.

'For goodness sake man, tell us what's wrong!' As the Chaplain spoke he prised, with some effort, Geoff's hands away from his face.

Geoff looked up into the Chaplain's face and mouthed something.

'What did he say?' asked Sammy, the look on his face now almost as bad as Geoff's. Things were going badly wrong, he just knew it, first the memory loss, now this. Sammy started to pace.

'Say that again Geoff, I couldn't quite make it out,' said the Chaplain, trying hard to ignore Sammy as he strained to hear what Geoff was trying to say. The reply from Geoff was barely audible but the Chaplain did manage to catch it this time. He turned away and faced Sammy, his face substantially gaunter, substantially greyer.

This was altogether too much for Sammy who began to get quite theatrical. 'He's dead, isn't he?' he wailed before the Chaplain had a chance to speak. 'I knew things would turn out bad – I just knew it.' Sammy's arms began to flail wildly as his pacing increased. 'No silver lining this time. Oh no, not this time. I'm never going to see the Light. Never. Never am, I…' Sammy's ranting was abruptly stopped short as the flat of the Chaplain's right hand caught him across the side of his face.

It worked, Sammy stopped his wailing and stared shocked and open-mouthed at the Chaplain who was already apologising. 'I'm sorry but it had to be done – Sammy?' But Sammy was speechless, shocked by what had just happened.

'Sammy?' The Chaplain's voice was soft, full of regret. 'You know I would never condone violence, but I had to do it, you were hysterical.'

As if in slow motion, Sammy's left hand went to the mark that was flourishing where the Chaplain had struck him. Amazingly it felt warm. Maybe it was the heat of retribution, Sammy thought to himself as he touched it; finding a minute glimmer of humour in the situation. He looked the Chaplain full in the face and saw that the man was hurting, maybe as much as he was in his own way. Sammy could see it in his eyes. The Chaplain was as genuine a man as one could be and he'd been acting like a jerk. Sammy turned to look at Geoff then returned his gaze to the Chaplain. He spoke quietly, he felt he should.

'What did he say?' he asked.

'It is serious,' said the Chaplain meeting Sammy's eyes as he tried to tell him as gently as possible the immediate lie of the land. 'But I don't know how serious. We called Geoff back before he had a chance to see.' He studied Sammy's face waiting for a reaction.

'And he saw what?' Sammy's voice was deliberate but calm. He was feeling a fool and wasn't going to let his emotions get the better of him again; not for a while anyway.

The tenseness surrounding them ebbed slightly and the Chaplain, feeling a sense of relief that things hadn't got any uglier, now felt Sammy was ready to hear what Geoff had said and seen.

'He said he saw Richard taking his tablets.'

Sammy's face reflected what he was thinking. He didn't understand. He'd been expecting and had steeled himself for something a little more dramatic. Seeing this, the Chaplain elaborated on what he'd said.

'What I mean is, is that Geoff said he saw Richard taking *all* his tablets, *at once*.'

'*All of them*?' stammered Sammy, shaken by the Chaplain's words.

116

'Yes.'

'But he'll kill himself.' Horror now filled Sammy's face as the implication of what was being said sank in. Now it was dramatic and far worse than anything he could have envisaged, but Sammy was determined the wild histrionics of earlier weren't going to resurface. 'He can't!'

'I don't think *he* is.' The Chaplain's words hung cold like a guillotine's blade.

'What – do you mean?' But Sammy's eyes grew wide as he spoke. It wasn't possible, surely he didn't mean? 'Would she?' he muttered under his breath.

'Sorry?' said the Chaplain, not quite catching what Sammy had said.

'She wouldn't – would she?' Sammy's eyes searched the Chaplain's face for some sort of answer.

The Chaplain, though, only knew as much as Sammy did, he remembered so little of Laura, of any of them. Shaking his head to say as much, his thoughts turned to Geoff again; maybe he could coax something else from him, some crumb of comforting thought. But such thoughts were driven from his mind when he turned to face Geoff.

Geoff, his hands back covering his face, was sitting where the Chaplain had left him, but he'd changed. The Chaplain stopped and stared, his mind floundering, all thoughts of Laura and tablets driven to the back of it. Geoff's body had become transparent, as if he was fading from existence.

What, by all that was holy, was happening? But deep inside the Chaplain knew it was the Transition, part of the journey to the other side. How, he couldn't say, he just knew. Could feel, if asked to put his finger on it, what was happening. He called to Sammy who was standing with his back to Geoff. He wasn't certain he should, considering the last few moments, but in reality what choice did he have?

'It's the Transition, isn't it?' said Sammy, sounding amazingly cool and collected as he drew alongside the Chaplain.

117

The Chaplain nodded grimly.

'Does he know?'

'I don't think so.'

'Should we tell him?'

'I don't think it would serve any purpose to do so. I suggest we let him go peacefully.'

Watched by the Chaplain and Sammy, Geoff did just that. Not appearing to notice what was happening to him, Geoff gradually slipped from sight and existence.

With Geoff gone, the others turned to each other knowing that bridges needed to be built. Sammy apologized for the way that he had acted. And in return the Chaplain pointed out that though Sammy was dead he was still only human. Sammy laughed and then laughed even more when he saw through the Chaplain, quite literally.

Soon after all that was left of the three of them was a barely visible and thoughtful Sammy. He was thinking about Laura and wondering if she had really done it, and what of the consequences if she had? He was also wondering where the hell he was going and hoping that when he got wherever that was, that it *wasn't* the "H" word.

CHAPTER 17

It was another dream, another nightmare. And in it someone had invaded Richard's body. He could feel them swimming about inside him. A strange alien creature that wanted his soul and would do anything to get it, even kill him. And now it was trying to do just that. Richard could feel the creature's hands slipping around his throat, getting tighter as it attempted to throttle him.

Terrified, Richard woke with a sudden start and immediately began spitting pills. As he spluttered, his mind tried desperately to grasp what the hell was happening. Choking the last couple of pills from the back of his throat, Richard slipped his feet over the side of the bed. He sat there sore and bewildered. Was he still dreaming? He didn't think he was. Then how the hell did the pills get into his mouth? Again, was he going crazy? Thoughts whizzing through his brain, Richard reached for the beaker sitting on his bedside cabinet and took a swig. It tasted bitter, the fluoride supposedly put there for your health (on which he had his doubts) but it was a heck of a lot better than the sour taste of the pills that was clinging to his taste buds. He swilled the water around his mouth and spat it back into the beaker.

What was going on? Richard's attention turned to the empty pill container. He picked it up and examined it, for what he wasn't sure. How the hell? He turned the little container around in his hands. But there were no answers, only more questions, and then he remembered the smothering feeling when he'd woken before. A horrible thought crept into his mind, the idea was unthinkable, but all the same was in the realms of possibility, however improbable. Could he subconsciously be trying to kill himself? No, the thought was preposterous; he'd never do anything like that, it wasn't in him; he'd have to be out of his mind. It had to be the dreams; he was getting caught up in the unreal reality of them. Acting the part he had in them, but then again?

Richard studied the container in his hand. The label didn't actually say anything about side effects, but? Maybe the pills did have something to do with it all? Maybe they were the catalyst for what was going on? And maybe in this last dream he'd been trying to get rid of them, but why in his mouth? So they'd be no good to use again? No, it was too ridiculous and there were way too many maybes. As Richard sat playing the maybe scenarios through his mind there rose another thought, a memory, to add to the mystery; the incident with the tea-towel raised its ugly – all cotton – head.

Maybe he should telephone the hospital. Ask for an appointment to see someone. Who? A shrink? And then what? Besides, he'd be long dead before he got an appointment. Why did he just think that? He meant – shit what did he mean? Richard's knuckles grew white as he tightened his fist around the plastic beaker, he didn't know what he thought. Perhaps he was going mad. Richard took another swig from the beaker, instantly regretting it.

'Damn!' he cursed, his face contorted. The foul taste of the water mixed with the discarded spittle was disgusting but it had an effect; acting as a sort of wake-up call. Richard spat it back where it had come from and decided enough was enough. What was the point of worrying. Perhaps it was just dreams. Perhaps it was the pills. Right now he wasn't about to have either and no way either was he going to talk to some quack that might tuck him up nice and neat with a room full of Napoleon Bonapartes. It was time for acting not glooming; he needed to pull himself together and get back on track. What he needed was things getting back to normal, something everyday, something constructive to take his mind off things.

Poor Freddie instantly sprang to mind. That's where he could start, bury his pal. That was normal – for him.

Richard stood up and looked at the spray of pills lying on the bed. It was about time he took back the reins of his life; time to try and forget the attack and the weeks in a coma. And that was another thing. He'd spent almost all that time in hospital asleep, so what did he do when he finally got out and home? Sleep, that's what. He was glad he'd had the dreams, glad he'd taken the tablets. Glad because now they were gone and he, whatever happened next, would be in control. Besides, if his head did start to hurt he could always get some more.

Having made his decision, Richard slipped on his slippers and headed for the bathroom. But even as he walked the short distance from his bed to the bedroom door a cloud was returning to bubble within his subconscious, waiting its chance to undermine his new found confidence; a cloud riddled black with uncertainty.

A fine drizzle was falling from a grey mid-morning sky when Richard stepped from the back door into the small brick-walled garden that was to be the last resting place of Freddie the goldfish. Richard carried Freddie, who'd been lovingly wrapped in kitchen roll and aluminium foil before being placed in his matchbox, to the place where Freddie's "forebeard" lay.

The ceremony, of sorts, that Richard performed at the laying to rest of his friend was simple and short. It was also done very quietly to avoid embarrassment, should a neighbour be lurking close by. He said a few words, mainly how sorry he was and that the next Freddie would be much better looked after etc, and then, with one swift scoop with a garden trowel, taking care not to disturb the graves of the other Freddies, Richard buried his latest little friend. A cross made of matchsticks was placed and that was that.

Now feeling a little foolish at his actions, Richard always did when he'd finished burying a Freddie, he got to his feet, looked around to make sure no one had seen him and scurried back to the dry warmth of the kitchen before the drizzle that was now quite heavy turned into the downpour that the sky was threatening.

Closing the back door behind him, Richard lifted the net curtain that covered its window of four small panes of glass and peered out at the little raised mound that was the latest Freddie. He sighed. He couldn't help it; the sentimental feelings that welled up inside each time a Freddie was laid to rest. Richard had told himself often enough that he was being stupid but it didn't work; a small tear would always form. When would he ever learn? Richard blinked the latest tear away and smiled at his foolishness. But as he lowered the curtain an uneasy feeling came upon him that this time would be the last, that there would never be another Freddie.

A slightly perturbed Richard let the curtain fall. He didn't know why he'd thought what he'd just thought but he decided he wasn't going to let it get to him, he wasn't going to mull over it, its meaning, if indeed it had one. Instead, with steely determination, he cast a critical eye over the kitchen and came to the conclusion that the place was grimy, layered in dust and in need of a good clean; something he hadn't noticed earlier – but then he hadn't felt in the mood to notice such things earlier.

Whistling a nameless ditty – somewhat badly – Richard made for the cupboard under the sink; he would need the cleaning gear. It wasn't going to be easy though, Richard was a pugger. While the house always looked neat and tidy, something his friends, particularly female ones, remarked on, inside every cupboard and drawer lay the sins of that feat. At last he managed to put his hands on what he was looking for, kitchen cleaner – spray on, no need to rinse – a cloth and a pair of rubber gloves.

The latter was his little secret. If Tom got wind of it, it would be goodnight "Randy", which might not be a totally bad thing, hello "Missus Mop" or whatever witticism Tom could come up with. Tom had always been good at making up witty nicknames, something Richard found near impossible to do, he lacked the imagination. But thinking about it Lackadaisical Laura hadn't been that bad an attempt. He paused and gave consideration to the subject of nicknames for a moment. Lackadaisical Laura and Dirty Tom, he mused – Richard had put the state of the kitchen down to Tom's misguided good intentions and Lackadaisical's idleness – Dirty Tom? There, he was crap, what the hell kind of a nickname was Dirty Tom? It didn't make any sense; had no rhythm. But Laura's on the other hand – Richard stopped short as something deep inside his mind shifted. Where did he know that name from? Lackadaisical of course, who else? But there was another, some other, Laura – in the shadows.

His stomach suddenly knotting, Richard fought against the notion. He knew no other Laura. Or was it that he didn't want to know another Laura? Richard donned his gloves. There *was* no other Laura, it was just that Lackadaisical was to be avoided and – and he was just getting a little confused with the nicknamed version and the real one, that was all. Richard liberally sprayed the nearest work surface, dousing an unwary spider in the process. After its careful removal, Richard began his cleaning in earnest; his troubled thoughts tightly suppressed. But for how long?

CHAPTER 18

He had been the first to leave, now he was the first to arrive and things, the things that he knew as memory, were only slowly starting to come back to him. Geoff looked around him, or at least he felt he did, he wasn't sure. If truth be told Geoff wasn't sure of anything at the moment, except that he didn't know where he was, or why, or how, he was where he was.

All around was black, and there was no sign of the others; He assumed, but didn't really know, that he was alone. Geoff tried to get some perspective on the situation he found himself in, but got nothing but a feeling of immense emptiness. He thought of his friends, his clearest memory, but it didn't help; his mind was kind of fuzzy. If he could just remember something, anything that might help him to understand.

It was a struggle at first, there in the black nothingness, but slowly, very slowly, there came to his mind, bubbling from wherever most of his memory was lurking, a recollection of his last moments with the others. He could see, in his mind's eye, the Chaplain and Sammy talking. Sammy was looking worried, concerned about something, was it him? Geoff concentrated harder. He now saw Laura. Oh God! She'd taken Richard's tablets. What had happened then? Horrified, Geoff found his mind trying to close in on itself, he couldn't let that happen, he had to fight it.

He struggled and won, he saw Laura again. She was inside Richard and emptying the container of tablets into his mouth; Geoff sensed she was crying. Then she was gone, but it wasn't his memory that had failed, he'd been called back at that moment. Called back before he could do anything, scream, shout at her. Anything to stop her doing the dreadful thing she'd been about to do. Geoff trembled in the blackness that surrounded him, at the thought of that last image of Laura.

Now his memory, perhaps a safety valve somewhere kicking in, shut Laura away. Geoff was stepping from the Shadow in a – hewrestled with what he had been actually feeling, he plumped for – distressed state. The others were waiting, they looked concerned, but how had they known? Then slowly it dawned on Geoff that the concern and worried looks had been for *him*. But why? His own worried look, of course, he'd just seen Laura trying to destroy herself and Richard, and maybe them all; of course their faces would have shown anxiety. They were only reflecting what he himself was showing.

But there was something else, something that, however his mind tried to cover it over, wouldn't go away. And it had something to do with him, not the way he'd looked, not what was etched on his face as he'd arrived back, but to do with him. Geoff tried and successfully turned his mind to the very last moments before the blackness that now enveloped him existed.

Sammy was distraught, his news about Laura obviously the cause, then the Chaplain hitting him. Geoff found this memory hard to believe but he was sure it was a true one. Sammy had calmed down and then, after some chatter between Sammy and the Chaplain that he'd not taken much notice of, the Chaplain had turned to face him. The very last memories then came a-tumbling, the Chaplain's face so pale, the resigned look on Sammy's. What had they seen? But no matter how he tried to hide it, to disguise the fact, he knew the answer. They had been looking at him, straight at him. Something to do with him had caused the looks on their faces, but what?

Geoff's mind wavered as fear and panic, together hand in hand, invited him to join them. He very nearly did but the blackness in that very instant, though so immense and empty to him, displayed something totally unexpected, a warmth, an influence of calm. It felt to Geoff as if it wanted him to relax and leave behind the despair he was feeling, to give himself over to it, to embrace its entirety, to join with it.

At first hewas reluctant, it was as if someone he didn't know was asking him to trust them and step out across a bottomless pit on to an invisible bridge. It was going to take an enormous amount of faith to do what he felt was being asked of him, something he wasn't sure he had. And as this was going on, in this all-encompassing blackness, in his mind Geoff wasn't totally convinced that he wasn't, himself, just a figment of some bizarre imagination.

As if glancing over his shoulder, the only way that Geoff could explain what he was feeling, he could see in his mind's eye the twin perils of panic and fear beckoning for him to come and play, laughing. Geoff looked away and slowly raised what he felt was a foot, feeling that they were joined, his foot and mind and vice versa, as if there was nothing in between, and like his mind it wavered there in its uncertainty.

Gradually Geoff guided this "figmental" foot towards the "bridge". He braced himself for the inevitable fall but it didn't come, he felt his foot touch something solid, as solid as solid was in the blackness, and followed. He now had the sensation of standing on the invisible floor of an immense cavern. Geoff dared to look again over his shoulder. He needn't have worried though; panic and fear had fled, gone with that first step.

The blackness now expressed itself as a sea of welcome that washed over him making him feel safe, safe in its vast blackness. And also safe in an unexplained knowledge that all he had to do now was to wait.

CHAPTER 19

Guilt, confusion, and curiosity were just a few of the things going through Laura's mind as she watched from within as Richard went about his chores.

The guilt which hung heavy like a leaden yoke across her shoulders because of what she had done. The confusion coming from uncertainty, had *she* woken Richard at the last moment or had she been prepared to sit back and wait for the inevitable end only for it to be cast aside by Richard himself?

But there was more than just uncertainty causing the confusion she was feeling. She had been watching a new world since the moment Richard had woken, spluttering the pills across the bed, it had been as though she was seeing her surroundings for the first time. Everything had become sharper, more lucid, "more organised" was the way Laura could best describe how she was seeing things now, but more than that, they, it, everything, had become so much more real. And now as she watched Richard's movements, his environment, it was with rapidly growing interest and curiosity.

With these new perspectives, though, came a price, more guilt and confusion, piling up on what she was already feeling, and questioning. Was she really so unfeeling that she could so easily push from her mind what she had done to Richard, to herself, the horror of her deed, with an *Alice in Wonderment* approach to what was going on around her? Everything so bright, so new, the need to explore, to touch; to take control of the cloth in Richard's hands and polish and clean, to put from her mind that which had gone before. How quickly she could forget, or was it just so much camouflage, a falseness put out to cover her tracks, a convenient amnesia?

No, it was none of these, she was certain. If it was it would surely be covered now, hidden away, no longer a memory. But she could remember and because of this and because of the new reality she was now existing in, she felt somewhere inside that the need to do what Richard was doing was not shallow. It was, in some way, a sign that it was time for her to try again, to try and contact Richard.

Richard continued his cleaning until the kitchen, by his standards and anyone else's, unless they were some sort of cleaning freak, was sparkling. He stepped back to admire his work.

'There you go, all done,' he said to himself with pride. 'Oops, not yet, you've missed a spot.' Richard had reached halfway towards the innocuous looking mark on the edge of the table before he stopped and thought.

He stood rooted to the floor as his mind shuddered. Did he say that? Richard wasn't totally convinced that he had, but he must have done. He gingerly reached the rest of the way to the offending mark and wiped it away. Of course, his thoughts turned to the pills and tea-cloth. Maybe it wouldn't be such a bad idea to give the hospital a ring; Napoleon here, how can I help you? He baulked at the thought; he was being stupid, it had to be side-effects from the pills. Once the last of them was out of his system things would return to normal. Richard dwelt for a moment on the word normal then quickly threw the cleaning gear back under the sink and left the kitchen.

In the lounge Richard sank onto the two seat sofa and pondered. The excuses he kept making were good but did he really believe them? And if not, what then? He gave the telephone a glance but swiftly moved on, his attention resting on the empty fish tank; poor old Freddie. Damn that girl. Which girl Richard? That damned Lackadaisical, that's who! Lackadaisical who? Richard didn't answer, he didn't want to.

Laura gazed thoughtfully at the room around her. Part of the reason she had so readily agreed to joining with Richard was the thought of seeing how the world had changed sixty years on from her death. The idea had excited her but, from her immediate surroundings; it was obvious that it had sadly regressed. She was impressed by nothing, apart from the sofa which Richard was sitting on, and that was only because of the black leather, she'd always approved of anything in black leather. The sofa itself though did nothing for her; it was too square – not enough curves. She found herself wondering what sort of man Richard was, the last chance for their joint Soul to find everlasting peace. From the décor, she plumped for boring. Most of it looked older than even she was. Richard, she decided, was most definitely not a man of action. Unless, she conceded, he had cleaning materials in his hands.

But who was she to condemn a man for his way of life just because *she* was feeling let down? One man didn't make a world. Laura once again got an urge to wander, to explore this world she was in further, to pass beyond the confines of the walls, to…. Laura managed to get hold of herself, curbing the wants in her heart and, in doing so, finding a small semblance of control which in its way surprised her. It was proper control, something which she hadn't so far achieved. Was she at last winning? Could she totally control her feelings and desires? She didn't think so, not yet, but it was a start.

The tatty old-fashioned sideboard opposite her caught her eye, she was sure her parents had had something like it, but then she realised it wasn't the sideboard that had called for her attention but what was standing upon it. A half empty whisky bottle stood waiting to be attended to. Laura licked her invisible lips; she sure could use a little tipple or two.

Rising from the sofa Richard walked across the room to the sideboard and poured himself a drink. He sure as hell

131

deserved one. At two fingers he stopped abruptly and wondered what the heck he was doing. He looked at the brown liquid in the glass and put it to his lips anyway. One swig and it was gone. He refilled the glass but this time instead of putting the glass to his lips he suddenly swung round and faced the sofa.

He didn't know what he'd expected to see, someone sitting on it maybe, but the emptiness that he found shovelled a little bit of sanity into his mind. *He* wanted a drink, that was all, nothing wrong in that, nothing to get paranoid about. It wasn't something to worry about; it was a perfectly natural thing that happens all the time. Brain sends message – nerves – legs – hands – mouth, Richard knocked the second glass back, – swallow – simple as that.

'Shit!' thought Laura as the whisky slipped down Richard's throat, its sensation playing down hers. Had she done that?

Amazingly the confusion that not long ago would have spread throughout her mind in a situation such as this didn't manifest itself, instead in its place Laura found clarity. It had been both of them, Richard and her working in unison. Neither of them forcing or holding back, they had worked as one. Laura felt as if a fog had lifted, but not a weight, the guilt hadn't gone with it, reminding her before she got too excited that all was not yet a bed of sweet-smelling roses.

As the second swig of whisky swept past Laura's tonsils, which managed to catch her unawares, snapping her from her thoughts in the process, she found Richard staring hard at the sofa. She sensed his feeling of bewilderment, but not only that, Laura's heart nearly missed a beat. Could it be possible?

Richard carefully put the empty glass down and stared hard at the sofa. He had no idea why he was doing so, he just was. And then, as if from nowhere, he decided he didn't like it. The colour was alright, likewise the leather, it was something else. Richard stared and thought and, that was it, funny he hadn't noticed before. The thing was much too boxy, too square, not curvy enough.

Other thoughts began trying to push and shove their way on to his train of thought. Trying to push past and get to the front, to the forefront of his thinking. One of these managed for a fleeting second to get through the melée, it was about poor old Freddie; it was also preposterous. Richard found himself wondering if he'd buried Freddie alive. The thought wanted him to check, go look just in case. But then as quickly as it had appeared it disappeared, eclipsed by another. Richard was now thinking about Lackadaisical – her real name emblazoning itself across his mind – Laura; but it wasn't. The name didn't belong to Lackadaisical, it belonged to another Laura. Some other Laura at the back of his mind he thought he remembered, thought he knew.

Laura felt her body become rigid. Or was it Richard's? She felt so close to him now. Both Richard's and Laura's bodies had grown rigid. Richard was still staring at the sofa. He seemed transfixed by it, as if it had some magical hold over him.

Laura felt Richard's breathing suddenly start to labour. It frightened her, something wasn't right; she could feel pain, Richard's pain. Richard's hand clutched at his chest, Laura could feel it pinching. Oh no, it couldn't be? Not now, not now that they were so close to a connection. It couldn't be happening.

Richard's head began to swim, slow at first, then faster until his mind started to blur in terrifyingly fast circles. He felt his chest; his heart was beating like a thing possessed. A trickle of cold sweat ran down between his shoulder blades.

This couldn't be happening. Not a heart attack. But it was the only thing he could think of that could be happening to him, him not being an expert on such things, not having had

133

one before. Richard fell onto one knee, grasping the edge of the sideboard as he did to steady his weakening body.

His chest felt so tight. Richard dropped onto both knees and balanced precariously against the weight of gravity, his hand managing to hold fast and stay the increasingly imminent crash to the floor.

But it couldn't be a heart attack – they were a thing of the twenties. The technological advances, the implants, no one had heart attacks anymore. A black mist began to swirl within Richard's mind, invading every corner, his consciousness now fighting a losing battle. Richard's hand lost its grip and, as if in slow motion, he slumped forward face first onto the carpet.

The carpet loomed large in Laura's frightened eyes, then blackness. She lay there feeling nothing but Richard's slowing heartbeat in her chest, seeing nothing but his heart in her mind's eye. She felt lost. Then nothing.

CHAPTER 20

Like Geoff, the Chaplain was slowly regaining his memory. He wondered briefly about the others, were they safe? Were they close? He tried to call but found he had no voice, or at least no real voice. He'd heard the words he'd spoken inside his head but not through his ears. So had he indeed actually called out? The Chaplain, for all his faults a sensible man, decided to leave that particular train of thought firmly in the sidings and turned his mind to the blackness surrounding him.

Where was he? He had no sense of actually being anywhere, just of existing. The Chaplain looked down, or what he deemed to be down, at his hands. He couldn't see them but he knew they were there, but they did feel different, strange. Next his feet, the same strange feeling. And then the whole of his body; he wished he hadn't. It was coming back to him now, what was happening. It was the Transition and his body, everything, felt alien to him, yet oddly familiar. He wasn't sure he liked what he felt.

The Chaplain, nervously reconciled to what was happening to him, waited quietly trying to feel what he had once been and what he was now, whatever that was! He knew the change had taken place but, into what, he hadn't the foggiest idea. It could be any one of the three. And then again maybe he did know, he just didn't want to admit it to himself; not yet anyway. Maybe he wanted to hold on until the last possible moment because – because it was scaring him shitless, that's why, but at the same time thrilling him, the whole thing was somehow exhilarating like an amusement park ride that was heading down into darkness and the unknown. And on top of all that was the knowledge that soon he would be alive again, able once more to taste life's simple pleasures that had so long been forgotten; regardless of the guise he would return in.

He'd decided, if there was time, and the Chaplain always believed that there was, that he wanted to take deep breaths of sea air. He would ask Richard to take him, and the others if they wanted to, to the coast. But not any old coastline, it would have to be a place that held both the beaches of his childhood and the later pilgrimages of his adulthood. He dearly wanted to visit Wales and little St. Davids, to see its Cathedral once more and then take a leisurely stroll along the length of Newgale's splendid beach. He wanted.

There the Chaplain's trip down memory lane abruptly ended as he realised that the blackness surrounding him appeared to be getting lighter. Or was it? Was his imagination getting the better of him? Could his mind in its present state be playing tricks? Why would it? To what end? The Chaplain managed to regain some composure and relaxed until he had cleared his mind of its clutter of questions and recollections. It *was* getting lighter, he wasn't imagining it, more so on what the Chaplain took to be the distant horizon.

As the world around the Chaplain grew steadily brighter he realized to his amazement that it wasn't the blackness that was getting brighter at all but that he appeared to be moving and getting closer to that distant horizon. The Chaplain tried twisting his body so that he could see the blackness that had enfolded him moments ago. Behind him it lay, brooding and still, like some great beast that lived and ruled in a night's dream but who could now only sit and wait for the new day to pass.

A shiver coursed through the Chaplain's body, a body that felt almost alive. Apprehension started to filter into its every fibre and the Chaplain tried to get some bearings. The light got ever closer, got ever brighter. It was coming faster.

Now it was so close it was as if the light with its mounting, almost terrible, brightness would sear from his head his very eyes and nothing the Chaplain did in an attempt to shield them would, he felt, be sufficient to escape its power. In pain, and feeling at the point of fainting, the Chaplain was engulfed.

Then it was over. The light that the Chaplain had so vainly tried to keep from his eyes had vanished to be replaced by another. This one though was soft compared to the other, bright but without the harshness. A lightness that felt more akin to the blackness he'd floated in.

The Chaplain, to his astonishment, blinked. Not a thing normally considered as a surprising event, but the moment was as far from normal as was possible. The Chaplain had been dead for well over a century, over one hundred years of non-blinking. He blinked again and then again. It felt wonderful, as wonderful as he envisaged the deep breath of sea air in Wales was going to be.

Then, causing a stern smile, he had a sudden recollection of the last time he'd blinked whilst alive. It too had had an element of surprise about it. It had happened in the last minute of his life as the bullet with his name on it ripped through his heart ending the misery of his time in the trenches. The smile wavered for a moment as sadness sought to overcome him but he fought it and at the same time was able to start his embrace of his new existence, this other chance at life. At least this *was* something the Chaplain was sure of. He *was* alive again, he *was* breathing, *could* feel the ground beneath his feet. Steady signs, he felt all was well. His feet!

The feelings he'd harboured in the blackness came flooding back. The fear of what he was to become had been lost in the coming of the brightness. But they were back now and the Chaplain was afraid to look down, afraid to confirm what he had already guessed – knew. He was alive in a different form, but which of them had his spirit been implanted in? Chastising himself for the stupid question, the Chaplain looked down.

It could have been worse but, on the other hand? The Chaplain wondered how Joe had come to the decision as to who was to be what, and if any, what part the real Joe had had to do with it. Realistically though, the Chaplain doubted he'd taken any part, apart of course from the obvious, but the choice regarding his situation was all the same quite ironic. Something the Irish-American policeman's sense of humour would have appreciated.

Smiling again, but this time the face muscles – although alien – operating without the tension of before, the Chaplain took his first steps back in the world of the living. Time for pondering was over, he had things to do and with each awkward step he took, the reality of life was coming back to him, bringing with it an awareness of just how little time he and the others had left. But even so, with the realisation that maybe he was wrong about there always being enough time, he was damned if he was going to let it mar his first day back on Earth.

Although, he thought as he scratched a particularly itchy spot behind his left ear, the trip to Wales was looking extremely doubtful.

CHAPTER 21

Whether or not it was the same inky blackness that the others were experiencing only Joe knew, and Joe wasn't around to say, as Laura's eyes opened to her dark surroundings.

Straight away, even before Laura began to wonder where she was, she sensed that she wasn't alone. Someone was close by. Laura ventured out a tentative hand but felt nothing, only then did she begin to wonder; faint echoes of memories returning to the far reaches of her mind. She tried a different tact and called out softly. There was no response, so Laura tried again, a little louder this time. A voice sounding as if it was almost on top of her replied.

'Who's there?' Richard's answer floated through the blackness like a raft on a vast ocean of nothingness.

She recognized the voice immediately as belonging to Richard. And with the recognition there came sudden realization. Laura was as near as it was possible to be near someone, she was still inside him. And although she could feel no beating heart she knew that Richard was still alive.

'It's me – Laura,' she ventured cautiously.

'Laura?'

'Yes,' she answered, wondering if she was doing the right thing, 'from the hospital.'

'The hospital?' Richard's voice sounded vague and confused.

'Yes.'

Moments of silence followed as Richard digested what had been said.

'Do you remember me?' asked Laura trying to prompt a response from that lengthening silence. Still Richard stayed quiet. Laura began to worry; maybe she'd overstepped the mark? 'Richard?' she said as softly as she could.

Richard, his voice slow and deliberate, answered. He'd just been hit with his own dose of realization. The realization that the bad dream he'd been trying hard to suppress hadn't been a dream at all but mind-churning reality.

'The girl with the dwarf?'

'Elf,' corrected Laura, 'but yes.'

'It wasn't a dream then?'

'No.'

More silence.

'Richard?'

'I'm still here,' he said, a little more aware, 'wherever here is.'

'Do you remember anything else?' Laura asked, taking the bull by the horns.

'I don't suppose you know where we are?' said Richard, deliberately ignoring her question. Other strange memories had surfaced in Richard's mind, memories that he wasn't sure he wanted to admit to Laura, or to himself, to having. Not yet anyway.

'No I don't,' replied Laura truthfully.

'Or how we got here?'

'Or what's happening?'

The "how we got here?" was also a mystery to Laura, however she thought she knew the answer to his third question. Then the infamous *but* reared its ugly head again, how to tell Richard what she thought she knew and how she knew it. She then realized that she was a little short herself on explanations for the latter. But back to the question, how did she explain to Richard that he was, for the moment, actually existing between heartbeats. She supposed that she would have to try.

'Do you remember falling?'

'Am I dead?' A small note of alarm registered in Richard's voice.

'I don't think so.'

'You don't think so?'

Shit, what did she say that for? 'I mean no. No you're not.'

'You don't sound too sure.'

Laura's hand was forced. 'You're in between heartbeats which means, I suppose, that technically you are still alive.' There was a pause as Laura decided whether to tell Richard what else she knew – in for a penny. 'I think it may have been the only way for us to make contact.'

'What are you?' Richard's voice had an eerie calm to it.

'You know what I am.'

Richard fell quiet again; of course he knew who, what, she was even if it didn't make a whole lot of sense. She was him and he was her. She was a ghost that came calling asking for help. Of course he knew. But he also knew that she brought death with her, and whatever things that were promised that would be coming afterwards, it didn't and wouldn't help him overcome the fear of that, it: the fear of his dying.

'When will I die?'

The question came out of the blue, taking Laura by surprise, but she decided that there was no point beating about the bush. The time for silly games, hers and Richard's was, it seemed, over. 'Soon – too soon,' she answered bluntly. As she spoke the guilt of her earlier actions started to filter back.

'When?'

Laura hesitated, but only for a second, 'The day before your birthday.' She could almost feel what was going through Richard's mind, so she told him, saving him the job of working it out. 'Sixteen days not including today.' She felt Richard's body tense around her.

'When?'

'Six-.'

'No, I mean when on the last day?'

Laura hesitated, things were getting a little heavy. 'I don't know.' She didn't, she hoped Richard believed her. 'It's a question I can't answer.'

'How then?'

'Another,' said Laura shrugging her invisible shoulders.

'What *do* you know then?' snapped Richard reacting angrily to Laura's seemingly convenient ignorance.

'The same as you,' she replied, her voice soothing, not reactive, 'sorry.'

And Laura really was. Only now was she beginning to understand a little of what it must be like for Richard, to have his world suddenly turned upside down. How hard it was for someone to know when they were going to die. In a way, up until this sudden blackness, it had been a somewhat unreal situation to her, feeling she was in a role, a role that needed to be played out.

'I really am sorry you know,' she said, emotion embroidering each word.

'I know.' Richard's words were surprisingly soft, free of the anger he'd just displayed. 'And so am I – it must have been difficult.' His voice flowed calm again almost regretful, the eeriness gone.

'Difficult?' Laura felt a little lost and slightly perturbed by his comment.

'Trying to get through to me I mean. It must have been hard.'

Laura gave a small sigh of relief. She'd thought for a moment he was hinting at the episode in the bedroom. If she was in his shoes that would have been one of the first things she'd have brought up. It was possible of course that he didn't know, but no, she didn't have that luxury, she knew he did; he just wasn't mentioning it. He was deliberately leaving it alone. Laura relaxed and smiled inwardly, maybe he wasn't so bad after all?

'Just a little,' she admitted.

'What now then?'

'What do you mean?' said Laura knowing full well what he meant. The trouble was she didn't have the answer, things kept changing. Things would come to her but not always. She hadn't expected the blackness. Laura didn't know what to expect next. She had a suspicious feeling, she didn't know why, that she was being kept in the dark, fed things on a need to know basis.

Richard picked up the hesitancy in Laura's voice. 'You don't know, do you?'

Laura shook her head and wondered how long a heartbeat took. 'No.'

There was a momentary silence before Richard spoke again.

'What about your friends, do you know where they are?'

To her astonishment and somewhat unexpected delight, Laura felt that she did. 'They're on their way.'

'You know that but you don't know where we are, why?'

'I don't know, I just do. What else can I say?'

There was nothing else she could say. And, as if twins born with a paranormal link, they knew as one that they were stuck in the endless black nothingness until the powers that be saw fit to deem otherwise.

Q: How long is a heartbeat?

A: As long as it takes to skip one.

A ridiculous question followed by an equally ridiculous answer; or a riddle? A question but no real answer, which summed up Richard's and Laura's present circumstances.

They were in a space that existed only in their minds; a place where nothing could be answered past their own limited knowledge. Outside of this place Richard's body lay face down on the carpet, his hand still clasped tightly to his chest. And Laura was still where she had always been since joining Richard, inside him; in the dark.

Without Laura, Richard would be lost. Without Richard there would be no Light for Laura, for anyone.

Answers would have to come from outside. And some were already on the way.

CHAPTER 22

To Sammy's immense relief there were no fires, and the impenetrable blackness he found himself in held no discernible traces of soul toasting heat. If this was Hell, it wasn't quite what Sammy had been expecting.

As he lay, stood, floated, Sammy wasn't certain what his present disposition was; he found his memory slowly returning. The fading! Where were Geoff and the Chaplain? What had become of Laura? It all came flooding back.

Laura? Sammy quickly came to a conclusion; she couldn't have gone through with it. Why else would he still be as he is? If she had, wouldn't he now be as one with the others, languishing in the "H" word, drowning their combined regrets and Soul in a river of unforgiving flame? And wouldn't Joe or someone from Upstairs have been there at the end, during their last moment, to say something even if it was just goodbye? Unless?

Unless, this *was* Hell or rather a doorway to it, the blackness some sort of waiting room. And behind some unseen portal the big red-horned one was waiting to surprise him, ready to invite Sammy the tramp to the hottest party around.

Twisting in the blackness, Sammy tried desperately to put these thoughts from his mind. This torment he was putting himself through, he was being stupid, dramatic, acting like a fool. But when all was said and done, wasn't that what Hell was all about, a place of eternal torment? Was this really it, the end, the far, *far,* end of the line? A thousand missed

145

chances, each one an avenue that ultimately joined the road to this black void he found himself in: the end of the road.

No – it *couldn't* be. Sammy fought against the drowning effect his thoughts were having on him. It was something he had tried but failed to do in the last days of his life on Earth. So why should he succeed now? Maybe if he tried harder? Found something in his thoughts to cling onto before he sank again without trace?

His dancing came to mind and with it the music, echoes of happier times. He swore he could almost hear the melodies of that bygone age sweeping through the layers of dark thoughts. No – wait – hold that thought – he *could* hear it.

A tune as clear as a bell was playing in Sammy's mind, flowing into his head through his ears. Sammy twisted again in the blackness, seeking to find the source of the music but it stopped suddenly. All was quiet then, as darkness attempted once more to invade Sammy's thoughts, it started again, the same tune as before. It was he, Sammy, that was making the music that sounded so blissful to his ears, that was banishing the darkness from his mind. Sammy couldn't believe it, he was whistling for the first time since his death.

Another song came to his lips, a song from his heyday. It had been so long ago; you didn't have heydays when you were dead. He was a little rusty but it was recognisable. Sammy tried another and another until he was in full flow and could almost feel his toes tapping along, almost.

This couldn't be Hell, thought Sammy as the tunes flowed, what Hell would allow such happiness? And something else was happening, with each tune Sammy whistled, however rusty, the blackness surrounding him receded a little. With each musical ditty that formed on Sammy's lips, so the blackness rolled back further to be replaced by soft, at first, but ever growing intensities of light. Light, glorious light! Sammy was now sure that his feet were tapping, tapping a tattoo to welcome the light.

146

But just as the blackness was all but vanquished and all around was on the verge of being all consuming light, something terrible began to happen. The tunes began to degenerate, lose cohesion. Sammy, afraid that the blackness would return, desperately tried other tunes; an easy one he learnt as a child during his piano lesson days, but it too failed to form as Sammy expected, becoming nothing but an incoherent warble. Scared, Sammy looked to the blackness expecting its return.

It didn't come; the light was holding its own, growing ever stronger, until Sammy was at last engulfed by its white brilliance. Confused and frightened, even by the light that seemed in its way so welcoming and warm, Sammy whistled again, whistled nothing but a nonsensical warble.

It didn't make sense. Why had he been given back this living gift only for it to be ripped from him in this way? Sammy's confusion and fear was now joined by anger.

Was it some macabre game? Someone somewhere having a laugh at his expense? Sammy tried to get a grip on what was happening to him. Unless – unless he'd been right all along, and this was Hell. Fear now had the upper hand and Sammy noticed a difference in his surroundings. The light that had been bright with welcoming warmth had started to change. It was becoming less comfortable, too bright, and worse still, too warm.

Another tune struggled from Sammy's lips as he attempted to fight against whatever was happening; panic beginning to set in as the light grew hotter and hotter against his flesh. He stopped his whistling, it was no good, he wasn't strong enough to fight, he would have to yield to the inevitable. What a fool he had been to even try and accommodate the notion that he would be spared. He'd been a failure in life and it was no more than he deserved that in death he should be rewarded for such.

With hope now but a fading memory, Sammy readied himself to succumb to his fate. He drifted as the light burnt against him and through the pain wondered if his life and death would flash before him in accusing retribution. Voices started drifting towards him. Or was he imagining them? The voices grew louder as the light intensified further. He wasn't imagining them, but whose were they? The damned no doubt, a jury of damned souls that would cast him as guilty before the charges were even read. Sammy's heart began to beat faster, he hadn't noticed it was beating until now, as the voices drew upon him: voices he still couldn't see.

'It's no good, he's gone I'm afraid,' announced one of the voices, a commanding one that sounded accustomed to making such statements.

Did they mean him? Sammy was on the edge of unconsciousness.

Another voice, not so controlled, Sammy thought he heard it sob. A third voice, soft and consoling.

'He's gone to heaven darling. It's for the best, he'll be much better off there,' it said. It sounded unconvincing to Sammy's tortured mind.

There followed the sound of a door opening and shutting and then the consoling voice spoke again. It had a more serious tone to it.

'What happens now?' it asked.

'We'll dispose of it if you like. We've an incinerator,' replied the "I've seen it all before" matter of fact voice.

Sammy shuddered as he heard the word incinerator. He was sure he was being toyed with but then as he prepared for the inevitable, if indeed you could when it was Hell you expected, he had the strangest feeling that he ought to be somewhere else. So, as easily as that, he went, and as he did, he heard the seen it all before voice change to one of surprise and disbelief.

'Well I'll be!' It exclaimed.

It was closely followed by the start of angry words.

CHAPTER 23

How long it had been since Richard and Laura had last communicated with each other, neither knew. It was also quiet in the blackness they still occupied, deafeningly so.

Laura felt Richard move, his spirit not his body, and wondered how long they had to wait, to exist in this uncomfortable black nothingness; the lack of comfort being their situation, not the blackness itself. She felt tempted to say something, anything, to break down the tension she felt building up inside her, around her. But she didn't, she'd already decided during their last conversation that she had nothing further to say. Nothing had changed.

Richard on the other hand had plenty he wanted to say but he was being stubborn. Why should he break the silence that had festered? It wasn't his fault that they were in this predicament.

He also had questions, reams of them, since the memory of his meeting with the Four had returned. Questions that wouldn't go away, questions like: Why was Laura with him and not Geoff? And ones of a deeper darker complexion such as: Why had Laura tried to kill him?

The latter stuck in his throat in much the same way as the pills had, trying hard to choke him. But Richard knew it was a question that would have to stay where it was; he doubted that even Laura had the answer. Richard instead decided he would wait and see if it would dislodge itself somehow. Maybe Joe, if he ever saw him again, would have the answer?

And that was another thing, who *was* this Joe character and what part did he play in everything? Richard shifted as he pondered this, causing minute uneasy ripples within himself.

149

Laura felt the ripples pass over her, causing her to wonder what was going through Richard's mind. She had felt him move, he felt uneasy. Maybe it was a sign that something was at last happening? Perhaps she should say something? Reach out?

She couldn't, she had a feeling that he was thinking of her. It was her that was causing the trouble in his mind; she could sense his confusion, his hurt. Oh God! Somehow she knew exactly what he was thinking, and he was right, she had no answers.

It was as if he was in a strange sleep, deep and restful, yet he was awake. Wasn't he? Richard stopped his shifting and, he felt, floated, allowing a certain peace to wash over him, relaxing him, his mind; the restful part of the sleep. Richard took advantage of this welcome respite in his wonderings and attempted to take stock of all that had happened to him. He needed to make some sort of order out of the jumble that tumbled through his head; to get a grip on things. To Richard's surprise he found it wasn't as difficult as he thought it was going to be.

He now floated in some vast black ocean that neither ebbed nor flowed. An ocean that was a constant, and from this constant Richard was able to draw a new found stability. The restlessness he'd been entrenched in went, leaving him with the realization that it had been him that had been causing it. He was his own worst enemy, or at least his thoughts were.

Without rippling waves, Richard's mind became clearer. He was able to cast aside his troubling baggage. Dig a way through the clutter surrounding him, until he was left with a single shimmering of introspection that hung like a welcoming lantern on a dark stormy night. Only one thing of importance, one thing that mattered, and like the lantern it was beckoning him on. And like the lantern it shone bright with a welcoming light.

The calmness that Richard found, or rather the suddenness of it, caught Laura unawares, causing her to flounder for a moment in its wake. When she regained her equilibrium she found something with it, fear. Laura could sense the light that Richard could see but she saw nothing herself but blackness. What should she do? Was *now* the time to make contact again; to re-establish their shattered lines of communication?

Laura knew she had to but she dragged her feet. She was afraid, not of the light she could not see, but that Richard no longer needed her. Or worse still, no longer wanted her. A chill went down her spine at the thought that he may have found a way to cut her off from his consciousness, the link between them severed, and with her left alone to float in the blackness that enveloped her until the end.

And then what? Would she ever know if it *had* come to an end? Would she remain forever more in eternal blackness, thinking and afraid? Laura couldn't bear the idea; her body was suddenly racked by a heavy sob. Was this to be her punishment? She thought she could feel a tear trickle from filling eyes. She was sorry, oh so sorry. Laura couldn't help herself now and another sob, greater than the first, surged through her. Surely they were real tears falling.

Then it was light and Richard was raising his bruised body from the living room carpet. The hand and arm that had lain trapped under his chest, coming back to life with the stab of a thousand pins and needles.

Reaching for the sideboard with his good hand Richard finished the job of getting to his feet. The clicking of his knees as he struggled into an upright position signalling that he was still alive. A smile of relief spread across his face but stayed only as long as the coughing fit that followed allowed.

He needed a drink. His eyes turned to the half empty bottle and glass standing on the top of the sideboard. It wasn't what he wanted; he had a real thirst, a thirst that belonged to a man long lost in some God forsaken desert. Only good old Adam's ale would quench the dryness he had in his throat, in his body. He needed water and lots of it.

Half walking, half staggering Richard headed for the kitchen. He took a glass from the drainer, filled it and, with hand trembling, put it to his parched lips. Richard gulped at the cool liquid, nearly choking in the process, but it didn't stop him. He drained the glass and quickly refilled.

He'd never known such a thirst. It reminded him of the summers when he was a kid, rushing around the park playing football for hours on end and then rushing home to stick his hot sweaty face under a tap, letting the cool water gush into his open mouth. But even that fell well short of the need for water he felt now.

The second glass was emptied and half a third before Richard felt his thirst slaked. He turned off the tap which had been running, as it had when he was a child, and placed the glass in the sink, absentmindedly running his fingers along its metallic edge as he did. Richard, feeling a little better, but with throbbing head, left the kitchen and went back to the lounge. The idea of a couple of aspirins had passed his mind but he'd had enough of pills to last him a lifetime; no, what Richard now had in mind was a drop of the hard stuff. He needed another drink, a real drink this time.

Apart from his head and the soreness that he felt in his chest, which was staying fairly constant, most of the aching was beginning to ease. What had happened to him? Richard stopped by the sideboard and picked up the empty glass. As he did he immediately got the feeling that something wasn't right. He stared at the glass inspecting it closely, then at the bottle. Putting the glass down Richard ran a finger along the sideboard's teak veneered top and examined his finger. It was covered in dust but that was to be expected, he hadn't cleaned in here yet, it would be dusty. But the dust had something to do with what he was thinking, with the sudden irksome nagging in his brain. What was the hell was it?

Then something clicked. Richard looked at his other hand, the one he'd dragged along the edge of the sink, there were traces of dust on those fingers too. But that couldn't be right; he'd only just cleaned in there. Ugly unease started to wriggle in Richard's stomach. Another click. Richard picked up the glass again, there was dust on that too, stuck to where his lips had been only moments ago. He quickly put it down, staring at it as if it were a ghost. Something was wrong, very wrong.

Afraid of the wild thoughts that were doing strange things to his imagination and with his stomach doing a frantic Irish jig, Richard reluctantly returned to the kitchen. He gingerly ran a finger along the sink again, the table top, the back of a chair. All returned the same verdict. It was if he hadn't touched them, as though they hadn't been cleaned for weeks.

His mind racing, Richard took a glass from the drainer and rinsed it, then, his steps urgent with purpose, returned to the lounge. He needed that drink more than ever.

Taking the bottle from the sideboard Richard took it over to the sofa and plopped himself down. With feverish fingers he unscrewed the top and poured. The glass shook a little as he drank sending a dribble from the corner of his mouth running down his chin. The liquid burned as he drank and the speed with which he swallowed might have choked a lesser man but Richard was getting used to choking and held his ground, quickly pouring another.

If he thought his head was throbbing before, it now felt as if it might explode. The refilled glass hovered before Richard's mouth. What was he doing? This wouldn't help; he needed to think. The urge to gulp this second glass was curbed, Richard managing to control it to a single sip.

So many thoughts were vying for space in his mind. He had to calm down, sort himself out. He took another sip, he could do this. Some of the thoughts he was getting bordered on the fantastic. Maybe he *should* give the hospital a ring? Another sip – a long one. What for? Things weren't right but it wasn't an illness, an illness couldn't make his kitchen dirty, conjure up dust.

Unless? Unless he was hallucinating; he could have banged his head as he'd fallen. It was the only thing that could account for the craziness going through his mind. The crazy notion of explanation for everything that was trying to get itself noticed. Richard got to his feet. There was a way to find out, to put this crazy idea out of his head for good. Glass in hand Richard went back to the kitchen.

An impulse drew him to look at the calendar that was hanging on the kitchen wall. But when he got there it told him nothing. How stupid was that, he thought, what had he expected to find, the days crossed out in blood maybe? Nothing had changed on it, apart from the layer of dust on top that is. There had to be something else. His watch! Richard's stomach did a neat flip. It had a date feature on it. He looked at his wrist but it was bare. Then he remembered, he'd taken it off when he'd gone to bed, it was still upstairs on the bedside cabinet.

As Richard stomped from room to room, from thought to anguished thought, Laura was going through her own torments.

Tossed back and forth in the blackness, Laura tried to grab on to something, anything, that might help her, steady her, as she bobbed helplessly. Laura couldn't understand what was happening. She could feel Richard as he walked, thought, drank, the light that Richard now existed in. But why still the blackness? Why was she denied what Richard had, what he was doing? Why wasn't she also in the light? Dread surged inside her. Were her worst fears truly founded?

Taking the steps two at a time, his aches and pains forgotten for the moment, Richard quickly reached the top of the stairs. The bedroom door was open, heart in mouth, he walked in.

The watch lay where he'd put it, but he felt almost afraid to go over. Afraid of what he'd find. But he had to know. Putting his fears aside, Richard crossed the bedroom floor to the cabinet and reached for his watch. He saw that it was also covered by a thin layer of dust.

Without looking directly at it, Richard picked it up, then hesitated, his thumb hovering millimetres from the dust on its face. With gritted teeth and with as much will as he could muster, he drew his thumb across the watch's face and looked. He stared down at it and felt his heart quicken as he did. It couldn't be!

CHAPTER 24

Watching from afar, yet only a fingertip touch away, a strange sensation even for one like him, Joe struggled against the temptation that wriggled like a serpent deep within him.

It was supposedly out of his hands now, the fate of Richard and the others, but he felt this temptation, this growing monster he had inside him, to at least try and intervene; to bring about a conclusion to the scenes unveiling before him. To meddle, as some would call it. Joe had tried to fight against it by looking away, but it was not an option that availed itself to him. Joe *had* to watch, to *feel* the suffering; the torment that Richard and the others were going through. That they still had to go through. Their torment belonged to him.

As Joe kept this unwanted vigil he found his body, his embattled existence, continually pounded by emotions, emotions that he could not control. Emotions that built up and then would spill forth making him tremble with incredible joy one moment and then quake with indeterminate fear the next. One moment his eyes would smile with a world of warmth and compassion, the next they would burn with flames of the coldest hatred. And when this emotion of naked hate came to him, Joe would wonder why, how could something so terrible live within him? Then he would weep for he knew why it was so.

The eyes it is said are the windows to the Soul. That if you look deeply enough you can see any man or woman for what they really are. But Joe had no need of such speculation, he could see someone's soul or spirit, or whatever their religion wanted to call it, as clearly as he could see the body which encased it. And within some that he now watched he saw the power of hope burning like a sun.

And with this hope also burned a determination, together helping to ease the burden Joe was carrying. The hope throwing its warmth onto the cold flames, the determination straightening his bent back, taking the pressure from his shoulders so that he could hold his head high again when all seemed hopeless.

It was not enough though. Not enough to completely straighten his back, to send the cold flames to oblivion. Of the five spirits fighting to reach the ultimate, one was weak. One that could, would maybe, turn the tide in a way King Canute could only have dreamed of. And this tide would be all consuming when, if, it came. It would wash all that is light before it and in its place leave a final eternal darkness. As Joe shuddered at the thought, the hope and determination in his mind dimmed. He felt weak and with the weakness came temptation stronger than ever. And the knowing was torment.

The scene before Joe's eyes changed and each of the five Spirits now came in turn to his mind alone, as through he was watching a small preview of a coming film, Joe watched fixedly.

A peaceful darkness appeared to Joe's mind, and encased within it, lay the young one called Geoff. He lay as if asleep, occupied in safe yet naïve ignorance.

Another image, comical if not for the seriousness of the task, came into view. In it the predicament of the Chaplain as he scurried from pillar to post, in his quest to find Richard.

Now it was Sammy, as nimble, if not more so, as he had ever been in the prime of his life. Joe watched with eyes of gleaming happiness as Sammy turned and twisted, pirouetted and swept low to the ground in his new found freedom. Sammy was dancing once more.

Still smiling, the scene changed again for Joe. But this one held none of the senses of serenity and happiness the others had brought with them. This one was dark in its content, sitting there like a rotten apple in the barrel waiting to taint and corrupt all within its reach, and bringing with it the temptation again.

The smile dropped from Joe's face. He couldn't! He had to fight as the others were doing. He had to stand up to the almost overwhelming feeling he had to help as he watched Richard dropping to his knees. He had to watch and do nothing as Richard fell forward onto his face clutching his chest.

Joe's face twisted as he felt Richard's pain and fear, his only solace the fact that it wasn't Richard's time yet. Richard could yet still rise and meet his struggle. But the end was very close. Closer than any of the five Spirits knew. Time was rapidly running out and all Joe could do was watch and wait and fight the demon within.

CHAPTER 25

Time had come to a standstill. Laura felt suspended, her surroundings, herself, devoid of all movement. No inner clock ticked, no outer noise came to her straining ears, a straining she could only imagine. Laura could not feel, see or hear, she could only think and her thoughts held no comfort.

When had it happened? How had it happened? No, that was the wrong question. How had it crept up on her? That was a better question, the one she wanted to ask. Laura strained and tensed and wondered if she was only imagining she was doing it. It was as if she was frozen in a coma and the world was continuing without her, only she didn't know it. All around time and people were ticking over, still going about their business. Everything still going on as it had always done.

Laura imagined she was opening her mouth to shout, to scream, to tell everyone that she was still there, still existed. But she had no idea if she had, was, did. It was a thing of nightmares. Laura imagined she closed her mouth and prayed it wasn't her imagination.

What did she do? What could she do? Laura played the questions over and over in her mind. There was only one answer though and no amount of thinking about it, mulling over it, would change it. She had to wait. However long it took, Laura had no choice but to wait and hope that it would have an end that she could emerge from.

With nothing but her mind for company, Laura waited. And as she drifted within the confines of her mind she did the only thing she could do, she thought.

Just how long could a heartbeat possibly last?

Sitting on his bed, Richard stared blankly at the watch he was holding in the palm of his hand. He hadn't been prepared for the truth and the moment it had shown itself to him he'd been unable to handle it. Richard's mind had ordered a shutdown. Would anyone else's mind have reacted differently to Richard's, when presented with such a terrible truth? To have staring up at you hard evidence that time had somehow moved on without you. That instead of a cushion between you and your fate you now found only a veil of gossamer standing between it and you.

Shock is a strange thing and can present itself in many different guises. In Richard's case it had surfaced as a bemused simpleton whose pleasure and wonder was at that moment staring back at him in the form of a faceless watch, faceless because Richard had taken it upon himself to ignore all things of proof.

The time on the watch was of little relevance, except to tell Richard that it was short. It was the date that had brought the fog to Richard's eyes. The undeniable truth that had glared back at him from the small box that lay where the number three would normally be set on a dateless watch. Inside the box lay a number that ordinarily would be resplendent in its anonymity, but now it stood brazen, daring any and all to deny its existence.

Richard hadn't been able to, but neither had he been able to accept. Thus the current impasse. Thus the bridge of predicament Richard found himself delicately balanced upon. A bridge that was never built to take such weight of thought as was in Richard's mind.

It slowly began to crack and sway, and as it did so the simpleton found that the truth it had sought to hide would soon be revealed. Enough was enough; he had no further part to play. The deceiver left and slipped silently into the shadows whence it came.

A sharp intake of breath announced the simpleton's departure and Richard's return. He found himself staring at the watch as a man of misguided passions might look at a blade that dripped with the blood of the innocent in the aftermath of his mistake.

Richard wanted to throw the watch, to cast it from his sight and his memory. But he didn't, he just stared at it all the harder, almost mesmerised by the number held within the date box.

An eight! that couldn't be right. But Richard knew that it was. The eight was real. The dust had been real. And if they were real then the thought he'd tried hard to suppress had to be real, had to be true. Somehow he'd lain face down on the floor of the lounge for two whole weeks. Fourteen bloody days had mysteriously disappeared. Gone like some unwanted dishwater down some sodding plughole. Richard closed his fingers around the watch until his knuckles whitened under the pressure.

But they weren't just any old fourteen days. They had been *his* fourteen days, *his* last days. His last days on fucking-Mother Earth! Burning with hopeless anger, Richard swung round, the watch leaving his hand and ploughing into the open bedroom door; shattering into pieces.

And in this fit of fury Richard at last admitted to himself that he knew. Admitted that he remembered the hospital visit of the damned, the conversation with the other Laura, the Laura that now, that very moment, was somewhere deep inside him.

Getting to his feet, Richard followed the path of the watch and made his way across the bedroom and out through the open doorway. He suddenly felt dirty, used, he was going to take a shower and then – well then he was going to try and find out why he'd deserved such treatment. Why his last days had been so cruelly ripped away from him? Richard slammed the bathroom door closed behind him.

Was it imaginary or did she really feel something brush against her? Something dark and inhospitable; something in a hurry. Laura dared herself to open her eyes. Then wondered how she'd feel if she found they already were. She argued the point; there wasn't much else to do, there in the blackness. There in the nothingness. But she argued none the less; there had been something. Her surroundings had changed, albeit for a fleeting moment, that is if she had really felt something. What the heck? Laura took the plunge and, whether mentally or physically, opened her eyes.

Things *had* changed. Her surroundings so black, now an ancient grey, like the stone of a ruined castle. But the greyness frightened her, more so than the blackness ever did. With the blackness there had been a stability of sorts, the grey brought foreboding, like the onset of a distant but forbidding storm. Things *were* still changing. Maybe an end was in sight? The thought both terrified Laura and, to her surprise, excited her.

But what if the end was to be a bad one? Better a bad one than none at all, she reasoned. Or it could of course be a good one. After all, what makes blackness lighten? White, and with white must surely come light. 'Was she right or was she right?' Laura softly laughed the laugh of a lunatic as she heard her voice echoing in the greyness.

Then there came a noise, a thud, the sound of something fragile hitting something solid and immoveable. Laura strained her ears and was delighted to find that she was able to. The greyness was now becoming even lighter; the grey after the heavens empty themselves of their dark anger.

Laura became aware of movement, her movement. She had the feeling that she was wandering, lost and wandering across a foreign plain that lay covered by a masking fog. Then there was rain. Laura held out her hands and felt the pitter patter of it against her skin. Her hair was now wet, warm and wet. The rain was warm. And then Laura realised that her eyes were shut again. She couldn't remember closing them. Slowly, fearfully, she opened them again. Water was falling on her, all around her. There was a mist about her face, her body. It was warm and wonderful.

Then Laura's wonderment came to a shuddering and abrupt halt. As if she'd been freefalling through a sky of her own making and the parachute had now suddenly opened, jolting her into the reality of her surroundings. She looked at her hands, and then her fingers. She felt for her hair that should have been lying bedraggled about her neck and shoulders but wasn't. Laura closed her eyes again and was grateful. The blackness had gone as had the grey and she knew that she was with Richard again, and she sensed he knew she knew.

CHAPTER 26

Sensed may have been the wrong word to use. In fact there was no may about it. Laura knew Richard knew she was with him, the moment she'd moved his arm to feel for her hair being a damn good clue. But he hadn't freaked out, so Laura was taking that as a good sign. She was also trying to stay as still as possible, for which there were a couple of very good reasons.

Laura, feeling heaps better for not being in any of the places her dark thoughts had conjured up for her while in the blackness, didn't want to rock the fragile boat she was in any more than she had to, and surprising Richard with any other sudden movements might just have that effect. The other reason was of a more delicate nature, the state of Richard's dress, or as was the case, the current lack of it. She certainly didn't want any surprises of her own!

The shower stopped and Richard, grabbing a towel, stepped from it. Laura closed her eyes, there were mirrors in the bathroom, and she was after all a good Catholic girl. Grief! It had been a long time since she'd said that.

Richard finished drying, and feeling a lot calmer, though he didn't see why he should, he went back to the bedroom to don clean clothes. A pair of jogging bottoms and a tatty but well loved sweatshirt. Richard had relaxing in mind, if he could; with a large stiff one, which would help.

Eyes still shut, Laura felt the softness of the sweatshirt against her skin – Damn it! – Richard's skin. She had to sort herself out. Laura made a mental note to try not to feel anything else until she and Richard were straight. If Richard wanted things straight, that is?

Dressed, Richard left the bedroom and made his way downstairs, feeling a tad more buoyant than he had been of late. To complement his present state of mind he'd had second thoughts about the stiff one and had decided on something a little lighter to go with his intended chilling session.

In the kitchen Richard took a bottle from an unopened six-pack in the fridge and eyed the rest lovingly.

'Soon you vill all be mine yah? Mit little lib-schlings?' said Richard intending the bottle in his hand not to be the last and speaking in what was possibly the worst attempt at a German accent ever. He closed the fridge door and looked at the bottle in his hand.

'You vill open up to me yah? For tomorrow…' The word stuck in Richard's throat. *Tomorrow*. Supposedly his last day on Earth if everything that had gone on was to be believed, and he was fast losing reasons to doubt it.

Richard sighed deeply and went to the drawer below the sink unit for the bottle opener. He had never been one to let things get him down, why should this be any different? But considering what *had* gone on recently, and what he *was* still going through, who would blame him if it did? No, he couldn't dwell on it, what was the point? And things had changed for him since the bedroom incident. He'd accepted things. He had decided to take what life he had left and live it to the full, take it on the chin – his way – and everything and everyone else could go blow as far as he was concerned. Besides, *if* all was true what choice did he have?

Richard found the opener, cursed when the beer turned out to be a "boy", shook the spill from his hand and went into the lounge flopping once more onto the old leather sofa. He took a swig from the bottle and sat quietly, contemplating.

He knew that things were going to get even more difficult for him as time passed – another swig – he just needed to get some steel into his backbone to help him cope. He felt calm but he needed to be calmer. He had to be in complete control when the time came to do what he now knew he had to do. The smashing of the watch, and to some extent the shower, although he'd almost freaked when his hand had gone to his neck of its own accord, had helped him to a modicum of accepting comprehension. But not for a moment did that mean that he agreed with all of it. No sir-ree! Richard had decided that he was going to have a few choice words to say to that Joe character when he next saw him. And Richard felt confident that he would.

Taking another swig, Richard casually cast his eye over the familiar things surrounding him. All of this was him. Everything had the stamp of his life engrained upon it. Richard looked at what was his life, something he'd taken for granted would always be there. And of course the day after tomorrow it still would, it was him that was leaving; him that was going to die. Richard took a long hard swig from the bottle and thought *shit!* It *was* going to be hard.

Richard searched the room for something to help lighten the mood. He found it on the far wall above the sideboard, the shelf of nick-nacks he'd collected over the years. His thoughts turned to Tom and he smiled to himself as an image of his best friend came to mind. What had that bastard called his home? Richard grinned as he remembered.

'To the "Emporium der Tat"!' Richard raised his bottle, toasting to the memory.

Tom could always make him laugh but how dare he call his home tatty; just because he happened to like old things. Liked the way things used to be. Richard loved his house, his home, just the way it was, and no amount of badgering by Tom or anyone else about joining the march of technology would make him change the way things were. Except maybe, and this was an exception he had explored, when it helped with the heating costs. But he supposed he wouldn't be needing the solar panelling he'd been saving up for after all.

Then the grin faltered as he wondered if he would ever see his old friend again. Stupid idea, of course he wouldn't, not in this lifetime anyway.

'To Tom the bastard, the best mate a man could have.' Richard threw another swig down his throat. The grin subsided but Richard stood his ground, fighting tooth and nail against the pressing despondency that tried to envelop him; to the victor a smile. 'Tom the bastard!'

It was hard but Laura had managed to keep herself to herself on the journey from the bedroom to the lounge. Even when, and she was proud of herself for resisting, Richard had opened the fridge and she'd spied a bar of chocolate nestling amongst its contents. How long had it been since she'd last tasted chocolate? Laura remembered being a constant slave to the stuff when she'd been alive, even though it and her thighs had never got along.

Now the chocolate was but a memory and Laura sat looking through Richard's eyes at the pitiful space he called his living room. It was no better than the last time she'd seen it. In fact she couldn't be sure that it wasn't worse. It looked dirtier for a start.

'And you're telling me that you know nothing about it?'

Laura scanned the room to see who'd come in, whom Richard had spoken to, but no one had. That could only mean. A shiver, as cold as the contents of the fridge, suddenly ran down Laura's spine.

'Well?'

A panic started to rise in Laura as she became aware of what was happening. What did she do? She felt embarrassed, as if she'd been discovered doing something she ought not. She'd expected to make contact, for Richard to speak to her again, but now the moment had come she decided she wasn't ready; she had to hide.

Hiding though wasn't an option, where was she supposed to go for Goodness sake? She was in the limelight and there was nothing she could do about it. Except answer, that is.

'Well? Did you?' insisted Richard, his voice calm and firm.

Laura tried to think of an answer but couldn't, mainly because it had just dawned on her that she had no idea at all what Richard was going on about. What was it he thought she should know? Laura was confused, she couldn't answer his question but at the same time felt that she should try, or at least say something. The door was open and she couldn't bear for it to be closed again. So Laura answered.

'No,' she said clambering out on a limb, in a voice that would have had the sharpest of ears straining to hear.

'You're telling me you know nothing about the dust?'

Dust? Laura was now even more confused.

'And I suppose nothing about my missing days.' Richard thought he was dealing with the situation quite calmly, but the slight rise in his voice indicated otherwise.

Sensing the change of tone, Laura decided she had to act. She still hadn't the faintest idea what Richard was talking about but she had to say something before things took a turn for the worse. She was going to have to admit to the fact, whether Richard believed her though was another matter.

'I…' stuttered Laura; it was harder than she thought it would be. And she was feeling strangely defensive about the nothing she knew. It was as if she was on trial. 'I don't know what you mean.' There she'd said it. Did she feel better? Not as you'd notice.

'The dust or the days?'

'Neither.' Laura didn't much like Richard's tone, it smacked of smugness; the type a copper has when he thinks he's got something on you. It made her angry. How dare he speak to her like that? But she had to keep her anger in check; she had the door to think of.

'But you were thinking how dirty the place looked.' Whether it had been the way Laura had snapped her answer or something else there was now a tinge of doubt running through Richard's voice.

She had been, Laura remembered that, but it still didn't explain anything. 'I don't understand,' she said in all honesty, 'did I upset you? I didn't mean to, it's just that I thought the place looked dirtier than before. Than the last time I saw it. Is that why you're angry with me?'

'I'm not angry!' retorted Richard indignantly.

Laura could have bitten her tongue.

'Well I am –,' he then admitted as he felt Laura's anxiety, his attitude mellowing, 'was – sort of – but not with you.' He had fooled himself into believing that he was calm and collected but in truth he was quite nervous, tense even, not quite a coiled spring, but…

'Are you okay?' ventured Laura softly sensing the change in him.

'Yes,' he said, his voice equally soft, but shaking, 'just give me a moment.' Richard glanced at the bottle on the sideboard but instead stayed with the one in his hand. He didn't feel much like moving at the moment.

Laura waited patiently as Richard collected himself together, and for the first time since coming out of the blackness she sensed the trouble he was feeling. Somehow it had managed to stay hidden from her. Maybe Richard's calm façade overshadowing it. But not now. She waited. Waited patiently for Richard to substantiate in his own words what she was now picking up. But surely it couldn't be true. If it was she could understand his anger and upset. Understand why he had acted the way he had. Understand his shock. But what she couldn't understand was *why* it had happened? What could it possibly achieve?

Richard finished his moment by finishing the beer. He then confirmed what Laura already knew.

CHAPTER 27

A compass may have been a good idea. Or a sign of sorts, a neon one maybe, or one with an arrow covered with brightly coloured light bulbs obligingly pointing, or even one a little less subtle, one that only a man of the cloth would be able to decipher and understand. Any crumb of a hint would have been helpful.

The Chaplain was not happy. Not happy with what he was at the moment, but beggars couldn't be choosers. Not happy with where he'd been dumped, in the middle of nowhere, but he couldn't really blame the poor creature whose body he now possessed for that. And finally he wasn't happy with how long it was taking him to find Richard and Laura, or the others when he came to think of it. And why hadn't Sammy and Geoff been there when he'd arrived? Surely it would have made more sense to keep them all together? Although he did have to admit to having the feeling that Sammy wasn't all that far away.

It was something else for the Chaplain to ponder as he mooched, a habit he found he'd inherited from his host and one he wouldn't want to wish on his worst enemy, and then mooched some more. The Chaplain was still mooching when he noticed that he was no longer alone.

A boy in his early teens wearing faded jeans and a tatty leather jacket was watching the Chaplain with interest. The youth, leaning on a fence, idly tossed and caught something in his hand, in his eye a malevolent gleam that transferred itself from the thing to the Chaplain and back again. Alarm bells started ringing in the Chaplain's head. Mooching forgotten, the Chaplain took stock of his surroundings.

Damn! His hosts habits had led him down an alley. Blind? Maybe not, but an alley all the same and a place best avoided. The Chaplain remembered how Sammy had described them, being something of an expert on the subject in later life, "Alleys are what alleys are, a shortcut to nowhere", he would say. And the Chaplain had had more than his fair share of going nowhere since his return to the land of the living.

With one eye fixed firmly on the boy the Chaplain began to carefully back away. No sudden movements. If he did this right no one would get hurt, the no one being primarily him. So far, so good, he'd managed to reach an open space that he took to be the road he'd turned to come in on. He had to time this right, the boy was moving. With one last glance thrown in the boy's direction the Chaplain turned tail and fled, straight into a gateless back garden.

How could he have been so stupid? He chided himself as quickening footsteps resounded from the alleyway. With increasing heartbeat the Chaplain looked for a means of escape. There didn't seem to be one, one way in, one way out, unless he jumped one of the surrounding fences. How fit was the old body he was in? Would it have the strength to carry him over? He didn't think so. There was only *one* way in and *one* way out and *that* meant going through the boy. The Chaplain tensed himself for the challenge, but if he had had doubts about the body he was in clearing a four foot fence what chance did it have against a near six foot teenage lad?

The boy entered the garden, too damned casually it seemed to the Chaplain, tossing aloft the object in his hand, the Chaplain's heart slumping in its pitiful chest as he saw just how big the rock was, almost as big as the boy's fist. If that hit him he couldn't see his adventure in the land of the living proceeding any further than the ground he was standing on. But the Chaplain, desperately trying to stop the old body from shaking and relinquishing the contents of its bladder, nevertheless bravely stood his ground.

'Wot yer doing in there yer mongrel?' smirked the youth, his body menacingly filling the only way of escape.

If things hadn't been so urgent the Chaplain may well have wondered what an Australian was doing down an English alleyway asking such bloody stupid questions, but they were and he didn't.

'No answer eh? Well just so's yer know whats it is I'm gonna bloody do to yer. I'm gonna bloody brain yer, yer lowlife bag orf shit!' The youth raised his arm and took calculated aim.

The Chaplain's eyes were now firmly fixed on the rock. He'd hurriedly devised a plan, a pretty flimsy one, but a plan all the same. It was simple, dodge and run. Forget the boy, think rock. When the rock was out of the equation then he would deal with the boy. Here the plan grew a little hazy.

The rock was let loose just as the Chaplain's bowels were trying to do likewise. He instinctively closed his eyes, something that wasn't in his plan. The rock flew hard and straight, and about a foot above the Chaplain's head, his eyes flickered open a moment later at the sound of breaking glass filling the air. This was promptly followed by the sound of a door being roughly thrown open and the eruption of a tirade of expletives the like of which the Chaplain had never experienced before.

Momentarily confused by not being dead or badly injured the Chaplain forgot about his assailant and stole a glance behind him. Standing in the back doorway of the house that the garden belonged too was what could only be described as a – and this was the only time the Chaplain had ever felt the description so apt – huge brick shithouse of a man.

Confusion now turned to realization. The boy had missed. It was time, apart from the dodging part, to put his flimsy plan into action. Steeling himself, the Chaplain turned, ready to evoke what power the old body he was in was capable of but, to his surprise and eternal relief, he found his way no longer barred. The boy had obviously taken to his heels. This

175

moment of triumph would have been long savoured if the Chaplain's wits hadn't suddenly fully recovered in the shadow that had fallen across him. With all the speed he could muster, and no looking back – salt and all that – the Chaplain followed the boy's example and legged it for all that he was worth.

Very hot, but not so much bothered, the Chaplain came to an exhausted halt in the midst of an expanse of trees and greenery that he assumed to be a small park. Park or not, though, the thing that endeared him most about this suburban oasis was not its botanic attributes but its total lack of people.

With no sign of the bane of his recent life in sight the Chaplain started to relax. He needed a rest, a damned good one, but as he stood panting in the shadows of a spreading chestnut tree and nicely shaped privet hedge, some sort of duck he thought, he found the need for a drink a higher priority.

The Chaplain scanned the surrounding area from his hiding place to ascertain if anything was close enough at hand to solve this problem. There didn't seem to be anything, but then from out the corner of his eye he spotted something promising. It stood tall and white and gleaming, and would have fitted in quite snugly with any thoughts the Chaplain might have had in mind to describe his idea of how Heaven might look.

Moving cautiously from bush to bush, tree to tree, the Chaplain made his way over to the marble fountain that gushed with an abundance of what he needed. He'd never drunk from a fountain before but then he'd never felt this thirsty before. The Chaplain sidled over to it and without ceremony, and only the merest of glances at his surroundings, stuck his face into the cool and amazingly clear water.

It tasted good and the Chaplain drank deeply from its depths which, and this was fortunate for the Chaplain who'd been too preoccupied with his thirst and tiredness to concern himself with such matters, sprang up from a natural underground spring and so was not inundated with man-made chemicals. Other cautions were also thrown to the wind, as he drank, he gave little if any heed to anything that might give rise to impending danger. And when a young couple ambled uncomfortably close, pointing and staring as they did, the Chaplain refrained from even the slightest of cursory glances. Deep inside he knew this was unwise and might prove to be foolhardy, but sometimes foolhardy ran hand in hand with thirst and tiredness and other longings and when this happened one rarely had a say in the ensuing stupidity.

His thirst finally quenched, the Chaplain shook droplets of water from his chin and re-entered the world of caution. He now eyed suspiciously the young couple who'd since wondered off and were now studying a signpost, but deeming them no threat, turned his attention to the rest of the park.

With no-one else within his line of sight, the Chaplain relaxed again, but just a little, and found that not only was his thirst gone but he'd regained his previously lost, albeit shaky, vigour. He in fact found that he actually felt better than at anytime since arriving back in the living world. The Chaplain thus concluded that either the water was in some way blessed with energy-giving tonics or that exercise was good for you after all. Whatever the reason, the Chaplain now felt good and at ease and, something he didn't have any answer for, strangely at peace. Which, he thought with a wry smile, was something that was evidently becoming par for the course, this not quite knowing how, what, why and where.

With this feeling of unexplainable peace flowing through him the Chaplain took the time to take a couple of steps back and for the first time really saw the fountain for what it was; a beautiful piece of art. It was so much more than he had first thought and the Chaplain found himself wondering how man with his many faults could achieve something so wonderful. He then remembered the works of Michelangelo Buonarrati, a personal favourite of his, and conceded that of course such people did and must still exist.

It was truly a piece of art, this fountain, a masterpiece of clean white marble that rose from its beginnings at the bowl base to emerge as two beautifully serene angels. One held a horn to its lips whilst the other drew before it a scroll from which to read. Heralds, thought the Chaplain, as his eyes caressed the marble's silky smooth whiteness before falling on the words that were inscribed in silver on the back of the scroll. Without really thinking about it the Chaplain read what it said.

"TWO ANGELS HOSPITAL"

As if mesmerised by the words, the Chaplain stood and stared. There was something about them that should mean something to him, he was sure of it, but what? Nothing was instantly forthcoming, he was certain he had never heard of the place. It was obviously a new addition, built sometime after his own days on Earth. But as he turned to resume his quest, a memory only just returning from the transition came to him. The Chaplain felt a twinge of excitement which gradually began to build. *He'd* been right about not knowing of the hospital in his lifetime, but he *had* heard of it; had heard of it *after* his lifetime. It was the *one*. The excitement the Chaplain felt grew. It was the one Richard had been taken to following his "accident". The place where they had first met. The place where it had all started. As the pieces fell into place something else came to the Chaplain's mind, something very important. Hadn't Richard mentioned that he lived close by?

Or had he? Again the Chaplain's head filled with questions and inexplicable doubts. One minute clear, the next foggy, it felt as if he was deliberately being kept in the dark about some things. *Had* Richard said it, or? "Par for the course" suddenly reappeared, splashed across the Chaplain's thought waves, giving cause to an inward smile.

178

What did it matter who had said what or how and how he knew what he did or didn't know? The Chaplain knew then that it was very doubtful that he would ever know the answers to many of the questions he'd asked. What did matter though was something else he had started to question. Something he had been close to losing. His faith. He didn't need answers, he just needed faith. With faith he knew that all would come right, that he would find Richard and the others, and that all would be well in the end.

The Chaplain's gaze returned to the angels' faces and he made a decision. Ending up here before these divine messengers in marble had to have been intervention. He had arrived here for a reason, one he could never hope to understand, but one nevertheless he'd take heed of.

Around the foot of the fountain lay a neat sandy coloured gravel path. From this four others sprouted in different directions across the greenery. There was only one choice, the one the angels were looking to. With his faith firmly in place, the Chaplain started to follow it

CHAPTER 28

At first there had been confusion. One hell of a lot of it. Then there had been disorientation. More hell. And finally there had come revelation. The memory of who he was, the surprise of what he was and finally the almighty relief that accompanied the realization of where he was. This time there was no Hell and Sammy was truly thankful for that.

For the rest of that first day, back in the land of the living, Sammy just sat back and watched. Taking in the world around him. The living breathing world he'd left so long ago. Watching as life busied itself. And as he watched something occurred to him, something that had eluded him his entire first time on Earth, the true meaning of life.

Even in the gutter Sammy had wondered what it was all about. More so he supposed than when his life had been mixed with the glam and glitz of his career. Sammy smiled sadly to himself as he watched and thought how ridiculous it all was. How he and others had strived, and he guessed were still doing so, to find the meaning of life when all the time it was right there under your very nose. Pity you had to die to discover that.

But that was then and this was now and now that Sammy knew, he didn't dwell on it. He had a pang of sadness for humanity but it didn't linger. Sammy had other things more pressing to deal with, namely Richard and the others. But, thought Sammy as he sat there watching, letting life, this new life of his, wash over him, one day couldn't hurt, could it? He was thankful for this second chance to taste life, albeit a short one, so would anyone begrudge him just one day? One day of soaking up life? So Sammy stayed put and spent his first day back on Earth as he pleased, just watching.

That night, even though his body felt on the verge of bursting with all the pleasure and excitement he was feeling, he slept, fitfully and without dreams. An ordinary night's sleep that people took for granted, not realising how lucky they were.

The next day came and Sammy awoke to herald the dawn. Taking in a deep breath of the wonderful morning air he watched with renewed awe as the night merged into day. He couldn't remember ever feeling as happy as he did at that moment, including yesterday. He was refreshed as never before and more than ready to face the challenge ahead. And then, as the birds around him sang their daily chorus of thanks to whatever deity they praised, Sammy decided it was time to go. To spread his wings and meet this challenge set for him. And how hard could that be? With him as he was now? With this rebirth of enthusiasm for life coursing so strongly through him, Sammy raised his eyes skyward and was gone.

But as Sammy left his resting place he was forgetting one vital lesson, or was it one he hadn't learnt even now, there was no Yang without Yin, no light without darkness, no good without bad.

By the fourth day of fruitless searching Sammy had been more than reacquainted with how hard life could really be. How life wasn't all moonlight and dancing. Gone were Sammy's recently acquired rose-tinted glasses. He now stood stooped and downhearted. A storm was raging overhead and hailstones were relentlessly battering the shelter he'd taken refuge in. Sammy felt, *was*, wretched, felt, *was*, miserable, but most of all he felt lost and alone.

It wasn't however a new feeling for Sammy. In his lifetime he'd tasted loneliness at its worst. And he'd swear, on any amount of stacks of bibles, that it wasn't just a word. Sammy believed that it was a creature that could creep up on you like no living thing could. A creature that existed equally happily in or out of the mind, trawling and feeding on the fear that it itself generated, giving no quarter to either the strong or weak.

Sammy shuddered and wondered if it was a draught that had caused him to do so, or the memories that were flooding into his mind. He remembered what loneliness meant. To sleep alone with no one to hold. To live alone with no one to share your thoughts. Just being alone. And then the worst loneliness of all. To die alone. And in that latter fleeting moment of thought Sammy was back in the cold gutter again, breathing his last wretched breath. Sammy shuddered again but this time he knew why.

Sammy huddled further into the corner where he sat, little realising that there would soon be another meaning of alone thrust upon him. This one sinister, and so brazen, that it would come upon you in the midst of others.

Since taking refuge Sammy had been watched. Eyes not unlike Sammy's had contemplated his every move from the deep shadows that existed in the shelter, but these weren't friendly eyes, these were filled with menace and suspicion and didn't like what they saw.

As the hail relented to be replaced by the softer patter of rain, a rustling from within those shadows drew Sammy's attention to the fact that he was not, as he believed, totally alone. Sammy peered hard into the darkness and saw that there were eyes staring back at him, cold relentless eyes that shone with malice. Responding to the menace that exuded towards him from these chilling pitiless eyes, uneasiness began to seep into his every fibre.

As if sensing this, the owners of the eyes shuffled from the shadows and sternly presented themselves before him. Sammy had the immediate feeling that he was being judged. The whole scene smacked of it. A Kangaroo Court and these cold creatures standing before him were to be his Judge, Jury and, Sammy's blood ran cold at the sudden understanding that had manifested itself in his mind, Executioners.

Sammy backed away but found nowhere to go. When he tried to ask why, in a voice that was barely able to suppress his fear, no voice answered but the silent contempt his question brought told him what he wanted to know. It was also there in their eyes. It was because he was different. Oh he was the same species. He was the same as them on the inside. His blood flowed as theirs; his guts would spill the same. But he was different on the outside. And when it came down to it, it was that and only that that was condemning him.

He had no way out as they bore silently down on him. He mustn't panic, he thought, panic would achieve nothing, but since when did panic ever listen to anyone? Sammy panicked and continued desperately looking for a way of escape even though he knew there was none. The eyes closed in, his fear inviting them ever closer. They surrounded him until all he could see was shadow, until all he could smell was what they smelled, his fear. Then they were upon him and Sammy grabbed the only option left to him. Sammy prayed.

For a fleeting second Sammy thought he was back in the blackness, that his new lease of life had been nothing more than a cruel dream. Then the pain set in.

As gently as possible Sammy laid his head, that he'd subconsciously moved, back onto solid ground. It felt to him as his senses kicked in as if every bone in his body was broken, every muscle and sinew torn and bruised. He now remembered the beating, falling, the blissful loss of consciousness. Sammy recalled how he'd welcomed it, urged it to do its job, and relieve him of his agony. He had never expected to survive and wake up where he'd fallen, still in the living world. Sammy's thoughts went back to the hateful, spiteful eyes; it was a miracle that he had.

His eyes, bruised and swollen but still able to open, suddenly grew wide and looked fearfully up as a new terror awoke within him. Were his attackers still there, watching him? Waiting perchance for him to come round so they could beat him some more? To finish the job? But there was no one there. Daylight now danced where the shadows once were, appearing through cracks in the wooden boards of the shelter. And with the shadows, it seemed, his assailants had also gone. Tears started to fill Sammy's eyes. Wasn't being alive wonderful?

Time moved on and Sammy, relieved at the lack of shadows, and assailants, but loath to count any chickens just yet, gingerly attempted to move one of his legs. The pain was intense, nearly causing him to black out, but he painfully persevered and to his relief found that it wasn't broken. Once rested from this self-inflicted ordeal Sammy repeated the process on other parts of his body. Each time slowly and carefully. Each time not slowly or carefully enough. But each time rewarded with a lack of broken bones.

Sammy now lay exhausted with the effort, his body tortured enough, but it was now the turn of his mind. He was thankfully in one piece, but for how long? And how long had he been lying there? Did the light that shone through the cracks belong to the morning after the night before, or had his attack happened days ago?

And Sammy would have worried more on this dilemma if it where not for a distant noise reaching the periphery of his hearing, bringing with it fresh foreboding to his breast and a sudden overwhelming urgency to his thoughts.

Were his assailants returning? No, the noise couldn't be made by them. This was something else. But either way Sammy decided it was time to move if he was able. In pain but now conscious that it was not the urgent pain of fresh injuries that he carried but the ache and soreness of old ones, old ones that were healing, he managed to roll onto his side, then with an almighty effort that brought stars to his eyes and bile to his throat, he got to his feet.

The noise was steadily growing closer and louder when Sammy realised he knew what the sound was. But wasn't it a bit early in the year for someone to be mowing grass? Less fearful now but still cautious, Sammy began to look for a new way out, he didn't think it wise to go out the same way he'd come in, and found a couple of loose shiplap planks, daylight pouring through a gap like a guiding beacon. Sammy limped towards it, his pain still very much prevalent but lessening second by second as stiffness eased, and awkwardly pushed his way outside. Making sure the coast was clear, Sammy left the shelter and staggered across open grass.

CHAPTER 29

At first he thought he was imagining it. A strange sensation unlike anything he'd ever experienced, dead or alive, was steadily enveloping him. The blackness was still there but now it had a different quality to it. Not so much warmth, not so comforting. It had to all intent and purposes lost its softness.

And now as it fully enclosed him he noticed it had a discernable coolness about it. An aura of coolness that toyed with the senses.

He moved and found that his movement was no longer smooth and liquid but awkward like a fish out of water. But there was no rise of panic within him. No sudden fear of this unsought change. Whatever was happening hadn't chased away the feeling of safety he'd been blessed with in the blackness.

More senses began to awaken in response to the aura. A metallic smell came to him, faint, very faint, but he was sure of it. And then another odour, much stronger than the metallic smell, triggering memories as it did. It brought with it images of his parents, his father in particular; of him smoking his favourite pipe.

The image, the last memory of his father he had, dissolved before his mind's eye to be replaced by a hazy light. A faint glimmer but light all the same. It puzzled him, why should he be thinking of light? He thought of reaching out to it, to touch it. But how could he? How could he touch something that lived only in his mind?

But it wasn't in his mind. It was no imaginary light; it was real and growing brighter as the realization struck home.

What was happening to him now? He was hearing voices. Voices he thought he recognised. But stranger still, one of them seemed to be inside his head, searching his mind. It wanted to contact him, communicate.

Confused, and feeling the safety he'd taken for granted only a few moments ago now rapidly slipping from him, he tried to call out, reply to the voices, but nothing came. Instead he felt as if he was being smothered. His throat, lungs, filling with something alien, gagging him as it did; threatening to snuff out his very existence.

Then the light was fully upon him. A terrible blinding light that tore into his eyes, ripping from him any last lingering shred of comfort the blackness had given him. Choking and shaking with fear, Geoff cowered helpless and naked before it.

CHAPTER 30

Because of the relentless pounding he had taken, was taking, from the demon within, Joe failed at first to notice the subtle changes that had started to take place within and around him during the fleeting moments directly after Richard's demise.

The first clue that eventually tipped the wink telling him something was different was with the awareness that he was no longer receiving glimpses of the Four. He tried frantically to retrieve them but it was to no avail; a veil had fallen over their exploits as each sought the end to their journeys. He then became aware of the easing, slow, but definite lessening inside of him of the demon's onslaught. Joe felt curiously and inexplicitly weak – manipulated? Then the battle ceased altogether. Abrupt in its moment, lacking in its reasoning.

Taken aback by this unexpected cessation of hostilities, Joe, alarmed, strangely hollow, draped in an unfathomable emotion of being lost, was given no time to claim calm repose before his being was rocked again. A new sensation that flowed over and through him shaking his already weakened state, causing him to reach out to steady himself, but the movement was checked as Joe suddenly came to understand what it all meant, what was happening. He stared down at Richard in that moment of lucidity as someone taking in the wonders of a tropical rock-pool for the first time.

Wonderment and awe swept across Joe's face as it came to him the reality that was Richard's existence. That was the essence of all existence.

The unnoticed glow that had been steadily growing about Joe became dazzlingly brighter, its source from behind him. Joe turned to face it and for the first time in his existence he blinked. He blinked with disbelief at what he was seeing. He blinked at the wonder of what he had just been given. If he had thought of it, if it had not been alien to him to do so, if he had been human, he would have pinched himself. Joe dropped to his knees.

The brightness grew brighter still, a dark nucleus forming within. A form within that could almost be described as human but not quite. And then, as if it had never existed, the light disappeared leaving behind it its dark nucleus. A dark form standing alone draped in an ethereal glow, smiling down at a kneeling trembling Joe.

CHAPTER 31

Like a Russian doll that sadly boasts only two pieces, Richard and Laura sat one within the other in total silence contemplating what had been, what is, and what might be.

They'd sat like this since Richard had confirmed what Laura guessed she already knew, that time had somehow marched on without them and had taken with it the last two weeks of Richard's living life. Cruelly, as though snatching candy from a helpless sleeping toddler.

When Laura's fears had been borne out as justified, she'd said nothing. Of course she'd wanted to say how sorry she was. How terrible she felt about everything including the way she'd been acting. What she'd done. But she'd sensed there was no need to. That Richard already knew all of this. And that the only thing that he needed from her, for the moment, was peace and quiet. A few moments, maybe more, of solitude, if that was possible, so that he could take it all in. Absorb all that had been thrown at him since the accident. Richard needed to process things, needed to get some kind of perspective, and only then would he be able to talk.

So Laura sat quietly, honouring Richard's wishes. She felt it the least she could do. At the very least what he deserved. And the seconds rolled on until she lost all sense of how long she waited.

'Laura?'

It was the second time that Richard had called her name.

'Laura!' said Richard a third time, this time sharper.

Down inside Richard, deep within her own thoughts, it slowly dawned on Laura what was happening. 'I hear you,' she at last answered, a little embarrassed.

'I thought for a moment you'd left me,' joked Richard, his attempted jest barely hiding his shaky relief that she hadn't.

'Not me. Ever the bad penny,' Laura quipped, her own relief at hearing Richard's voice barely under control. 'What can I do for you?' God, she thought, she hoped that hadn't sounded as aloof as it had to her.

'I...er...I was wondering if you'd like a piece of chocolate?' Richard sounded a little hesitant. Laura wondered if that was her fault, her nervous aloofness the culprit.

'Um – okay, please,' replied Laura not quite sure what to make of the current, getting-to-know-you situation she felt brewing. 'Are you okay?' Damn it! Why the hell had she said that? From cold aloof bitch to interrogator in one swift size ten step. Nice one Laura. But Richard, to her surprise, laughed.

'As good as anyone with only one more day left on Earth.'

Laura felt herself rise as one with Richard from the sofa. At the same time Richard felt Laura's presence slump within him.

'I'm joking,' he said quickly, hoping the possible glibness of his reply hadn't been taken the wrong way. 'I'm fine, honestly,' he tried to reassure her, and perhaps himself. The slump took an upturn. 'Chocolate it is then'

As Richard strode towards the kitchen and the heaven in a bar laying beyond the fridge door – no thighs, no worries – Laura felt a wash of relief roll over her. It was as if Richard had had a minor personality transplant. He was, and she'd swear to this, well almost, happy. She doubted she would be in his situation, but it was true, for him, he was fairly buoyant. Why the sudden change? But she wasn't complaining, it was better this way, she even found herself beginning to like the man more. Laura hoped it would last.

The small light inside the fridge blinked a welcome as the door was opened, and then continued to do so.

'Blast it,' said Richard tapping the light's plastic surround. 'Must be something loose, I'll have to -.' Richard stopped what he was saying. Do what? Mend it tomorrow, his last day on Earth? Pop down to the DIY store on Sunday, when he was dead?

Laura held her breath, waiting for what had to be the inevitable. But she worried unnecessarily; Richard composed himself admirably and reached for the bar of chocolate as if nothing had just happened.

'Then some beer?' he asked, catching Laura on the hop.

'What?' Laura had expected a collapse back into depression from Richard but he seemed completely unfazed by the moment.

'After the chocolate,' Richard explained.

'Oh – right. Yeah – that's fine by me,' Laura answered, once she'd found solid footing again. She was also still struggling to come to terms with the chatting to Richard like old pals scenario that had gradually arisen.

'Good,' said Richard, closing the fridge door with his backside.

Richard ambled back to the lounge, hands full of chocolate and beer, and returned to the sofa.

'And then,' he continued as he sat down, 'I thought maybe a vid?'

Still baffled by Richard's behaviour and amiable mood and the upturn in their relationship Laura missed the connection and was therefore a few seconds out of sync. 'A what?' she said, not quite catching up.

'A DVD. Funny how we still call them vids though,' mused Richard as the thought struck him.

Laura was lost now; she didn't have the slightest clue as to what Richard was talking about.

'I'm sorry,' she said, 'call me thick, but I've got no idea what the hell you're going on about.'

'A…' Richard started, but then a penny dropped. 'You bloody idiot!' He sensed Laura stiffen up. 'No, not you, me,' he said quickly. 'I'm the idiot. You've no idea what I'm babbling on about, have you?'

'I just said that.'

'Here I'll show you.'

Depositing the munchies on the seat beside him, Richard scrabbled from the sofa and went to the sideboard which he opened revealing a stack of some thirty to forty DVD's. 'There,' he announced triumphantly, 'take your pick.'

'I still don't understand,' said Laura staring blankly at the pile of plastic containers.

Reaching down Richard pulled a DVD from its rack and turned it so the front could be seen. On it was a black and white picture of Humphrey Bogart leaning on the title of one of his films.

'It's a film?'

'That's right; I've got the whole collection of Bogey's films. We can watch it if you like, or maybe you'd prefer -.' There was a pause as Richard swapped Bogey for another film. 'Tar-rah – a colour one.' Richard held the new one out for Laura to see. It was one she'd never heard of. 'I don't suppose they had that in your day?' he added as an afterthought. Sometimes Richard could be as dull as dishwater.

'What do you mean, my day?' snapped Laura, on the defensive. 'I'm not bloody prehistoric you know. Eighty four I died, not thirty four.' She had also just caught up on what Richard had been going on about before. '*And* I bloody well know what a bloody video is.'

Enthusiasm very much on the wane, and realising his stupidity, Richard clung dumbly to the DVD in his hand before finding his voice again. 'Sorry,' he said quietly, 'Of course you know. I know. Feels like I've always known.' If he could have looked Laura in the eye he would have done. 'I only have to think and I remember.'

It was true. There was a connection between them that stretched further than their understanding. Somehow Richard had memories that didn't belong to him. Memories he didn't want to pry in. But maybe they were there for a reason. Richard placed the DVD he was holding on the top of the sideboard and reached back inside to the rack.

Inside Richard, Laura was now feeling awful. She wished she hadn't snapped like that, she hadn't meant to. She felt as if she'd chastised a small child just because of his excitement.

'Sorry yourself,' she said.

'We keep saying that.'

'I shouldn't have – .'

'Its okay – it's my fault. I shouldn't have tried putting you to the back of my mind.'

'Do you know everything about me?'

'I don't honestly know. I get flashes if I think about it – you. I try not to though, it's private to my mind.' Richard waited a moment before asking the obvious. 'Do you get anything from me?'

'Sometimes, but it's the same for me, I don't try.'

Richard emerged from the sideboard with another DVD in his hand. It was a Laurel and Hardy compilation.

'I thought this might be more up your street. It's the nearest to silent movies I've got.'

Laura was moved and at that moment would have even forgiven him his taste in décor. 'The chocolate first though.'

That afternoon, on the penultimate day of Richard's life on Earth, Richard and Laura become more then just the strangest of relations, they became friends. And with a new understanding and a mutual agreement between them to try as hard as possible not to sift through each other's memories and thoughts, however tempting it might seemat the time, they sat and did what friends did best.

They ate the chocolate, which Laura extolled as being mankind's greatest ever achievement, laughed out loud at the antics of Stan and Ollie on the small "Silver Screen", and drank the whole six-pack dry with gusto.

As the afternoon merged into early evening and the television announced the end of the last Laurel and Hardy film with the familiar "Dah-di-dah – Dah-di-dah", Richard and Laura began to talk. Both were fairly mellow by now, largely thanks to the beer, and soon small talk gave way to earnest discussion.

With mutual agreement in place, each had things to ask each other. Their lives, their loves, Laura acted just a little "surprised" to hear that Richard had had little success in this area, and what the future, if there was to be one, might hold for them.

There were good times, bad times, Laura's struggle in London as a "wannabe" actress, and unfortunate times, Richard's first attempt at sex, "lust said" said Laura covering her ears with Richard's hands and then apologising in fits of laughter. And sad times, but the sad time brought up by Richard was not his imminent demise but the unexpected realization that in the afterlife he wouldn't be with his family and friends like he had always believed would be the case. Laura had tried to reassure him that she, the Chaplain, and the others were his family in a way, but she knew what he meant and for a while the room went silent.

It didn't last long though, Richard deciding he just didn't have the time to dwell on things he couldn't change, and the earlier happy ambience returned, bringing with it lighter hearted conversation.

One foray into their particular likes and dislikes concerned the world of culinary delights and Richard had been amazed to find Laura had never sampled the delights of a good curry. Rising from the sofa, and feeling a little hungry due to the topic, and other things which he'd forgotten about for the moment, Richard headed to the kitchen and the freezer. Once there he pulled from it a boil in the bag chicken Balti for two, Richard always had one for himself as there never seemed quite enough otherwise, complete with rice and naan. The naan Richard explained, to an adequately embarrassed Laura, who'd openly wondered how boiling it could possibly work, needed to be placed under the grill.

With Laura staying prudently quiet during the cooking process, much to Richard's amusement (which hadn't helped to enhance her now slightly sullen mood) the late dinner was soon ready. Together with more lagers from a replenished fridge Richard sat himself, and Laura, down at the kitchen table, his saliva glands already clocking on for overtime at the sight and smell of the feast.

'It won't taste like any boil in the bags from your time,' said Richard, as he prepared to place the first steaming forkful into his mouth.

'I won't know, will I?' Laura reminded him, her frame of mind now taking a turn for the better as her own senses began to get caught up in the gorgeous aroma wafting to her from the plate.

'You'll just have to take my word for it then. This is your authentic Indian cuisine, all the way from the East. Not something concocted in a factory or wherever it was it used to be made in your time.' Richard popped the food into his mouth; not too much though, just in case she didn't like it. 'Well?' he asked after he had swallowed; the spices playing on his tongue and throat.

'It's delicious,' relayed Laura after a few seconds of savouring the moment. The chocolate had been heaven, but this? Laura had never tasted anything so good. Or at least she couldn't recall having done so. 'Now some pickle please.'

'Chutney,' Richard corrected, 'but its plain old Mango I'm afraid.'

'I'm ready,' she giggled.

Richard laughed out loud at Laura's childlike response and placed a small dollop of the chutney on the edge of the naan, again a small amount just in case, and took a bite. And yet again his fears were unfounded, Laura loved it. The curry, the

197

naan, the "pickle", she loved it all, and in no time the plate was clean.

'That was good.'

'Glad you liked it. Shall we?' said Richard gesturing to the door leading to the lounge.

'Why not?'

Leaving the dirty dishes in the sink, something he wouldn't normally think of doing but, considering the situation, Richard, although he suspected he might see to them before the night was out – old habits etc –, bottle in hand, left the kitchen and went into the lounge.

By now the amount of beer he'd consumed, even though he, technically, he felt, was drinking for two, was taking its toll. As he bent forward to open the sideboard for another film a moment of light-headedness nearly had him carpet bound face-first again. He managed to steady himself with a bit of help from the sideboard but his hands were no longer as dexterous as they had been before the Indian and beer dinner and so his attempt at retrieving a film resulted in the stack collapsing. As the DVD's poured onto the floor in a heap Richard broke into a fit of giggles.

Richard now dropped knees first to the floor, but this time there was no pain or blackness to greet him, just belly laughter that was bringing tears to his eyes. Laura, herself a little worse for wear due to the drink but not nearly as bad as Richard, began to laugh as well. And if asked in that moment why, they wouldn't have been able to say, but maybe it was laughter for laughter's sake.

Laura was still giggling away, taken along on the ride of nonsensical cheer, when she gradually became aware that the tears she felt rolling down Richards's cheeks were now no longer ones of laughter.

'Richard?' she ventured, a modicum of sense returning, curbing her laughter as it did.

'I…I'm sorry,' he spluttered through a juddering sob. 'It's just…' There was a sort of half gulp as Richard fought to control another sob that filled his throat.

'What is it?' Laura could feel herself welling up now, even though she had no idea what was wrong.

Leaning forward Richard picked up a DVD from the top of the pile and held it up, pointing to the title.

'I don't understand,' said Laura looking at it.

'I don't either,' Richard admitted, feeling a bit silly. 'It just struck a cord somehow,' he explained. 'I don't suppose there's gonna be a guardian angel somewhere that'll save the day for me?'

'Oh,' said Laura as the film title clicked. 'You've got me,' she proffered brightly. It was pathetic but the best thing she could have said. Richard studied the disc case in his hand and managed a tiny smile.

'You're prettier too,' he sniffed, wiping tears from his cheeks with the back of his hand.

'You'd better believe it.'

With the atmosphere in the room getting back to how it was before the hysterics of laughter and tears, Richard got to his feet and shuffled over to the sofa.

'Didn't want to see another film anyway,' he said, sitting down. 'Did you?'

Laura said she didn't, and without another word spoken between them they settled down into a mutual silence, one that was contemplative but not in any way melancholy.

How long this steady silence would have continued is anybody's guess but end it did, shattered, after a few minutes, by the ringing of the telephone.

Richard went to look at his watch, but of course it wasn't there and the words "who can be calling me at this time of night" died on his lips. He lifted the receiver and spoke; he didn't recognize the voice on the other end.

'Hello, this is Tom Welburn of the Parks Football Association. May I speak to a Mister Richard Ross please?'

For a moment Richard was at a loss, the F.A. ringing him? How did they know he was home? He'd told no-one he'd left the hospital. It had to be some kind of wind up. Richard decided to play along for the moment and let this Welburn character, if that was his real name, prattle on, then he would tell him where to get off. If by some coincidence it was the F.A. then all the better.

'Speaking,' said Richard.

'Ah, Mister Ross, as I said I'm Tom Welburn, nice to make your acquaintance, you may call me Tom, and I've recently taken the reins so to speak from Winston Singh as this area's area co-ordinator.' Slight pause for any forthcoming congratulations; none were. 'And hmm, noticed that you haven't officiated for us for a while. I'm afraid everything's in a bit of a mess at the moment, Mister Singh wasn't the most organised of people it seems.' A moment's stilted silence. 'So, ahem, if there's a particular reason for not doing so, or you no longer wish to officiate at the Parks level, then maybe we can discuss it.'

Richard was hanging on to the phone as if he'd never seen one before and hadn't realized "Tom" had stopped talking.

'Mister Ross?'

'Mister Ross!'

'Er-sorry-yes, sorry what?

'The other reason I'm ringing, Mister Ross is to ask if it's at all possible for you, if you do wish to continue that is, to officiate at a match scheduled for tomorrow afternoon. I'm sorry it's short notice but I've been let down last minute. It's a semi-final thingy – two local teams.'

It had all been going in one ear and out the other; Tom Welburn may well have been talking double Dutch as far as Richard was concerned, until then.

Match? It now fully clicked that the call was for real and he understood what it was that "Tom" had been droning on about. Tomorrow?

Tomorrow! What was being asked of him? Tomorrow! His last day on Mother Earth, and the prick wants him to waste it officiating – what sort of bloody word is that – reffing a bloody footie match? The bloke must be stark staring bonkers.

And Richard was just about to tell him so when Laura intervened.

'Wait...think about it for a moment before you answer. It could be happening for a reason.'

'What?'

'Sorry, did you say something Mister Ross?'

'Not you. What do you mean?'

'Mister Ross?'

'Sorry.'

'What do you mean, for a reason?' whispered Richard, even though this time he was using his mind rather than his mouth.

'It could be something to do with what you have to learn. *The Lesson*.' Laura quickly explained, whispering herself.

Richard had all but forgotten the reason why he was in the pickle he was in. He stared blankly at the phone as he wondered what to do next.

'You'll have to say yes,' interrupted Laura, going against their agreement and reading Richard's mind, 'just in case.'

Richard didn't seem to notice her indiscretion though as he found himself glumly agreeing; the idea sobering, dispersing much of the drink's effects.

'You're right, I suppose.'

'Sorry? I didn't quite catch that Mister Ross.'

'Yes – okay.' There, he'd said it, even though he wasn't totally convinced it was what he wanted to be doing on the last day of his life, as well as the fact that he'd sworn he'd never ref another match as long as he lived; there was irony there somewhere.

'Good. Much appreciated. It's at Robertson's Recreation ground, three o'clock kick off. Oh – and its Roach versus a

201

team called Valley. Thanks again. Bye.' Welburn's goodbye was short and sharp, mission accomplished.

'Are you alright?' asked Laura, sensing Richard was struggling with more than just the inconvenience of the football match.

'Yes, but?'

'Something's up?'

'It's something about the names. I just can't – I don't know, I'm sure I've heard them before somewhere.' Then it came to him, the memory suddenly emerging like a terrible cloud, disengaging itself from mists that drifted in his mind, bringing with it a coldness that played down Richard's spine and a damp clamminess to his hands. With slow deliberation Richard replaced the phone.

'It's…the same teams,' he said, his voice slow, hollow.

'As what?' said Laura, puzzled by the deep and subdued vibes she was getting from Richard. They were also scaring her a little.

'As before. The attack.'

Laura struggled to understand.

So Richard spelt it out for her. 'It's the same two teams that were playing – that I was reffing – when I had my little *"accident"*. I'm going to die on the bloody pitch, aren't I?' Richard's voice raised an octave as he spoke.

'I'm sure…'Laura started to say; though she didn't really know where she was going with it.

'My last bloody day on Earth is going to end with me laid out in the middle of some two-bit bloody excuse for a football pitch.' Richard's mood took a swing towards anger.

'Richard…' Laura tried to voice concern but Richard cut her short as he continued with his rant.

'Surrounded by morons and half-wits who have trouble dressing themselves let alone playing football.'

'Listen!' Laura pleaded.

But Richard, his face contorted by a bitter twisted snarl, took no heed. 'Well sod all of them. I won't go. Sod the match; they'll just have to ref it themselves. Hit themselves too, until they're all bloody senseless; that won't take *bloody* long.' Richard spat the last expletive with considerable venom.

Laura was becoming worried. Richard sounded on the verge of losing it and there was nothing she could do about it. She had tried but he wasn't listening, she just couldn't seem to get his attention – unless?

'And I bet that bastard Welburn knew what he was doing, Singhy wouldn't have asked me.'

Laura decided he needed a slap, a hard sharp one, but how could she? Considering where she was? But Laura, whatever anyone else might think, was not a quitter at heart; she decided she at least had to try. As if of its own accord Richard's arm began to move ever so slightly away from his body.

But Richard, in too much of a lather, a photo-fit of what he thought Welburn might look like had popped into his mind, foiled the plan without even noticing as his fists clenched in anger. He wished with all his might that the pompous ass would appear in front of him that minute, he'd teach the bastard a thing or two.

'Richarddddd!' The scream would have brought the walls of Jericho down if they'd still been standing. Richard clamped his hands to his ears as it threatened to beat his eardrums to a pulp, but it proved a useless exercise. Laura had chosen a different course of action and was slapping him the only way she could, and slapping him hard.

At last the beating stopped and Laura, hoping she hadn't overdone it, spoke Richard's name, though much quieter this time. She waited a moment, her ears ringing, before continuing. 'Are you okay? Talk to me.'

'I think I'm deaf,' came the muted shell-shocked reply.

Laura had the sudden urge to laugh, nerves maybe, but the situation of a moment ago seemed somehow comical now that

Richard had stopped his ranting and raving, but she managed to control it.

'I'm sorry…I just wanted you to stop, you were scaring me.'

'Me, scaring you?' said Richard, still rubbing his ears.

Richard felt what he took to be an affirmative nod from deep within him which brought along with it an insight as to just how frightened Laura had been by his behaviour of the last couple of minutes.

'I guess I was acting a little insane,' he said, his voice hushed.

'A little,' Laura gently agreed, not wishing to push the point.

Richard reached for a lager and opened it. He wanted something stronger but he took what was at hand. 'I guess I should apologise?' he said after taking a swig. 'Letting things get on top of me like that.'

'There's no need.'

'I feel I should.'

'If you feel the need then.'

'It's just, you know, the thought of dying. Dying like that, on a bloody football pitch of all places. Where's the dignity in that?' Richard started downing the beer.

'But you might not. Who says you're going to last that long?'

'Well thanks,' choked, laughed Richard, beer bubbling from his nose.

'My pleasure,' laughed Laura nervously, she hadn't really meant it as a joke, but if it helped…

'What do we do now?' said Richard wiping beer from his top lip.

'How about the film with the angel in it? I know its not Christmas but, hey-ho'

The DVD was by the side of the phone, James Stewart and entourage staring up at Richard; he must have absentmindedly brought it over with the beers.

'How about giving it a miss?' smiled Richard picking it up. He was fast mellowing again, the mad moment of a moment ago rapidly forgotten as his mood improved. He'd deal with tomorrow when it came. As for now he might as well start again and try and relax and live what was left of his life the best he could. Or at least that was what he was trying to tell himself. Richard finished the beer and tossed the DVD Frisbee-style across the room towards the open sideboard. It missed.

'Oops,' said Laura as it cracked against the wall.

'Over-rated anyway,' joked Richard as it fell to the floor. He of course wasn't going to admit to anyone, even under threat of torture, that it was one of his all time favourite films. Besides, now wasn't a good time to be reminded of the fact that what he himself needed was a miracle. 'Now, where were we?'

CHAPTER 32

The Chaplain had not gone too far from the hospital grounds when he found he needed to stop and rest again. He blamed the unusually warm weather, although it was in truth only unusual for him. Things had changed since his time on Earth, the weather being one of the major changes.

Unknown to the Chaplain, since the year 2022, the shift in seasonal temperatures had been quite dramatic, and it was now fairly normal in Britain for March to herald the start of what the Chaplain would have called summer and for it to come in like a hot lamb and go out very much the same, mild and in the seventies mostly. There was the odd sudden violent outburst, as had happened a couple of days back with a thunderstorm and hail. Of course not knowing this meant nothing to the Chaplain as he stood gasping air and wishing the body he'd been endowed with could have been just a little bit younger.

Resting but briefly, (he was of the mind that he'd already lost enough time through dallying what with one thing or another) the Chaplain gathered his old body together and resumed his journey, heading along the small street he'd entered that had lain directly opposite the hospital gates and the gravel path he had been following; he'd taken this as another sign that he was on the right track.

Keeping to the pavement's shadows as best he could, the Chaplain found, as well as the obvious benefit of the cooler shade, there was something of comfort to him in that the houses along the way reminded him of his first life on Earth.

It was not the houses themselves of course, he reckoned on them being post World War Two, way after his time, but the red brick that they were built of. Red bricks that sparked memories of warmth and happiness and things long dear to him. These houses had character, were homes, unlike the grey and drab monoliths he'd seen standing by the roadside on his way to the hospital which had spouted people like a disturbed ant colony and which lacked such qualities.

Red brick houses joined together in an almost unbroken line, the odd alleyway, which the Chaplain would steer well clear of, occasionally interrupting the symmetry but, in their own way, adding to the street's identity. Each red brick house with its own little piece of England in front, some unkempt in appearance, but most boasting hours of loving care.

Stopping by a small wall built from the same red brick, the Chaplain took a precious moment to sniff the air. It smelled sweet and clean, cleaner than the Chaplain had expected, sweet with the faint scent of flowers wafting from some unknown garden, flowers the Chaplain could not quite put a name to. It was a wonderful moment and brought back memories of the long lazy summers of his youth. But as wonderful as it was, he had to move on, continue his dogged search.

Ten minutes later he stopped again, but this time it wasn't to rest, or marvel, it was because the street, and with it seemingly the Chaplain's theory that the marble angels had divinely intervened, had come to an unexpected end. Before the Chaplain now lay a small, but significant, T-junction which led onto a similar but much longer street than the one he was in.

Which way now? The Chaplain looked skyward for inspiration, left or right? But there were no signs, no magical writings amongst the sparse clouds to guide him; the decision obviously rested squarely on his narrow shoulders alone. The Chaplain pondered on the possibilities and then did the only thing he could do under the circumstances, he prayed, called heads, and then tossed a mental coin – left it was. The

Chaplain crossed the road, heading for the shadowed part of the street, and with reservations aplenty, set off along it.

As he followed the new street, certain doubts began to surface in his mind and the Chaplain found himself wondering if he was on nothing more than a wild goose chase. He had been wandering for ages now and still had no real clue as to Richard's whereabouts. And as for the angels and divine intervention, what a silly old fool he'd been.

But faith still bubbled within even though for the moment he felt it was better placed in him. If he couldn't count on help from Upstairs then it was obvious he had only himself to rely upon.

It was therefore lucky for the Chaplain that the coin he'd tossed had been replaced in mid-spin with a double headed one.

At the same time as that so-called piece of luck was borne on the Chaplain's narrow shoulders, another so called piece of luck was being meted out, and not so far away. And the fortunate recipient of this luck had just happened to pass out through the hospital gates as the Chaplain had been pondering his choices.

How Sammy knew it was the Chaplain disappearing from view around the corner, especially considering he'd not as yet been acquainted with the Chaplain's new form, was anybody's guess. But know he did, and as quickly as possible Sammy made after him.

It wasn't easy though, the Chaplain's stride affected by the heat and old age as it was, was still much longer than Sammy's. Also, the effect the physical battering had taken on him had given him a big minus where fitness was concerned.

But these weren't his only worries or hindrances. There were other concerns that made catching up with the Chaplain more imperative than it already was. Sammy had dangerous enemies, worse than the ones that had attacked him, natural enemies that wouldn't think twice about putting him out of his misery, but enemies that would shy from the presence of the Chaplain. So as Sammy endeavoured to catch up, he too kept to the shadows, but for different reasons than the Chaplain.

Half hopping, half limping, the ragged specimen that was Sammy soon found it hard to keep up, let alone make a dint in the distance between them. And each time there was a chance, the Chaplain resting or, on occasion, relieving himself, he found his hopes dashed by one thing or another, as if the Gods were conspiring against him.

He'd toyed with the idea of shouting a couple of times but had, on having second thoughts, held his tongue for fear of drawing the attention of the enemy. Besides, he'd thought, he doubted that the Chaplain would have understood him. And as for using his mind, he'd tried that first and – nothing. It was as if the lines of communication they'd formerly enjoyed had been cut.

Unless – unless the Chaplain was ignoring him, but Sammy couldn't see the sense in that. It *had* to be something to do with the forms they had adopted; it was the only plausible answer. So Sammy, in the fragile safety of the shadows, and with little or no other options open to him, continued with his half-hopping, half-limping dance of pursuit.

Down the street went the Chaplain and behind him followed Sammy. Then another, and another, turn after turn, until Sammy felt almost dead on his feet. He desperately needed to rest but he dare not stop, not even for a second lest he lose sight of the Chaplain or worse still, it left him open to attack. It would be dark very soon and then they would be everywhere, the enemy. Hunting, torturing and killing as was their bloodthirsty wont.

Sammy shivered at the terrible thoughts, and moved deeper into the shadows. They, for the moment, offered some refuge from prying eyes and, as they had for the Chaplain, brought with them a certain familiarity and comfort.

As Sammy fought against his fears and his fatigue the Chaplain, still some way distant, took that precise moment to suddenly break from his relentless march and pay, with what seemed like great interest to Sammy, urgent attention to something at the foot of one of the lampposts that adorned the pavements on either side of the street. On seeing this, Sammy saw the chance of at last making up some distance between them or maybe, if luck was with him, even catching the Chaplain up. Throwing caution to the wind, Sammy broke cover and moved as quickly as his aching body would let him. It was a big mistake.

In his blind rush to catch up Sammy completely ignored the dark gaping mouth of an alleyway that lay in his path, and its possible implications. As he reached halfway across, a shadow sprang to life and a terrible black shape spewed forth from the alley's dark depths.

Just too late, Sammy realised his mistake, he tried to dodge but the shape was too fast. Sammy hit the ground hard. Winded, fighting for breath, disorientated, Sammy tried to get back to his feet. But he couldn't, he was pinned to the ground. Sammy twisted with what strength he had left, fighting desperately for his freedom but his assailant was too strong. His body, now succumbing to all it had been through in the last few days, finally gave way to pitiful resignation. It was too weak to fight, too weak to escape, this was the end. Through sunken eyes, Sammy at last turned his face to his attacker, up into the sadistic eyes of the enemy.

It was too much, he didn't want to die again, not yet, not this way. Sammy turned his face away from his attacker's evil stare and looked desperately to where the Chaplain had stopped. Maybe his friend would see what was happening? See and come charging to his rescue. But to Sammy's despair the street was empty and the Chaplain was nowhere to be seen. Sammy felt the enemy's hot breath on the side of his face and he knew that once again he was alone. He prayed his end would be a swift one.

211

CHAPTER 33

'You could have told me earlier,' groaned Richard as he rummaged urgently through the cupboard under the sink.

'I didn't *know* any earlier,' defended Laura, a little of the Irish finding its way back into her voice, 'I'd have told you if I had.' It was true, she hadn't known until a few frantic moments ago. It had just sort of crept up on her, into her mind.

'Wouldn't have had so much to drink,' grumbled Richard delving deeper, his head almost completely hidden from sight, 'could have found it a lot quicker.'

'What you looking for?' asked Laura, the agreement not to pry still holding fast, even with the amount of alcohol that had been drunk.

'I told you.'

'You did not.' argued Laura, which was a trait of hers when drinking, as was returning to her linguistic roots, though she wasn't as far gone as Richard.

'I di…ow! There was a resounding thud as Richard attempted to remove his head from the cupboard. 'Bloody hell!'

'I wish you wouldn't swear like that.'

'I wish you – you'd…' Richard bit his tongue and rubbed his head as he pulled it clear.

'Wish I'd what exactly?'

'Never mind. Just give me a hand up, I've got it.'

'And just how am I supposed to be doing that then?' If Laura had been corporeal she'd have been standing over Richard with hands on hips, much as her mother might have done when chiding her as a child.

'With…oh, bloody hell!'

'Stop it.'

Richard decided to stay where he was, seated in the middle of the kitchen floor, and held his trophy aloft. 'Knew it was there somewhere,' he said, grinning at it in triumph.

'Does it work?'

'Course it does.' Richard flicked a switch. It didn't. 'Bollocks!'

'Richard! I won't be telling you again.' What she thought she'd be doing instead though was a mystery.

'Okay – I'm sorry, but I can't help it. I always swear more when I've got more than a few drinks inside me. It goes with the territory, Jekyll-Hyde, Hyde-Jekyll. You know what I mean.'

'What?'

Richard picked himself up and started rummaging anew in a drawer. 'I'm sure I've got a new packet somewhere in here.'

'Maybe I could help if I was made privy to what you're looking for.'

'It's obvious isn't it? And how can you help anyway?'

'The good Lord gave me eyes didn't he? And don't be so rude, I'm only trying to help.'

'Batteries,' replied Richard sulkily. He'd had enough for the moment. Enough of Laura, of looking for things, and most of all, of the feeling he had. He'd definitely had more than enough alcohol. He wasn't feeling at all well.

'Under your hand.'

'What…oh.' Richard picked up the unopened pack and split two from it. 'It's old but it'll do the trick.' He tried the switch again and this time the torch flooded into life. 'There, told you.'

'Good, can we go now? I don't know how much longer he will last.'

Richard opened the backdoor and stepped into the back garden, the sudden rush of fresh air not helping the nausea he was feeling. He played the torch around the garden until its beam found Freddie's grave. As he made for it, fighting the effects of the drink, he couldn't help but wonder at the craziness of what he was doing. He'd been taken aback by what Laura had told him moments ago and hadn't really believed what she was saying, still didn't maybe, but here he was, armed with a torch and garden trowel, preparing to dig poor old Freddie back up. It was crazy, he told himself, but what the hell? Was it any crazier than anything else that had happened to him the last couple of weeks?

He got to where Freddie was buried – all the Freddies were buried, and stopped, trowel poised. Richard played the torch's beam on the spot.

'Are you sure about this?' he asked, still not convinced, not wishing to disturb Freddie for nothing.

'As sure as anything,' answered Laura anxiously. 'Please hurry.'

'Okay then,' said Richard kneeling. But he still wasn't happy. He began to dig.

It didn't take long. Richard removed the soggy matchbox from the earth and slid it open, playing the torch on it as he did. He didn't know what it was he expected to find but was relieved when all he did find was the aluminium foil he'd used to wrap Freddie in.

'Quickly!' urged Laura, from a position Richard could only describe as from somewhere over his shoulder. 'He might be dying.'

Keeping tight-lipped, Richard was certain she was losing the plot, he carefully unwrapped the foil expecting nothing but poor dead-as-a-doornail Freddie. But, as he prepared to remove the sheet of kitchen roll, a sudden movement from within drained the colour from his cheeks.

'He's alive,' squealed Laura. Richard was sure he could feel her clapping with joy within him. 'Quick, inside with him.'

The urgency in Laura's voice and the wriggling that was going on in his hand had a sort of cold water effect on

Richard, bringing him back, well almost, into the realms of sobriety once more, and before he knew it he was running back inside.

Richard couldn't believe it. The whole idea of Freddie still being alive – did fish do comas? – had sounded insane when Laura had mentioned it, but now there was only one thing on his mind, to get Freddie back into his tank as quickly as possible.

It had all come back to him since leaving the blackness. The others, what was happening, his role in it all. But something was going terribly wrong. Geoff gasped, trying to suck air into his empty lungs, but to no avail. He knew what dying felt like, he'd done it before, and now he was doing it again.

Richard brushed the backdoor aside crashing it against the wall. Had he thrown the water away? Through the kitchen. He couldn't remember, he didn't think so. Into the lounge, Laura in his head all the while telling him to hurry. The tank thankfully was still full, a bit slimy, but water was water – he guessed – to a fish. Freddie wriggled in his hands. Richard reached the tank and gently slipped Freddie in.

Then, as if by a miracle, Geoff felt his bursting lungs relax. Air was filling them again, he wasn't going to die. He wasn't going to let the others down. He still had a part to play.

Geoff lay still for a few moments then, feeling life fully touching him again, he began to embrace his new lease of life.

For a while Freddie didn't move. He just lay there on his back on the water's surface, slowly mouthing O's. But just as Richard started to think that all had been in vain, to curse the alcohol he'd drunk and his sluggishness, Freddie flipped and started to move arthritically through the water.

'He's alive. I can't believe it.'

'Told you,' said Laura smugly. 'Now we just have to get in contact, shouldn't be too hard.'

Laura's words sank in at a leisurely pace, fairly dawdling, but they got there in the end.

'What do you mean, contact?' said Richard cautiously, having just acquired the unnerving feeling that there might just be a little bit more to the miraculous recovery of Freddie than first met his eye.

'It's not exactly Freddie,' Laura started to explain.

Richard was afraid to ask, so didn't. He went to the sofa and sat down. Laura, sensing a certain reticence in his mood, thought better of continuing for the moment and kept quiet, he'd come round.

Keeping one wary eye on the tank, Richard grabbed his half finished beer and drank. He now knew for certain that the drink was the problem; he hadn't had nearly enough as he should have.

'It's Geoff,' chanced Laura, finishing her explanation after patiently waiting for Richard to finish the bottle he had in his hand.

'The elf?'

'Yes.'

'Why the hell didn't you tell me this earlier?' Richard tipped the bottle and waited for Laura's answer as the last dregs of beer funnelled into his mouth. As he did, Freddie manoeuvred himself to the front of the tank. The bloody thing was watching him, Richard was sure of it.

'We had an agreement, remember, so I thought you knew. Besides, I forgot in all the excitement. The others must be close by, you see, I'll ask him.'

'Whoa-there!' said Richard, so suddenly that he made Laura jump, and, technically, himself. He was still getting his head around events. 'Nothing was said about anyone being a goldfish. I mean it…it's…' Richard stuttered to a halt. If the truth was known he couldn't be certain about that last statement. Certain things were blurred around the edges, as if he were blinkered against seeing the whole picture.

'I feel the same,' Laura confided.

'About what?' asked a suspicious Richard.

'Not seeing the whole picture, of course.'

'You read my mind – what about the agreement?'

'You were moaning just now.'

'That's because I'm going slightly insane, having just dug up my dead goldfish of one day that turns, in a blink of an eye, into one of two weeks. And who now happens to have the persona of a dead elf.'

Laura could see why this could be upsetting for Richard.

'You knew things were going to be strange. I admit Geoff being a goldfish threw me when I first knew but Joe did say that we were all needed one way or another. You knew that.'

Richard had to concede this point, but…

'Yes, all right, but a goldfish? What next, the Chaplain arriving as a cauliflower or something?' When Richard did manage to be sarcastic, he did it well. 'Or…let me think, what do I have in my garden that I can dig up?' Laura sat tight. 'More Freddies of course. An abundance there but the tank may get a bit overcrowded. No – wait.' Richard took a swig from the bottle but only glugged air. He gave it a disdainful look before carrying on. 'How about a dandelion? I've plenty of them. I could sit Sammy in a pot and have a good old chat with him. I could actually talk to plants. Move over Doctor Dolittle I say, yer ain't seen nothing yet!' Richard stared hard at Freddie. 'I think I need another,' he said, flourishing the empty bottle close to his face for Laura's benefit.

Inside, Laura was seething. Richard might be right on a number of things but there was no need for him to aim his sarcasm at her. It wasn't her fault; she was after all, to all intents and purposes, in the same metaphorical boat as he was. They all were. Beggars couldn't be choosers, and she didn't suppose for a moment that Geoff was happy with his present predicament. Richard to her mind was being childish and unfair and awkward.

In the kitchen Richard, who was doing his best to ignore what Laura thought, was taking the last six-pack from the fridge. He had made his up mind to drink the lot, whatever the consequences. "Waste not, want not", was his motto of the moment. And if he was still standing after they were gone there was always the whisky.

'Do you think that's wise?'

'Mind your own business and stop reading mine.'

'But all that drink. Enough's enough.'

'And who's going to stop me?'

'Me, if I can.'

'You and what army? Unless of course you're going to hit me with a wet fish?'

As his mind had recently taken steps, a little while ago, while on the sofa, to shake itself free from the shackles of its shock-imposed near soberness Richard found this last remark hilarious and, as is the wont of the self-amused fairly pissed, he cracked up. He then laughed himself all the way back to the sofa.

Anger now near to boiling point, her infamous temper bubbling dangerously close to the surface, Laura decided enough was enough; it was time to get rid of what she now saw as the major hurdle standing between her and the Light. The threat had to go, however drastic the measure.

But before she had a chance to do her woman scorned act, the drink, or Richard, was saved by the bell. The front door bell.

CHAPTER 34

The enemy was enjoying the moment, Sammy could feel it. He could sense the sadistic triumph his attacker was wallowing in, and knew that no amount of praying was going to save him from a death that was going to be slow and torturous.

It was as if this new chance at life he'd been given had suddenly become a cruel parody of his first. Here he lay, his last moments, with his head in the gutter. If only…

'If only what? That's the trouble with you Sammy; you're always feeling sorry for yourself. Especially when you're alive.'

With eyes widening saucer-like, Sammy stared up in disbelief at his attacker. How did this creature know his name? What new torture was this? A lecture before he died?

'It's not him idiot, it's me. Keep still, I'm almost with you.'

Sammy's saucer eyes swivelled wildly in their sockets. Surely that was the Chaplain's voice. Sammy tried to see past his attacker's bulk but it was screening all but the immediate street either side of him.

'I told you not to move.'

'Is that really you Chaplain? Help!' It was a pitiful contribution.

'Just a few feet more, hold on.'

Sammy noticed the enemy start to shift uneasily atop him. The creature could sense something: something that should have stirred deep-seated primeval fears within it.

But other primeval stirrings were more prevalent, the creature shook the feeling off, choosing to ignore its warning instincts, returning its eager attention to its prey. But it saw something, or rather the lack of something, in Sammy's eyes; the fear was going. It was then that it knew what the something it had sensed was. It was the old enemy, closer than it should be. A mistake had been made, too preoccupied with the catch, the fun. Too late, Sammy's attacker turned. The Chaplain was upon him.

His heart pounding ten to the dozen in his puny chest, Sammy saw his chance and with what strength he had left twisted free from his attacker's grip, managing to roll completely into the gutter. He lay there and watched the struggle on the pavement, powerless to help, unable to aid his friend: the Chaplain was on his own.

The fight, to Sammy's relief, went the Chaplain's way. The enemy, although powerful, had not been looking to win, just escape, and at the first opportunity had done so.

The Chaplain, his face scratched and bleeding, went to where Sammy lay and bent over him. 'Are you all right?' he asked, his expression unable to hide his despair at Sammy's battered condition.

'Are you?'

'Just scratches, I'll be fine. Can you get up?'

It wasn't easy but Sammy managed it. 'Thanks,' he said, once up. 'I guess I owe you one. It's a good job you saw me when you did, else I'd have been a goner.'

'I didn't.' The admission was said slowly and almost painfully. 'I heard you praying.' The Chaplain had a very guilty look on his face as he spoke.

It took a moment or two for what the Chaplain was trying to say to sink in. 'You heard me praying?' said Sammy, giving the Chaplain an incredulous look. 'But I was saying it quietly to myself, how could you...' Realization of a sort started to set in. 'But I've called out to you much louder than that before.'

The Chaplain now looked decidedly sheepish. 'I know,' he admitted, 'I just didn't feel it important enough to stop. The search,' he tried to explain, 'I believe I'm quite close now.'

'And a couple of hours ago, were you close then?' snapped Sammy, anger rising.

'Well…no, I don't suppose so. I was…'

'Well, thanks for nothing.' Sammy started to shuffle angrily along the pavement. He didn't know where he was shuffling to but as he was heading towards the lamppost that the Chaplain had been showing such interest in, it seemed as good a direction as any.

As he did, the Chaplain played through his mind everything that had gone on since he'd first become aware that Sammy was following him. But whichever way he played it, it ended with the same result. He'd been wrong. He had thought Sammy would be a hindrance. He'd had no right. The whole point of them being where they were was so they could be with Richard, together.

'I'm sorry,' he said, head bowed, as he followed the limping and dishevelled tramp along the street.

'Forget it.'

'But I was wrong.'

'We all make mistakes.'

'Yes…but.'

'It was your call, you just happened to make an extra bad one, that's all.' With the fright of the attack slowly fading, Sammy began to enjoy, with maybe too much relish, the upper hand he had over the Chaplain. He wasn't going to let him off lightly. 'And nearly getting an old friend killed in the process,' he added, rubbing salt.

'I said that I'm sorry.'

'Yeah, we can all say that.' Sammy's mind wandered back to the attack. The Chaplain deserved all that was thrown at him. He had let him lay there, suffering at the hands of the enemy, could have spoken earlier but didn't, left him to stew in the enemy's cruelty, now it was the Chaplain's turn.

The thought burned brightly in Sammy's mind but the intensity of it also burnt inwards, bringing the truth and realization of what he was doing out into the open. He was being cruel, not with the intensity of the enemy, but cruel, as the sum of the word. Did the Chaplain deserve that? He'd said his piece to the Chaplain, made it clear how he felt. Everyone did make mistakes, why was he trying to make him suffer so much for it, he was alive wasn't he? *Thanks* to the Chaplain. He was acting as badly as the enemy.

'But I guess you mean it.' Everyone deserved a turn of the cheek now and again.

'I do.'

'Enough said then.' And anyway Sammy was glad to be with his old friend again. 'Now, where do you reckon Richard is hiding then? You said you felt he was close.' As far as Sammy was concerned, the whole episode was now closed. 'Something to do with the lamppost perchance?' Let bygones be bygones.

'Well – not really,' said the Chaplain hesitantly.

'But I saw you sniffing about, something was interesting you.'

They arrived at the lamppost. Sammy leaned heavily against it, surveying the surrounding area, but he saw nothing that gave any clues as to Richard's whereabouts.

'I don't see anything,' he concluded, looking to the Chaplain for answers.

The Chaplain pointed.

'Where?'

'There.'

'I don't see – oh. Pooh! You?'

'Afraid so,' said the Chaplain regretfully. 'It is I suppose, par for this particular course.'

'Bummer!'

'Yes, shall we move on?'

'I don't mind if I do,' agreed Sammy trying to wrinkle his nose now that the reason for the Chaplain's interest was no longer a mystery, but finding it physically impossible to do. Sammy decided on the next best thing and moved away a lot quicker than he'd arrived, pain or no pain. 'It must be worse for you?' he said, as the Chaplain drew along side.

'In what way?'

'You being a Vicar and all.'

'Chaplain.'

'Yeah, but it must be worse.'

'I suppose so.'

Two more streets went slowly by without the slightest whiff of Richard or his whereabouts. The Chaplain led the way, Sammy, his limp steadily worsening, labouring a little way behind. This went on for a while until the Chaplain, concerned by Sammy's clear deterioration, called a halt.

'Are you all right old chap? You're looking a little green around the gills.'

'I haven't got gills, and yes, as well as can be expected I suppose. That brute back there was a bit of a heavyweight.'

'Let me take a look.'

'I'm okay, stop fussing.'

'I don't think you are.' Without giving Sammy a chance to resist, the Chaplain stepped forward and gently poked him in the side of the ribs.

'What are you...look I don't...hey...ow!'

'Thought so, you're bleeding.'

'What...where?' demanded Sammy, trying to see.

'Your side.' The Chaplain looked grim. 'Looks like the *bastard* stabbed you.'

'Chaplain!' said Sammy, honestly taken aback by the Chaplain's rare and sudden profanity.

'Well...' said the Chaplain, slightly embarrassed by Sammy's response to his outburst, but not regretting it in the least.

'Is it bad?'

225

'Doesn't seem so, but you are steadily losing blood. How do you feel? Honestly now.'

'A bit sick, come to think about it.' Sammy actually looked to be thinking about it.

'I'm going to have to carry you.'

'Go on with you, I'll be okay. I can still dance you know,' joked Sammy, forcing a thin smile. He then went on to prove the matter and duly fell to the pavement in a heap.

'And what was that, the Bump?'

'What's what?' said a dazed Sammy struggling to get to his feet, coughing rather badly as he did.

'Nothing, just a dance Laura told me about once.'

'Yeah? Well I haven't danced me last waltz yet,' coughed Sammy, his eyes glowing with defiance.

'Corny as well as croaky, eh?'

Sammy gave another thin smile and promptly slumped back to the pavement. He no longer possessed the strength to stay up or get up.

'May I?'

Sammy had to finally admit defeat. 'I suppose so, but don't bloody drop me, pardon my French; I've had enough ups and downs already this lifetime.' Assured that he wouldn't be, Sammy allowed himself to be picked up. 'Not too heavy?' he asked as his feet left the ground.

'No,' said the Chaplain who was startled at just how light he was – too light perhaps. 'No problem at all.'

'Good. Then upward and onward dear fellow.'

It was getting very late as the onward continued to lead them down street after street. Sammy had long fallen into an exhausted sleep and the Chaplain's doggedness, which had seen him through thus far, was beginning to wane. He felt almost asleep on his feet but he knew he had to keep going, something deep inside was telling him he had to, regardless of how he was feeling. That to stop now would be nothing short of a disaster. He felt in his bones that he was close and getting closer, but it was getting hard, oh so hard. And of course there was Sammy, his dear friend, who he could sense was getting weaker by the minute. The Chaplain grittily marched on.

Yet another street and with it the near collapse of the Chaplain, his resolve almost in tatters, wondered, how long? With eyes that were sore and watery he blinked several times as he tried to read the signpost holding the street's name. Why he was bothering though, was a mystery, he hadn't bothered with any others. His tired eyes cleared a little and he began to read.

It couldn't be? The Chaplain blinked again to make certain he wasn't seeing things and nearly dropped Sammy in his excitement as he read the sign again. "Eden Street". Surely not?

'Sammy! Sammy? Wake up.'

'Wha-what's up?' stirred Sammy from a wonderful dream that had mirrors and bells in it.

'I think we are here.'

'Where? What – was I asleep?'

'I think we are nearing journey's end.'

'Why's that?' asked Sammy as the effects of sleep fell away and the Chaplain's excited words began to sink in.

'Read the street sign. I think it may well be one of dual purpose.'

Turning as best he could, in the position he was, Sammy read the sign.

'Well?' the Chaplain enthused.

'I don't get it.'

'It says Eden man. I'm thinking as in the garden of.'

'You think Richard's maybe Adam?' Sammy may have been a little groggy but he was coherent enough to know when he didn't know what the Chaplain was going on about.

'No-no you silly man. Eden wasn't just a garden; it was also a place of great delight and contentment.'

Sammy thought this through but was forming his own thoughts on the meaning of the street name.

'And I think that if things run true to course, as I think they will, we may just find what we are looking for at number seven.'

'Seven?' thought Sammy. Surely the Chaplain wasn't thinking what he thought he was thinking? That would just be too corny. He couldn't be. But it *was* exactly what the Chaplain was thinking.

'Seven – Seventh Heaven – Eden,' explained the Chaplain. 'It makes sense.'

To Sammy though, the sign had other meanings, two of them, firstly it was more likely the street was named after a Prime Minister than the biblical garden, secondly the Chaplain was more tired then he realised.

'Come on, let's see how far away we are.'

Sammy tried to put his thoughts across but the Chaplain was having none of it as he walked a little way up the drive of the corner house to see its door number. It was number ninety seven.

Great, thought Sammy, they would have to travel to the other end of the street before the Chaplain saw how daft this all was.

'It can't be that far,' said the Chaplain, who, in his excitement, only half listened to what Sammy was thinking.

'We haven't looked on the other side yet,' mentioned Sammy, thinking he ought to.

'Don't need to, the odd numbers are all on this side.'

'What are we up to now?' Sammy queried, trying to show at least a little of interest.

'Eleven. We're nearly there.'

Sammy could hardly wait, and he wasn't being in the least bit sarcastic, the buffeting he was taking as the Chaplain trotted stoically up one path and then another was taking a sorry toll on his body.

'And do you have to check every door number?' queried Sammy who understandably couldn't see the point in it.

228

'Better safe than sorry,' replied the Chaplain, nudging open another gate.

Sammy still didn't understand and tutted under his breath. He decided to shut up and let the Chaplain find out the hard way. Besides, he wasn't listening to any suggestions he made, so why waste his effort? It wouldn't be much longer anyway, though Sammy was wondering how long before what? Maybe it wouldn't be long before the Chaplain collapsed in a heap. A more likely ending to this goose chase, he seriously doubted Richard would be at the end of their search. No pot of gold at the end of the Chaplain's rainbow, unless of course fool's gold.

'Number nine. This is it Sammy, the next house is the one.'

Sammy, prompted by the Chaplain's enthusiasm, twisted to get a better look as the Chaplain pushed the gate open. The house certainly didn't bring to mind feelings of great delight or contentment, with its shabby paintwork and dusty-looking curtains, unless it was empty and he could somehow persuade the Chaplain to hide up and rest in its overgrown garden.

'I wonder if they will be surprised to see us?' pondered the Chaplain gazing at the slightly askew seven as if looking upon an ancient relic of great religious significance.

'There's only one way to find out.'

'You're right, I'd better knock.'

'There's a bell there.'

'Good idea.'

Was it? Sammy wasn't so sure. Maybe there was lurking behind the door of shabby number seven a different ending than finding Richard, or the Chaplain collapsing. Maybe the house was occupied. Inhabited by an old lady and a horde of the enemy, waiting to rip him and the Chaplain to shreds, too many for the Chaplain to stand up against. Sammy's cough made a hacking reappearance.

'Maybe we should wait, think about it,' urged Sammy between rasps.

'About what?' said the Chaplain pressing.

'What might be *inside*.'

The button pushed easily, considering its rusty condition, in the house a dull brrringing reverberated along the hallway.

'What do you mean?'

'Never mind,' muttered Sammy. It was too late now. Sammy tensed himself for the horde's onslaught.

CHAPTER 35

With her anger for the moment grudgingly restrained, Laura prodded at the rapidly diminishing speck of soberness, she was amazed there was one, that at that moment was struggling, mainly due to the Geoff the elf, who was now Geoff the goldfish previously known as Freddie, conundrum, to keep afloat in Richard's befuddled and pickled brain.

'Are you going to answer that? It could be the others.'

'Could?' Richard mused. 'I thought you'd be able to sense them, like poor old Freddie…oops, Geoff.' Sarcasm dripped from his words like grease from a slab of back bacon. 'Anyway, I expect it's just some Jehovah's Witnesses or the like come to tell me how it's not too late to save me and my soul.' Richard took a swig from his freshly opened bottle. 'And everyone else that bloody owns it.' He then chuckled to himself. 'Bit late though, I say.'

Bit late, period, thought Laura, ignoring Richard's drunken self-pity and thinking of the time. She didn't believe any religious following, however zealous, would be calling this late at night. But that said, Richard did have a point, if it was the others, why wasn't she sensing them? Laura decided she had to know either way, but first she would have to change tack if she was going to uproot Richard from his alcoholic and downright stubborn stupor and get him to the door. She'd had an idea.

'It might be your friend, Tom,' she said, tossing a carrot that reaped immediate effect.

Somewhere in Richard, a nerve was struck and he visibly straightened. He'd not given Tom much of a thought these past few hours. How he missed old Tom. But wait a minute, as he was *now* thinking about him, how could Tom possibly know about him being out of hospital?

'It's two weeks, remember,' said Laura nipping neatly into and filling the questioning space that was forming in Richard's mind.

It was now fifteen-all on the making a point front.

The bell rang a second time. 'But what will I say to him?' said Richard, putting the bottle down, his mind going into blind panic. 'How do I explain what's going on?' Richard stared at the dark hallway through the open lounge door as if it were the gateway to Hades.

Laura didn't know, but then again she wasn't really bothered. She was almost certain that Richard's friend wouldn't be standing at the door once opened, that it would be the others. Time was surely too short for it not to be them? But that still didn't answer why she couldn't sense them.

Steadying the bottle, he had nearly knocked it over at his first attempt at standing up, Richard got to his feet. Heart in mouth, he walked as straight as he was able to into the hallway. Just inside, he looked with mounting trepidation towards the front door. Was it Tom? Or if it wasn't, he wished his head would stop spinning, and it was the others as Laura kept bleating on that it might be, was he prepared? Prepared for the reality of the unreal? For what would be the final realisation and the sealing of his fate? Or was he just babbling? He clicked the hall light on at the second attempt and moved towards the door.

Richard heard Laura in the worried depths of his mind urging him on, encouraging him to open the door. His hand hesitated on the latch. He could do this. He clicked off the deadlock and turned the knob. The door slowly opened.

Laura held her breath.

There was no immediate answer so the Chaplain tried again. And again the ringing of the bell reverberated in the house.

'Sounds empty,' said Sammy, brightening up.

'No, I hear something,' said the Chaplain, instantly pouring cold water on Sammy's hopes.

'Maybe they were in bed,' suggested Sammy.

The Chaplain stepped back, suddenly aware of just how late it was. For a moment doubts clouded his mind, perhaps he had made a mistake, that it was the wrong house. He was tired. 'Maybe we…' he started.

'…should go, quickly?' Sammy finished, happily latching on to the worried signals emitted by the Chaplain.

'Try again in the morning?' Sammy had begun to notice his surroundings in more detail. Bushes, wild and unkempt like the garden, dark and forbidding, making the garden a perfect place for an ambush.

'But I think I hear someone coming. Listen, I'm sure I do.'

The hall light suddenly came on, bathing the Chaplain and Sammy in an eerie yellowish glow.

'I don't like it,' moaned Sammy.

But the Chaplain wasn't listening; he was watching the door slowly open. 'Richard?' he ventured when it stopped moving after a couple of inches.

The door opened but not very far. Richard had forgotten to take the security chain off. He tried peeping through the gap but couldn't. Cursing himself for not installing the peephole he'd always promised he'd put in one day, he unclipped the chain and cautiously pulled the door open.

Laura had chosen to close her eyes while Richard faffed about with the door. She didn't know why, it just seemed like a good idea. And now, with eyes still firmly shut, she felt the cool of the night touch Richard's skin, goose bumps rising on her own. He'd opened the door.

'Who is it?' she whispered, the lack of any sense of it being the others keeping her eyes shut tight.

Richard, who was standing in the doorway with his mouth open nearly as far as the door itself, didn't answer. He couldn't, he could hardly believe what he was seeing.

233

'Richard?' Laura wondered whether she should risk a quick look when he didn't answer this second time. She decided she should.

Now both Richard and Laura were looking out into the night, mouths agape. Outside on the doorstep, looking both embarrassed and bemused, the two visitors standing there exchanged glances, then proceeded to speak, a little hesitantly.

'I...er...that is we, were wondering – if you would be willing to spare us a little of your precious time?' said a smart-looking young man of no more than twenty-two.

'If that's not too much trouble,' added the young man's clone-like companion.

Richard said nothing as he closed the door on them.

'Who were they?' asked Laura as the young men mumbled something and went on their way.

'Mormons,' said Richard, shaking his head in disbelief, 'bloody Mormons. I need my beer.'

'Who's there?' croaked a voice verging on the ancient.

'It's us,' said the Chaplain.

'I said who's there?'

'I don't think it's Richard,' said Sammy stating the obvious, to him anyway, as the old lady repeated the question.

'But it must be,' said the Chaplain, hardly able to, or want to, believe that the omens he'd been following could possibly be wrong, even though he had wavered earlier.

'It's an old lady,' murmured Sammy, half to the Chaplain, half to himself, his earlier fears apparently about to bear fruit. He nervously eyed the shadowed crack of the open doorway. Any moment now the enemy horde would be at their throats. 'I think we should go,' he swiftly added.

'I'll call the police if you don't go away. I will.'

The door suddenly slammed shut, to Sammy's relief, and the old lady's voice shrank away into the depths of the house muttering something about a special button as it went. The hall light went off.

Eden – seven – the angels pointing – it all fell into place. The Chaplain stood at the front door still staring at its number. It had to be the right place, it just had to be.

Sammy gave the Chaplain an urgent nudge. 'Come on Chaplain we've got to go. We don't want the Rozzers involved,' he said, still eyeing the bushes with distrust and apprehension. It was as good an excuse as any to get away from the house.

'The what?' said the Chaplain in a half daze.

'The Police,' said Sammy, 'We've got to go.'

Still encumbered by the disappointment of his errant revelations, the Chaplain reluctantly turned and walked from number seven's door. 'But I was so certain,' he said, stepping from the garden path on to the pavement. 'The signs were all there.'

'Maybe you were looking too hard,' Sammy empathised. He knew all about failure.

'But…'

'Sssh…someone's coming.'

The Chaplain and Sammy quickly slipped back into number seven's shadowy garden as voices carried along the street.

'Is it the Razors?' the Chaplain whispered as the voices drew closer.

'Rozzers…I don't think so. Sssh, here they come.'

Down the street strolled two smartly dressed young men. They were in deep conversation.

'He was a bit odd,' said the first in an unmistakable American accent.

'It takes all sorts,' said the other, offering up some sort of explanation in a deep southern drawl. 'Mind you, I tend to find the Brits all the same. Gee! I hope that doesn't sound kinda racial?'

'Naw, most of them are odd one way or the other, but that fella, well. Standing there, his mouth open like that not saying anything just staring, you'd have thought he'd seen a ghost or something.'

'Strange you should say that. I don't know why but I thought he looked as if he'd been half expecting one.'

'How d'ya mean?'

The young men stopped outside number seven.

'Well it…nah…forget it. I guess I'm a bit tired, imagining things.' Feeling a bit foolish the young man with the southern drawl turned his attention to number seven. 'Shall we?' He swung the gate completely open, the bottom of it dragging on the path.

The young men hovered for a moment, then decided against it.

'Naw, let's go. I've had my fill of nutters for one day. I'm hungry too, and it is kinda late. Let's call it a day.'

'Yeah, why not?' The southerner went to close the gate but it stuck, one of its hinges seizing, not before time. He looked at his watch, it was very late. 'Probably call the Cops anyway.'

The young men moved away, continuing their conversation about the quaint Brits as they went, and disappeared down the street.

When they could no longer be heard, the Chaplain and Sammy emerged from their hiding place. The Chaplain seemed excited about something.

'Did you hear what he said?' he said, almost bursting with new purpose.

'Something about food? Good idea if you ask me.' Right on cue, Sammy's stomach rumbled for added emphasis.

'No. That someone was expecting a ghost.' The Chaplain's eyes rolled in their sockets.

'They were joking,' said Sammy, missing the eyes but sensing the Chaplain was on the verge of going on another hare-brained omen chasing expedition.

'Maybe not. And there's only one way to find out.'

'Let's not,' pleaded Sammy, his fears substantiated, the food he desired, not.

But the Chaplain was already on the move. 'This way,' he said, dodging past the broken gate.

The last dribbles from the latest bottle were just trickling down Richard's throat when the doorbell went again.

'Hell's bells! Can't a bloke get pissed in peace any more?' Richard slammed the empty bottle down in temper and exasperation. 'If it's those flipping Mormons again – I'll – I'll.'

'What?' said Laura, not the least bit interested in what Richard was or wasn't going to do, just in the mood for downright bloody-mindedness. She was feeling down, she'd been so sure it was going to be the others at the door earlier.

'I'll,' Richard stuttered, 'bloody well tell them what's happening to me. That'll show them.'

'Do you think that's wise?' Laura spoke with the air of one who didn't really care. Though that wasn't strictly true, she did care, it was the feeling of being drained that had hold of her, drained by all that had gone on, the disappointments. So much so that her anger had now all but disappeared, apathy creeping in to fill the void.

'I don't care. A man needs to drink in peace sometimes and people need to be told.' Not making a whole lot of sense Richard got up and made for the front door again.

Laura closed her eyes and wondered if it was possible for her to go to sleep with Richard stomping around her? What did she have to lose? She may as well give it a go.

As Richard reached the door the bell rang again, quite insistently this time, which didn't help to temper his temper one little bit. He was going to give those Mormons one heck of a bloody big piece of his mind. Grabbing the latch Richard tore the door open, nearly pulling it from its hinges as he did.

237

'Bugger off!' he stormed. 'I've had e-fucking-nough...' But his voice trailed off as he realised he was shouting at nothing but thin air. 'What the...' he started, his anger quelled momentarily by the conspicuous lack of Mormons.

He then froze as a familiar voice popped into his head, saying his name, threatening to throw the last threads, the fragile equilibrium of his shaken world of normality, into final doubt and turmoil.

It wasn't Laura's, he could sense her shallow breathing, she was sleeping. Sleeping! This minor but annoying revelation as to Laura's present disposition didn't help as he tried to grapple with the *craziness* that was at that moment trying to engulf his sanity.

Laura had *gone* to sleep; that *was* crazy. Was it crazy? Someone in your body, nodding off, yes it *was* sodding crazy, as crazy as crazy shit can get. But it wasn't only crazy, it was also downright rude.

This vaguely familiar – no, it was no good denying it – this familiar voice that was in his head speaking to him saying his name; that *was* crazy too. Not as crazy though. Yeah right, not as crazy, who was he kidding? It *was* just as crazy, more so maybe. If only his body would let his eyes confirm it.

But he didn't want to confirm it. It was him that was causing his own paralysis. He didn't want to look down, to where he felt the voice had come from. But he had to.

And looking down, as his self-imposed paralysis gave way, was a sight, which was *even fucking crazier*, which had an instantaneous sobering effect – total this time; the greying of hair type – and which was threatening to show him the door to the funny farm and firmly strap him down.

'It's us,' continued the voice. It sounded exuberant yet tired. 'May we come in?'

Temporarily dumbstruck by what he was seeing Richard stepped lamely aside and let his visitors through to the hall.

'How did – what?' he mumbled. Richard, who maybe should have got used by now to strange occurrences unfolding before his eyes, had got his voice back but was finding it hard to string together a coherent sentence.

'Someone said you were looking for ghosts,' explained the Chaplain chirpily.

'What?'

'Looks like he's found them,' Sammy chipped in, basing his opinion on the bemused and befuddled look etched across Richard's face.

As Richard struggled to come to terms with what he was seeing, Laura started to stir from her nap. She'd been hearing voices.

'Is Laura about?' The Chaplain's question had a fresh and innocent air about it, like a young child enquiring about a playmate.

'Is that you, Chaplain?' Laura inquired dreamily. She had heard the Chaplain's voice, but still existed in the vague limbo between the end of sleep and full awareness, and thus was not yet comprehending its significance. 'Is Sammy with you?'

'I sure am, a bit worse for wear, but the same old Sammy. You can put me down now Chaplain – gently. Thanks.'

Not quite, thought Richard as he watched an aging black Labrador gently drop a bedraggled bundle of budgie from its mouth on to the hall carpet. Richard regained a little of his senses. The scene was crazy, granted, but there was a poignancy about it that seemed to be making it all right somehow. It was in that moment that Laura fully regained hers.

'Chaplain!' she suddenly squealed, causing a reaction from Richard that a low flying jet would have done had one just screeched overhead. 'It is you!'

Partially stunned by this sudden explosion of noise in his head, Richard failed to notice, until it was too late, that his body was making an involuntary movement towards the floor.

239

'Wai...!'

But the protest was way too late and Richard found himself kneeling beside the Labrador hugging it like a long-lost relative. Beside him the budgie was trying its best to stare up at him doe-y eyed.

'That's enough!' said Richard regaining a little composure, thanks to a couple of sweeps of soft wet tongue washing across his face. 'I want my body back *now,* thank you.'

'Sorry,' Laura apologised, smoothing down a metaphorical apron. 'I was just so happy to see them.'

Richard stood up and wiped his face. He wasn't angry, he could understand. In a way he was feeling the same. Seeing them, whatever the guise, was a relief. He looked at the two, pathetic crossed his mind for a moment, creatures standing in his hallway with a mixture of foreboding and increasing wonderment, and, if he was to admit to it, a growing fondness. Richard smiled, at last it was sinking in.

Here he was standing in his hall with a dog and a budgie who in reality, yes he could admit that, were two long dead people. But not just any old dead people, these were his relations of sorts. They were him and he they. And in the lounge swam another and in his body a fourth. And these four were but a few of many that existed. A multitude of former selves, though each unique in spirit.

He was sure no one would have blamed him if he had given into a bad case of insanity, but that, albeit very close at times, was not going to be the case. Surprisingly Richard (Randy) Ross was feeling completely sane and frighteningly lucid. The arrival of the Chaplain and Sammy had not in the least effected him, as he thought they might. He felt calm and collected, but most of all he now accepted that he was only a small part, though a fairly important one, of something much bigger than he was. He had a job to do and he was ready at last to face up to it, even if it was going to be the death of him.

'Are you okay?'

With Laura's words of concern breaking his train of thought, Richard became aware that everyone was staring at him, including Laura, which was an odd sensation. He didn't think he could ever get used to having someone sharing his body.

Richard answered with a certainty that was almost unnerving, 'Yes…yes I am, thank you for asking. And I think I'm about ready to hit the sack. But first I think we'd better deal with this little chap.' he bent down and gently gathered Sammy the budgie up in his hands.

As Richard tended to Sammy's injuries, which weren't as bad as first thought – superficial cuts and bruises – Laura reluctantly took a self-imposed back seat. She was happy to see her old friends, of course, and was looking forward to hearing of their adventures, but she had something important to tell them and didn't want it accidentally slipping out in the midst of idle conversation. In truth she was worried as to how they were going to react to it. So she had decided it was best to wait until Richard was asleep before divulging her news, so she would be able to give her friends her full and *divided* attention.

Richard finished playing doctor, then fed and watered the weary travellers as best he could, Sammy proving difficult until an errant pack of grass seed lost since last summer came to light. When he had finished, Richard felt more than ready to hit the sack. But first Laura had a favour to ask of him. Richard agreed, thinking nothing of it.

Less than ten minutes later, whether due to the alcohol he'd imbibed or the weight he carried on his shoulders, or both, Richard was sound asleep. Dead to the world the moment his head hit his pillow. On the bedside cabinet, Laura's favour, Geoff was happily swimming to and fro.

Laura waited until she was sure Richard was in deep sleep, then called to the Chaplain and Sammy to join her. As quiet

241

as church mice they wandered into Richard's room. The Chaplain gently clambered on to the foot of the bed, Sammy perched himself on the headboard, his wings, bruised from the terrible beating he'd taken in the shed, healed enough to allow gentle flight again. Once they were settled, Richard began to stir.

Under the control and guidance of Laura, Richard continued to move until he was in a sitting position. Happy with this, she looked at each of her friends in turn, studying them, preparing to drop her bomb.

'Tomorrow!' was the Chaplain's incredulous response as the shrapnel from Laura's bomb blast fell among them. He could scarcely believe what he was hearing. 'It can't be true, it's preposterous. We won't have time.'

'Is it true?' asked a fearful, but calm Sammy.

'I'm afraid it is,' confirmed Laura, turning Richard's head towards him and smiling grimly.

'But what happened? Where did the time go?' stammered the Chaplain, utterly confused. 'It's only been a handful of days since we arrived back in the land of the living.' He looked hard at Richard. 'You must be wrong.'

'Is it?'

'What do you mean "Is it"?' said the Chaplain, puzzled by Laura's remark.

'Is it really only a few days?'

The Chaplain wanted to say of course it was, he knew what he was talking about, but something held him back.

Laura went on to explain what had happened to her and Richard, again looking at each in turn for their reaction. Only Geoff, who had been confined to the blackness the whole time for whatever reason, seemed to be taking everything in his stride. She then offered an explanation as to what she thought might have happened to them.

'Time's different here,' she said, then paused. She spoke as a teacher might speak to a classroom full of first year

242

pupils. 'And I don't think any of you fully realize just how quickly it was passing. You forgot how it is on Earth, among the living.'

The room became quiet but for Richard's steady breathing. The Chaplain got to his feet and climbed from the bed, padding across the bedroom to the window. The curtains were drawn wide apart, allowing him an uninterrupted view of the dark night sky with its multitude of tiny stars. Staring up into it had always helped the Chaplain, when alive, to put things into perspective. Laura's explanation was shaky, the Chaplain knew it, he knew Sammy knew it, Geoff he wasn't so sure about; he appeared to be on another wavelength to them. She had dodged the whole issue of the blackness, but why? What was to be gained by papering over the obvious: that they had been held captive within it for whatever reason? It didn't make sense, yet Laura had seemed so resolute. Maybe she didn't know.

He gazed awhile, he thought awhile, then turned back to face the others. He'd decided that he would play along, they all would; wait and see what developed.

'I thought I did,' he said reflectively, 'I thought I remembered.' The Chaplain looked past Richard's mortal eyes and deep into Laura's. 'But it's now obvious to me that I was under a misapprehension. Something I can now recall as being quite easy to do.' The Chaplain paused thoughtfully before continuing, a rueful look on his face. 'One can sort of take things for granted when one is alive.'

There was a murmur of agreement from the headboard.

'And so,' said the Chaplain slowly, 'what happens now? *Have* we still time?'

Laura could only answer that question by briefly reiterating what had happened since Richard's two-week blackout. All listened, perhaps more carefully than they had before, and when she'd finished everyone was clear about their position. There was little more they could do, other than

243

play out the final act. And the ending, when it came, whether for good or bad, was in the hands of fate, and Richard.

CHAPTER 36

Apart from Richard no one got much sleep that night. Laura's news gradually turning from the initial shock into resignation, then an anxious mounting excitement at what the prospects of the coming day might bring.

In between, to keep their nerves from jangling too much, each told of their respective journeys to Richard's house. Laura had laughed, so heartily that Richard had nearly woken up, at the Chaplain's indignation at being called a mongrel, and had explained to him that, from her experience, that was what Australians called anyone they didn't like. The Chaplain had been relieved to hear it, which made Laura laugh even more.

Geoff, though, didn't contribute much. There was only so much one could say about being wrapped in foil and kitchen roll. The others had agreed, but, on sensing a degree of despondency from the fish tank, (the water bizarrely acting as some sort of sensory amplifier, giving away Geoff's feelings however much he tried to hide them,) they banded together and bucked him up by admitting that they didn't think they could have handled his situation half as well.

Then there was Sammy's story.

'And there must have been at least a hundred of them, tall as trees…'

'Bonsais?' interrupted Laura, trying to keep Richard's face straight.

'And black as night,' Sammy continued, doing his best to ignore her.

'How did you see them then?' asked Geoff who, unlike the others, was completely enthralled by Sammy's tale.

'Their eyes,' said Sammy narrowing his. 'Cold and mean they were. And then they made their move.'

'What did you do?' Air bubbles escaped from Geoff's mouth as he excitedly swam up and down the front of the tank, mouthing as well as thinking his questions as he went.

'What could I do? I fought back as anyone would,' preened Sammy. Literally and in attitude. 'The first one went on his knees, then another. I could see the fear shining in their eyes as they realised they had a real fight on their hands.'

'Then what?'

'Then blackness!' Sammy closed his eyes dramatically and fluttered his wings. 'And deathly silence, one of the devious beggars had crept up on the blind side and had got me good.'

'However did you survive?' asked Laura sweetly. Richard winked at the Chaplain.

Sammy didn't seem to notice and continued undeterred with his story. 'In my last moments of consciousness, as the blackness threatened to leave me helpless and at the baying mob's merciless mercy, I rolled from beneath them and left them fighting themselves in the darkness of the shed. It was the last I remembered.'

'You're a hero!' extolled Geoff, his tail flipping through the surface of the water.

'Well I think we all agree on that,' said the Chaplain, giving Laura a sideways glance, 'but what were they again, the ones that attacked you?' – a return wink.

'Hawks of some kind I should imagine. It was dark.'

'Not rooks or sparrows then?'

'I don't think so,' said Sammy, turning defensive. The Chaplain couldn't know the truth, could he? Sammy quickly thought this over. No he couldn't. He'd been nowhere near. But Sammy, however hard he tried, couldn't quite fully convince himself that the Chaplain didn't have some knowledge of what had really happened.

'You were very lucky then,' said the Chaplain. 'Very lucky indeed, don't you think Laura?'

246

'Oh yes. And brave, you must be one of the bravest budgies I know.'

Sticks and stones thought Sammy, at last latching on to the Chaplain's and Laura's gently mocking banter, but still, it might be a good idea if he did quit while he felt he was ahead. At least Geoff was impressed.

'Now tell us about the other creature you fought off,' said Geoff with impeccable mistiming. He had, which now incurred grave misgivings and a look of ignorance on Sammy's part, been privy to an earlier, quicker, version of Sammy's slightly exaggerated exploits. 'You know,' he encouraged enthusiastically, noticing Sammy's blank expression, 'the one that appeared from nowhere and attacked the Chaplain. Go on; tell Laura how you saved him.'

'Yes, why don't you,' agreed the Chaplain, his face a mask of bemused interest.

'I…I,' started Sammy wondering how he was going to get out of this one, his feathers well and truly ruffling, when as luck would have it he was rescued from this particularly uncomfortable fate by the tones of yet another bell, this time the ringing of the alarm clock.

Saved by the bell, must be something about this house, thought Laura, smiling to herself, as Richard began to stir. Still smiling, Laura relaxed and gave way.

Richard reached out, stopped the alarm, stretched, and then, just as he went to settle back down again, his eyes suddenly opened wide as if a bucket of ice had been dropped down his back and he sat bolt upright. From the bottom of the bed the Chaplain's soulful eyes stared back at him.

'What?' said Richard, his mouth then shaping into an O and dropping open as he remembered; it hadn't been a dream after all.

Looking at Freddie or what had been Freddie, full recollection of his situation struck home again. But this time there was no panic, no needing a stiff one. This time there was the return of the calm he'd experienced before going to bed.

247

'Are you okay?' enquired Laura softly, apprehension in her voice.

'Huh? Yeah. Sorry, forgot I had a dog, that's all.'

That morning, their last one on Earth, was understandably quiet but not in the least strained. Richard, and this caused a mite of concern amongst the Four, seemed to be coasting through it as if he didn't have a care in the world. Shower, dressed, joke, the tank back in the lounge, light hearted banter, breakfast and then the ironing of the "Little Hitler Starter Kit", as Tom liked to refer to Richard's ref's kit, went swimmingly. The Four wondered if it wasn't all a little too good to be true.

But with the last hiss of the steam iron, Richard, sensing their doubts and worries channelled through Laura, decided to put their minds at rest. And at the same time get answers to questions he wanted answering himself.

'There,' he said cheerfully, 'finished.' Richard unplugged the iron, putting it on the table, put away the ironing board and hung his kit on a hanger, which he then hung on the back of a chair, all in cheery silence. 'And now dear friends, ghosts and relatives, or all of the above,' he said turning to the Chaplain and Sammy, each of whom had hardly left his side since he'd got up, and, smiling, continued, 'I think we have something to talk about.' As Richard spoke he felt a slight uneasiness shift deep inside him.

'Don't worry, it's nothing bad,' he reassured through a private channel. He felt Laura relax. 'Good.'

'Now everyone, what say we go into the lounge? And Chaplain,' the Chaplain stopped in the doorway, 'please keep off the furniture.'

Laura giggled to herself as the Chaplain turned tail and strutted indignantly, nose in the air, into the lounge.

'Perhaps I should tell him I was only joking?' chuckled Richard; he hadn't meant to upset him.

'No...well, maybe,' laughed Laura, who knew she shouldn't, but since the serious stuff with the others had been got out of the way, found she couldn't help it. The poor old Chaplain had gone through enough already, she didn't mean to laugh, but it wasn't just the Chaplain's reaction, it was also the black studded dog collar that he wore with its white name plate (which was sadly blank), it got her every time, obviously Upstairs had a sense of humour.

As Richard entered the lounge to join the others, Geoff already there of course, swimming quite happily in his tank, he felt a tension in the room. An air of anticipation mixed with trepidation. He set himself down on the sofa.

The Chaplain, sitting on the floor and eyeing Richard with the sort of look that said he wasn't sure as yet just how to take the man, was the first to speak. He wanted to know what Richard knew about the coming day.

'Well, Chaplain,' said Richard leaning forward, 'if you mean do I know when I'm going to die, I'm afraid I'm going to have to disappoint you, I don't.' The Chaplain exchanged a quick glance with Sammy who shifted uncomfortably on the table lamp he was perched upon. It was obvious they had been talking between themselves, perhaps when he was in the shower. 'But,' continued Richard when the Chaplain looked back, 'if you're asking me what's going to happen today, to the best of my knowledge, then all I can say to you is refereeing. I've to ref a football match today and that's my only insight into what the day will bring – other than my death of course.'

Another glance was exchanged but this time Sammy, albeit with nervous reluctance, spoke.

'I think the Chaplain,' Sammy paused for a moment, the black dog sitting unmoving in the centre of the room, the focus of his attention, 'the Chaplain,' he continued, 'was meaning more on the lines of are you prepared?'

'Did I?' shot the Chaplain, frowning at Sammy. Sammy did another uncomfortable little dance.

'To die? or for everything?' replied Richard coolly. Inside him Laura baulked at the questioning and felt increasingly awkward, but she kept quiet. It was Richard's show after all, he would have to deal with it.

'Both – I think.' Sammy shivered, ruffling his feathers, glad to be rid of the burden he hadn't wanted.

'Well? Are you man?' The Chaplain was brusque, butting in before Richard had a chance to answer.

But Richard didn't let the Chaplain's attitude upset him. He could see past the Chaplain's manner to the fear that lay behind the questions and the doleful brown eyes that stared up at him.

'No.' The answer was blunt but, before another exchange of glances could take place, Richard added. 'But I have come to terms with it.'

The exchange now took place and when the Chaplain's gaze returned Richard saw his eyes were different. The dread was no longer evident, or considerably lessened, in its place was mostly relief.

'It's all I can say,' said Richard almost apologetically, trying to help them understand, 'I'm only human.'

This was almost too much for Laura – Richard having to apologise for his humanity. But she held back again, she had to. For hadn't she, not long ago, had ideas and thoughts the same as, some even worse than, the Chaplain's? So Laura kept quiet. She was in no position to judge.

A silence now followed that screamed awkwardness. Sammy kept his eyes well away from Richard's, fidgeting on the shade rim as he did. On the floor the Chaplain was now lying on the carpet doing his best to behave like a dog, his eyes darting every so often in the nonchalant yet uncertain way dogs have. Laura would have left the room had she had a choice.

It lasted a full minute before Geoff, who'd been staying quietly in the background taking things in, broke through it, like a chick finally escaping its shell, sure of his motive but uncertain as to how he was going to be met.

'Can I say something,' he asked tentatively. No-one said anything so Geoff saw it as a cue to continue. 'It's just that I want to know about today?'

'Haven't you been listening,' hissed Sammy, almost furtively, afraid that the others might hear, what Geoff was saying, which obviously they had,

'I know that,' said Geoff wondering as he spoke why he was now whispering, 'I meant with me?'

Laura could no longer contain herself. 'That's a bit selfish isn't it?' she snapped. 'Poor Richard's got the world on his shoulders and you want to know about you!' The silence was well and truly torn asunder.

'Thank you Laura, that's nice of you,' said Richard slightly taken aback, but genuinely touched all the same, by Laura's words. 'But I think Geoff's talking about something else.'

Laura immediately started regretting what she'd said, or rather, how she'd reacted. 'But...I,' she managed to say before becoming totally consumed with embarrassment, and meekly retreating out of thought's way.

'He means himself, as a fish.' Richard continued, purposely not pursuing Laura's outburst and embarrassing her further.

'I don't understand,' admitted Sammy who'd flown across the room and onto the edge of the fish tank. 'What do you mean?' Sammy stared into the tank at Geoff who blew a couple of bubbles and stared back.

'Think about it. It's why I wanted to talk. But its not just Geoff, it's all of you.'

The Chaplain's ears pricked up.

'I still don't get it.'

'I think what Richard and Geoff are driving at is the match this afternoon. Am I right?' said the Chaplain, catching on.

Richard nodded.

'The match?' said Sammy, still fogbound.

The Chaplain got to his feet. 'As mad as it sounds,' he said, the bit now firmly between his teeth, 'the most important thing, apart from Richard's death of course, excuse me, and the going into the Light, which goes without saying.'

'And the Lesson,' interrupted Geoff.

'And the learning of the Lesson,' repeated the Chaplain, 'which I was coming to, er hum, is the match and how *we* are all going to get there and get away with being there? Especially Geoff.'

'Exactly my point,' agreed Richard when the Chaplain had finished. 'How are we going to do it?

CHAPTER 37

By two thirty that afternoon things had been sorted out and Richard, still alive and trying hard not to think about it, was donning his referee's kit.

'Aren't you going to change there?' asked Laura as he started. Her question was idle, a stab at small talk, mainly to keep her mind off things to come.

'What's the point? If I'm going to die at the match I'll not be changing back into civvies,' answered Richard philosophically.

Laura was about to make the point that he might not, when Richard was called from downstairs.

'You ready yet?' came a voice from the foot of the stairs. 'Time's running!' It was the Chaplain sounding like an irate taxi driver, but then who could blame him – he was as nervous as the rest of them.

Richard started down the stairs.

'Who's a pretty boy then?' chirped Sammy perching on the newel post. Nerves take people, and budgies, in different ways.

'Who rattled your cage?' Richard joked, stopping to admire his handiwork, 'any problems with the flying?'

Sammy the budgie had been treated to a new hair colour, or in his case, feather colouring. Inspecting his work, Richard had to admit that it wasn't perfect but, at the end of the day, whenever that was going to be, he hoped Sammy would be high in a tree and away from close scrutiny. Richard was *almost* certain that there was at least one tree within spitting

253

distance, wind assisted in some cases, admittedly, of each pitch in the park.

Sammy fluttered up the stairs and back again. 'Doesn't seem to be,' he said landing back on the newel post. 'But I'd rather have been another colour.'

'You know black's the only boot polish I have.'

'I know, but it reminds me of the rooks.'

'Thought it was hawks,' the Chaplain quipped, quick as a flash.

'That's what I meant, hawks – rooks, all the same.' Sammy did an uncomfortable pirouette above the foot of the stairs then disappeared into the lounge where Geoff was waiting, where he would be appreciated. Landing on the edge of the tank, Sammy had a little smile to himself as, out in the hall, he heard Laura chastising the Chaplain for being mean to him.

'You ready Geoff?' he asked, looking into the water. Geoff was gliding through it close to the surface making slow "Dar-dar – dar-dar – dar-dar" noises. 'Geoff?'

Geoff stopped his shark impressions and swivelled around to face the little black budgie. 'Suppose so,' he said glumly. He swam to the side of the tank and looked out. 'It looks a bit claustrophobic, that's all.' He was looking with profound doubt at the idea Richard had come up with for transporting him to the match.

'It is a two litre job,' said Sammy trying to be helpful. 'And the water'll be cleaner.'

'Suppose so.'

'And you're not going to be painted.'

Geoff cheered up a little.

'You ready Geoff?' It was Richard.

'Ready as he's ever gonna be,' said Sammy, winking at the nervous goldfish.

'Right then.' Richard picked up the coke bottle and took it into the kitchen. He returned with it half full of water. Luckily for Geoff, the old shaped bottle his time had known had long been discarded, for one jug shaped and with a wide lipped neck.

Gently scooping Geoff up with a ladle, Richard transported him to his new home.

'There, how's that?'

'Not too bad I suppose,' admitted Geoff, inspecting it.

'I'm glad to hear it, but it's blackout time now, I'm afraid.' Apologising, Richard picked the bottle up and popped it and Geoff into his sports bag. It was then Sammy's turn.

'Sammy.'

Sammy hopped across the sideboard but stopped short of hopping into the bag. 'Do I have to? I can follow the car.'

'It's better this way,' said Laura taking the words out of Richard's mouth.

'But…' pleaded Sammy.

'She's right Sammy,' agreed the Chaplain who was looking on, 'we have got to stick close together, you know that. If something was to happen to you, what then?'

Reluctantly Sammy hopped up and settled on the edge of the bag's open maw. Pausing there, he tried one last desperate attempt at getting out of it, pointing at the possible dangers that the bottle could bring, rolling on him for one.

Smiling, Richard produced a towel from behind him which he wedged beside the bottle. Sammy's fate was sealed.

'Right,' said Richard glancing at the time on the DVD player. It read 14:41. 'Time to go I think. Everyone ready?' As the question slipped from his lips he felt a sudden quiver, of something he couldn't quite put his finger on, move deep inside him, deeper than Laura. What it was, fear, anticipation of the unknown? He wasn't. But no one else felt it, of that he was certain.

Laura said she was, everyone agreed and the Chaplain wished everyone the best of faith.

The journey to the park usually took about fifteen minutes but today, for some reason, nervous energy, Richard surmised, they got there in nine.

People were already on the pitches, limbering up, taking part in shooting practice, lighting up, the usual. Richard parked in the small purpose-built concrete car park, turned the engine off and sat for a moment getting his breath. It was getting hard, very hard. Harder than he thought? he didn't know. His legs were pretending to be jelly, no, they were jelly.

'You going to be okay?' asked Laura, fully aware of Richard's anxiety.

'Yeah…I will be.'

'We're all with you, remember that,' said the Chaplain from the back seat, trying his best to sound reassuring.

'It's going to happen here, isn't it?' The full reality of what was soon to occur started to hit home. Richard gave a thought to the condemned prisoners of old, before the death penalty had been abolished. This is how they must have felt as the cell door swung open for the chaplain or whoever to come in and give them the last rites; to take them to their last place on Earth. Richard shuddered at the thought. But he was different, he was guilty of nothing, but he supposed, neither were some of them. And what, when all was said and done, did guilt have to do with dying? Death could come at any time, to anyone, for any reason, and today it was coming for him, during the match.

'We don't know that for sure,' Laura gently reasoned, knowing full well that she wouldn't actually bet against it.

'Oh come on. If someone tried writing this in a book they'd be laughed at. It's so obvious, it's corny.' Beads of cold sweat were starting to form on Richard's brow as he spoke.

'You have got to calm down, Richard, get a grip, or you won't be able to referee the match,' advised the Chaplain, reassurance no longer being tendered, Richard's anguish catching.

'Learn the Lesson you mean.'

'That's unfair. You know that is not what I meant.' But the Chaplain wondered if Richard's words held some note of truth.

From inside the bag Sammy was chirping, he wanted to know what was going on, he sensed the tension, a bubbling anger close to surfacing, but the lining of the bag was muffling the thoughts of the outside world from him.

Somehow Richard managed to motivate his hands to unzip the bag, probably with a little help from Laura. Sammy popped his head out.

'Problems?' he said, looking from Richard to the Chaplain.

'What's happening?' asked Geoff, who'd been doubly insulated, as daylight poured into the bag.

'No problems, just gearing up to go to the pitch – aren't we Richard?'

As Laura spoke, feeling began to return to Richard's legs and sense to his brain. Where the hell else could he go? It was going to be hard but the Chaplain was right; he wasn't going to be the only one out there. He wouldn't die alone on the pitch if that was to be his fate. Laura would be with him and the others wouldn't be far away. He was ready, or as ready as he supposed he ever would be.

Richard went to reply but found he was voiceless, his mouth and throat as dry as a desert, his tongue like sandpaper attaching itself to the roof of his mouth, then he realised he didn't need to speak, his thoughts, unguarded, had rung out loud and clear for all to hear. But he still had a problem, turning in his seat he leaned into the backseat and grabbed the bag. He took the bottle from it. 'Sorry about this Geoff,' he said in his mind, 'but I'll be needing my voice on the pitch.'

Richard unscrewed the top and put the bottle to his lips bracing himself. It wasn't going to be a pleasant experience.

As the bottle tipped Geoff, fearing a Moby Dick turn around, began to swim frantically uphill.

The first mouthful, although distasteful to the mind, wasn't to the palate and did the job. Richard could feel his mouth and throat returning to normal. Another for luck. Richard took another mouthful but instantly regretted it, spitting it out into the passenger seat foot well.

'What the heck,' he sputtered, trying to get the bits out of his mouth.

'Sorry,' said Geoff as he jiggled about in the bottle, 'I was scared.'

Ignoring the giggles coming from within, Richard replaced the lid, grimaced and spat again, this time through an open window. It hadn't been the taste, that had been negligible, it was more the thought. But he did see the funny side and smiled along with the others' laughter.

The laughter gradually subsiding, Richard glanced at his watch, one he kept aside especially for refereeing; it was almost time for the match to start. His legs back to normal, himself, almost likewise, he felt ready. Gathering the bag, Richard left the car and resolutely started on what he felt sure would be the longest walk of his life.

The pitches were marked with numbered pegs which made it a little easier finding the right one, but as Richard approached the first, it dawned on him that he had no idea which pitch he was supposed to be on.

'Trouble?' asked Laura, sensing something was up.

Richard ground to a halt. 'Er…no, not really, just looking for the right pitch,' he replied doubtfully.

Pitch number or no pitch number it still shouldn't have been a problem finding it, he knew the teams, worse luck, and some of the faces, but there was one, a big one; the park and pitches were packed solid with teams. He knew he'd find them in the end, but when?

'Time's getting on you know,' nudged the Chaplain.

Richard didn't need the reminder though, he'd looked at his watch close on a hundred times since leaving the house; or so it seemed. Richard looked at his watch again anyway; it read a minute to three. The Chaplain wasn't wrong. Richard recalled how his mother had always gone on about him being late for his own funeral. It now looked like he was going to be late for his own death as well. Richard started to walk a little quicker.

As he reached the second pitch someone called out to him. A voice he felt he should recognize. Stopping, Richard turned and was faced with a man who he could only describe as being a bit of a dandy, hair-wise at least, running towards him in a referee's kit; the man's foppish coiffure, blonde and under a ton of hairspray bobbing as he did.

'Mister Ross. Richard?' said the man, offering a pudgy hand. Richard nodded and reciprocated. 'Great – Tom Welburn,' he introduced. 'I'm sorry, but I meant to get back to you with the pitch details as soon as I remembered I'd forgotten to give them to you,' he rambled on breathlessly, 'but then, as I picked up the phone I thought "why not?" It's been a little while now since I've had a little run out, so to speak.' He tittered at his weak attempt at humour. 'So here I am, all yours, ready and willing.' Richard looked blank. 'Assistant Ref, I'll be on the line for you.'

Bollocks! Was the first thing that sprang to Richard's mind as he weighed up the arsehole standing before him in a kit that was at least one size, if not a couple, too small. That, he felt, was being kind to the man.

'Who is it?' asked the Chaplain, sniffing in Welburn's direction.

Richard quickly explained.

'Problem?'

'I hope not.' Richard glanced at his watch again, which didn't go unnoticed by "Dandy" Welburn.

259

'Don't worry,' he said looking at the Chaplain. 'I contacted the teams this morning to inform them of the situation. Nice dog, yours?'

'Situation?'

'That we may be a little late.' Welburn patted the Chaplain who curbed his urge to growl. 'I put the match back to three fifteen.'

So that's why I haven't seen the teams, thought Richard. 'Which pitch?' he asked as he diplomatically guided the grumbling Chaplain away from Welburn's hand.

'Thirteen.'

'Figures.'

'Sorry?'

'I said, unlucky for some.'

'Oh…yes. Quite.'

'Then, lead on Macbeth!'

'Pardon?'

'Nothing.'

By the time Richard arrived at pitch thirteen the teams had started milling around on it. He felt a knot clench in his stomach as he approached. Would they remember him? Stupid question, of course they would, but he held out hope.

'Hey ref! How's the head? Eyesight any better? Ha-Ha!'

It took but a few brief seconds for him to get verification and for his hope to nose-dive into oblivion.

'Thought you were dead!' rang another voice.

Oh-yes, they remembered all right. Head down, and with the Four offering encouragement, Richard made his way to a spot some fifteen feet from the half-way line where there sat, he was thankful to see, though he couldn't recall ever seeing it before, a large holly tree. He set the bag on the ground. He knelt down beside it as a couple more "witty remarks" flew over his head.

'Boys will be boys – eh Ross?' said Welburn, rubbing his stubby hands together like some cherubic version of old Fagin.

'Richard,' corrected Richard, wondering if the man was for real.

'What are they on about anyway? You had some sort of accident?'

'Don't know,' fibbed Richard, wishing the man would go away and leave him alone. He had an idea.

'You couldn't do me a favour could you? Check the nets and pitch for me while I change the battery in my stopwatch.' The little white lies were starting to come easily.

Welburn sucked the bait in like a good one and happily sauntered off towards the nearest goal. Once he was well away, Richard opened the bag.

'You'll have to lay here Chaplain, beside the bag. I'm going to wedge Geoff between your paws.' Richard carefully removed the bottle from the bag and placed it in front of the Chaplain.

'I can't see properly,' complained Geoff as the water levelled.

'This better?'

'Much, thanks.'

'Chaplain?'

'I'm fine.'

With two satisfied customers, Richard turned his attention to Sammy who was waiting patiently on the towel in the bag. Richard motioned to the tree that was almost directly above them.

'Can you make it?'

Hidden from Welburn and the milling players Sammy hopped from the bag on to Richard's fingers. He surveyed his seating arrangements.

'Do I have a choice?'

'That or the bag I'm afraid.'

'Fair enough.'

'Off you go then.' Richard got up, one eye on the pitch.

'One thing before I go though.'

'What's that?'

'Good luck. Good luck to all of us.' Sammy then, while Richard made sure the coast was clear, fluttered up into the tree's branches.

'That goes for the rest of us too,' said Laura as they watched Sammy go.

'Thanks,' said Richard, still watching the spot where Sammy had entered the tree's greenery.

'He'll be all right,' said the Chaplain, as if reading Richard's thoughts; which of course he more than likely had done.

Just then, just in time to stop things turning into a syrup-fest of emotions, Welburn arrived back at Richard's elbow.

'All checked,' he chirped brightly between enthusiastic pants.

'That was quick,' muttered Richard suspiciously, while eyeing the flag that had mysteriously appeared in Welburn's hand.

'I'm not one to hang about, and, besides, it's almost time for kick-off.' Welburn stabbed excitedly at his watch with a stubby finger.

Obviously a little while since he'd officiated anything but the seating at dinner, thought Richard as he watched Welburn waddle back to the pitch, the man's enthusiasm finding its way to the flag he was now waving with gusto. But thoughts aside, this was it. Richard felt the knot, which he hadn't realised had gone, return to his stomach – or had it simply worsened?

'Good luck,' the Chaplain proffered as Richard started towards the pitch.

'Thought you didn't believe in luck?' teased Laura.

'With that man in the vicinity I thought I might make an exception,' said the Chaplain nodding towards Welburn, who was now practising, with exaggerated motions, assistant refereeing signals.

Smiling grimly, Richard left the Chaplain and the others and walked to the centre spot. He checked his watch, put his whistle to his lips, and blew to start the last match of his life.

The whistle went to end what was a thoroughly uneventful and in some ways anticlimactic first half in which, through boredom rather than concentration, Richard had at times almost forgotten what fate had waiting in store for him – almost. As the players trooped off for their halftime orange, which in some cases was the phone not the fruit, (it was never too early to put your drinks order in) Richard breathlessly sauntered over to Geoff and the Chaplain.

'How's it going?' asked the Chaplain, opening an eye as Richard arrived. The Chaplain had never been one for football when he had been alive, more a cricket man, and had spent most of the match so far with his eyes closed, soaking up the sun. His mind on the other hand was wide open and alert.

'Exciting!' Laura enthused, who'd found the whole experience of being chauffeur driven around a football pitch quite exhilarating.

'Knackering,' panted Richard, dropping to his knees, 'should have brought something to drink.' The day, which started bright and warm, had grown steadily warmer.

'Why didn't you?'

'It wasn't high on my list of priorities this morning.'

'Maybe someone would give you some if you asked?'

'You could always take a swig from my bottle,' offered Geoff, peering from within its confines. 'I've managed to keep my bowels under control since – you know,' he added helpfully.

'Yeah – thanks for that Geoff, but I think I'll pass, okay?'

'If you're sure?'

'Couldn't be more so.'

'What are you going to do then?' asked Laura, sounding quite concerned.

'If you were in a desert you wouldn't be saying no,' chipped in the Chaplain.

'But I'm not – look, just forget I mentioned it,' said Richard growing slightly irate as the drink thing threatened to blow out of proportion. 'I've survived without a drink at halftime before and I'll do it again.' The words tried to stick in his throat as he spoke. 'It's no problem, really,' he finished quietly.

'Sorry,' said Laura after a moment of awkward silence, 'I guess we were trying too hard. We're all a bit nervier than we thought.'

'Yeah,' Sammy agreed, hopping warily onto the lowest branch. 'I guess we were all expecting something to have already happened.'

'Sammy!' scolded Laura.

'I didn't mean…'

'It's alright, you don't have to explain. I wanted to blow for halftime quarter of an hour ago. It's pretty tense at times out there when I remember.'

'And eerie,' added Laura before she could stop herself.

'What d'ya mean, eerie?' said Richard, surprised by Laura's strange statement.

'Well…' she said reluctantly, afraid to add to what had already left her big mouth.

'Go on,' urged the Chaplain, intrigued but loath to probe her mind.

'It's…it's just that it's all sort of déjà vu out there – but not for me exactly – for you, Richard.'

Richard was more than slightly puzzled by Laura's comments, as were the others. 'How do you mean? I haven't felt anything.' He frowned.

'I think you're being shielded somehow, don't ask me how, I don't know. I just get this feeling.' Laura paused for a moment, not sure whether she should go on. 'I shouldn't really say any more.' But she did, she couldn't stop herself. 'I think it's got something to do with the last match.' It was blurted out, almost against her will, she felt, but the feeling though was fleeting, squeezed near instantaneously from her consciousness and memory.

'The match I was injured in?' said Richard, thinking aloud.

'I don't know – could be.'

'I don't understand, why should you get the feeling instead of me? It doesn't make any sense.'

'It could be…' the Chaplain started, before thinking better of it.

'Could be what?' Richard didn't like what was going on around him. It was as if he was being excluded from some loop the others were sharing.

'I can't say. I…' The Chaplain hesitated, realising the danger.

'Why?'

'You do not – would not, understand. I don't know.'

But it was too late for denials, a light had clicked on in Richard's brain. 'You mean the Lesson don't you? But I know the match has something to do with it, unless, unless it's a sort of re-run.' Richard came to a startling conclusion. 'Another go at getting something I did wrong, right. One of my decisions was wrong. Or something I didn't do because of the attack. That's it, isn't it?'

'I didn't say that,' said the Chaplain, horrified by what Richard was saying, panic rising in him. 'We are here to observe, watch each other, not to interfere.' But the Chaplain was afraid that that had already been done.

'But say we can help. Say that's the reason we were put here all along,' reasoned Laura, trying to find a bright spot in the gloom that was rapidly descending on them all, trying to make good the mistake she may have made.

'I don't think so, Joe was specific in what he said,' cautioned Sammy, who was throwing his own caution to the wind by hopping closer to Richard and the others.

265

'But he's not going to tell us is he?' argued Laura. 'He wouldn't be able to.'

'I don't like it. It feels wrong,' said the Chaplain.

Sammy and Geoff agreed.

'But we could be making a huge mistake,' Laura continued, but then her argument suddenly flagged, 'but I suppose it's not down to us.' She'd made her argument, the argument she wasn't quite sure of, and backed down. 'It's Richard's decision.'

By now Richard had got back to his feet, his brain humming, his mind spinning. They all had a point, but Laura's was most compelling. The idea wouldn't have been there in the first place if they weren't supposed to use it, surely. But what was it? What was the lesson he was meant to learn? Richard thought hard, back to the match so long ago. To his surprise it sprang to mind easily. This seemed to Richard yet another reason to listen to Laura's argument.

With almost crystal clarity the match played like a film through his mind. But it was disappointing in its lack of clues. In the end there wasn't that much to it, the match, for all of Richard's worries at the time, had virtually run itself. But having said that, there were two things that had stuck out; two things that may or may not have been what he was looking for.

The first, he realised, he'd already done differently. In that first match he'd blown early for half-time, this time he hadn't. But surely that couldn't be it, be the thing that would send him and all his relatives into the Light? It seemed so trivial, too easy. It had to be something else, the only other thing that his memory of the previous match had thrown up: the *penalty*.

But what about the penalty? Richard racked his brain, trying to get the clarity to total crystal. He hadn't actually awarded a penalty, had he? But he had reached for the red card which meant that he would have done given the chance. Or would he have? No, he remembered, he'd pointed to the spot. What the hell was it he was supposed to have done, or not done?

'Richard. It's time.' The excruciatingly cheerful voice of Welburn rang out, bringing Richard back with a start to the here and now.

'What?' said Richard, not sure for a moment where he was.

'It's time for the second half. The teams are waiting.'

Through momentarily blurred eyes, Richard looked over to find himself under the scrutiny of twenty-two plus impatient neo-simians.

'Come on yer wanker!' shouted a fat one, one of many, but one of the ones that Richard remembered from the last match. 'We've got pubs to go to!' This was met by what Welburn would have described as roguish laughter.

Like a man pulled reluctantly from sleep, Richard stumbled toward the pitch, frantically collecting his wits as he went. He blew for the start of the second half, but thoughts of the penalty stayed with him. It had to hold the key to the Lesson, or at least be a part of it.

The second half was being played much like the first, little happening, but with Richard sometimes feeling as if he was in a dream, sometimes swearing that it was the first match being played over again. But at those times he would feel Laura in his mind sharply reminding him that it wasn't, urging him on, feel an eagerness for the final lesson to be learnt building inside her. It was an eagerness, though, that frightened him; an eagerness that bordered on fervour, growing relentlessly, as if blindly following orders, a thing unable to veer from some pre-destined course. Then it was gone again.

Five – four, three minutes to go.

Richard felt his pulse quicken as the minutes melted away. It was nearly time, but for what? In Richard's heart sprang the sudden hope that they were all wrong, that his last minutes on

Earth weren't going to be played out on the football pitch after all.

Two – one.

It was nearly over. Relief was all set to creep over Richard when he felt Laura suddenly tense inside of him. Then it happened.

The roles were different. In fact the situation was about face, this time it was the Nomads who had suddenly woken up and were racing towards goal. Richard started to have doubts, maybe the penalty had nothing to do with anything. Then *what*? He was on his own, lost, maybe they all were? But inside him he could feel Laura bristling with mounting excitement. Richard became frightened, he felt as if he was losing control, but had he been in control? It felt now as if Laura was trying to force the issue, willing something to happen.

Richard's mind began to swim, the knot in his stomach, which had been there on and off all day, taking on a life of its own. Richard was sure it had exploded, he felt his knees go inexplicably weak but he held on, or did he? All around him voices were shouting; his head was hurting.

'Penalty ref!'

In slow motion the moments before the penalty shout played themselves through his mind. The Nomad's player had broken clear, dodged past the keeper; it had been an open goal. He'd shot, he'd cursed. The shot had been handled and stopped on the line by the fat number seven, who had "darted" on the pitch from behind the goal where he'd been taking a quick leak.

'Acci-dental ref-er-ree,' pleaded fat number seven arranging his shorts. 'Never saw it coming. Ball to hand ref, ball to hand.'

It was time for a decision, a choice to be made. Richard knew it, he recalled the penalty plea in the other match, what did he do? What, if anything, had he learnt? Another voice was screaming at him, but this one wasn't on the pitch or along its lines, this one came from within him. This one belonged to Laura.

'No way a penalty,' she was yelling. 'It's a goal kick. You mustn't give a penalty Richard.'

Richard felt dizzy, he knew she was talking nonsense, his head was throbbing, but should he listen to her?

'Come on ref, fatty did it on purpose. Anyone could see that,' shouted the Roach manager.

'Oi – you wanker! Who're you calling fatty?'

The voices swirled around Richard as he desperately struggled with what he should do, so much could depend on his decision.

'It's no penalty,' screamed Laura, her voice harsh. 'It must be the lesson. You don't give the penalty. Are you bloody listening to me?' Laura sounded out of control.

As Laura screamed her views and abuse, the voices of the Chaplain, Sammy and Geoff entered the fray. It had to be his decision, they were saying. Whatever he did, it had to be his choice.

The pain in Richard's head was now agony, nearly all consuming in its intensity, but he had to think. He needed to think. What the hell did he do? Laura was pushing him, the others pleading. He just wanted it all to end.

Then the voice of an angel.

'Blow Richard, it's the only way.'

No – not an angel, the voice was Laura's but she was no longer screaming, she had somehow regained an equilibrium of reason that cut a swathe through Richard's despair, lessening his pain; *maybe* it was the voice of an angel.

Richard put the whistle to his lips and blew. For good or bad, right or wrong, he'd made a decision.

Then there was all consuming darkness.

CHAPTER 38

The light was faint to begin with, as were the voices. What was happening? Richard tried to remember. Then, like a burst dam, all came flooding back. His whole life tumbled before him, unfolding in a sparkling cascade of memories, until it came to what had been the last moments of his life.

It played much slower now, not quite in real time but close enough. He was on the pitch, about to make a decision. Laura was screaming things to him. His head felt as if it was going to explode, then darkness, but only for a second.

Richard was now watching himself from outside his body, not floating above exactly, but hovering close, coming to a decision. His hand was shaking as he held up the red card to the fat number seven. He'd awarded a penalty to the Nomads.

Back inside himself again, watching the penalty being taken, there were sparks of light flashing before his eyes, he didn't feel very well. The Nomads' striker strode purposefully to the ball, striking it hard and low and just past the outside of the post. He'd missed! Richard felt his body surge with relief as the ball went wide then, as the grass of the pitch suddenly sprang towards him, surge with panic.

He was laying on the ground his lungs breathing their last, but instead of continuing panic he felt at ease, a restfulness enveloping him. He was dying but he was at peace with it. Richard stopped breathing but his surroundings remained clear. He was dead, he knew he was, but he could still see the grass, the odd churned up sod, the goal, and a crowd of people gathering around.

In that moment, if he'd been able to, Richard would have smiled. The irony of it, he thought, as the crowd milled

271

around, not him, but the fat number seven. Richard recalled wondering what could have happened to the fat number seven. Wondering if maybe he'd suffered a heart attack. A prophetic warning to the other players perhaps? Richard's eyes glazed over and saw no more, except the illusion of a darkening fog.

'Richard!'

The light was no longer faint and the voices were clear enough for Richard to ascertain that he knew their owners.

'Richard?' repeated the Chaplain, his voice heavy with concern. 'Can you hear me?'

Richard answered that he thought he could, but then wasn't sure if he actually had, the voice that he'd taken as being his own sounded distant, disjointed.

'It'll take a little getting used to,' said another familiar voice. It was Sammy. 'We all felt a little odd and disoriented when we first arrived.'

Arrived? The explanations were throwing up more questions than answers. Richard slowly opened his eyes, afraid the brilliant light surrounding him might damage them, but the light, so bright, was not in the least harsh. The Chaplain, Sammy and Geoff were gathered around him, but it took a second or two for Richard to comprehend the change in them. Back to their old selves again, no longer the bedraggled creatures that had watched from the sidelines as he had breathed his last.

'Welcome to the other side,' said Geoff, dressed in elf garb again, a half smile on his face as he bowed, moving his arms outward in a gesture of welcome.

But apprehension continued for the moment for Richard as he looked about him, past the others. Fully aware now of what had happened to him, where he was, in the sense that he now existed in the afterlife, Richard touched his chest. It was still, the final confirmation. No beating, no regular familiar rising, it felt strange, yet, perfectly natural. The fear and unease he'd felt on awakening was now gradually dispersing, allowing Richard to take in his surroundings with a new perspective. But as he surveyed it, a place that his mere mortal sphere of consciousness could have only comprehended as a translucent globe of whiteness, he sensed that something was wrong. The picture was not complete.

'Where's Laura?' he asked.

The answer, as far as the others in the globe were concerned, was easy, they didn't know. The Chaplain tried to explain the situation. They'd arrived, the four of them, in the orb, together, only an instant ago. There was no news of Laura, whether the Lesson had been learnt, or if they would be going into the Light; the orb *not* being *it* they'd assumed. In a nutshell, no-one knew anything.

'But it feels like I've been here for ages,' Richard protested.

'That's because you are new,' explained the Chaplain. 'You now exist in a different sort of time than that of the living. You will get used to it.'

Richard wasn't so sure.

'Think of it as a kind of jet-lag,' Geoff suggested helpfully.

Richard sat up and placed his head in his hands. He still had so many questions but for now he didn't need the stress, he would rest, wait, see what happens next in this new world, this alien space.

How long he waited or had to wait, wondering his fate and that of the others, he didn't know. To him a thousand years could have passed, to the others an hour, a minute, a nanosecond. But the waiting did finally come to an end.

A section of the orb grew darker, the shape representative of a doorway, until the space was filled with a blackness that stirred memories in the orb's occupants. Out of this blackness stepped a form that all but Richard recognised.

'Roberta?' said the Chaplain as recognition rapidly turned to surprise.

Another form appeared beside Roberta, lingering for a moment in the blackness before stepping into the orb.

'Laura!' exclaimed a delighted Richard, his pronounced exuberance catching him by surprise as much as anyone by its intensity of feeling. But to Richard it was like finding a long-lost friend again. A very close long-lost friend.

But before Laura could respond, Roberta stepped forward and raised her hand.

'I have come to tell you of your fate,' another surprise; her voice no longer guttural like that of an animal but soft and clear and yet commanding, 'but before I do, I know you all have questions you feel need to be answered. Am I right?' Her face had a graveness about it.

A consensus of eager nods greeted her and Geoff started the ball rolling with something they all were wondering, though perhaps which was not top of their own personal lists. 'Where's Joe?' he asked.

Roberta answered with swift but cryptic surety. 'Joe is no longer with us. He's gone to a better place.'

'But he's our Guardian Angel. He said he'd look after us, that he'd always be there.' Geoff's voice trailed off, his face a mask of uncertainty.

'Did he?' Roberta's question, simple, searching.

Geoff quietly retreated behind the others, his thoughts confused as they had ever been.

As he did, Roberta's expression of stern authority fell away and a smile gently spread across her face, pity in her eyes. 'I think I should explain,' she said, her voice softening considerably. 'And for you to fully understand what I am about to say, I will start at the beginning.'

Roberta explained that she and others like her had been the first creatures to inhabit the Earth. It was their task to pave the way for the mortals and immortals that were to follow.

Each mortal arrived as a blank canvas, ready to learn the Lessons of life to enable them to throw off the yoke of their mortal coil and transcend to the Light and a wondrous new life of immortality.

And for each mortal there was linked an immortal. The immortals though were not blank like their counterpart the mortal. They were creatures steeped in an equal division of the knowledge of good and evil. But as with the mortals, they were also there to learn, but to learn but one lesson. Good over evil.

Once the lessons were learned the link between immortal and mortal would be broken, each then receiving their reward. The mortals with immortality. The immortals with a taste of mortality before they themselves attained acceptance into the Light.

But of course the lessons were not easy to learn. And to make things harder for all, the evil half of the immortals were given a lust for power. An ultimate power of having a Darkness to rival the Light. Where it could subjugate mortals and, in time, fulfil its dream of power: of rule over all mortals and immortals alike.

Joe was an immortal, explained Roberta, whose evil had managed to hold sway against good almost to the end. The ending would have been bedlam had his evil succeeded. A place where the impossible thought would have been pushed aside, touched and replaced by the unthinkable. And to that end, Joe's evil had exerted pressure on what it believed to be the weakest link in the relative chain. That link had been Laura.

But just as evil looked to have triumphed, as Joe's heart turned almost completely to black, both he and Laura fought back. A small remaining spark of good had managed to hold fast against the overwhelming threat of evil swelling at its door, gaining precious moments for one last act of defiance. Joe's good had called out to Laura, strengthening the link, telling Laura what she must do.

'Joe's act had seen his redemption and for you and your waiting brother and sister spirits it laid open the way to the Light.'

The orb seemed stricken with silence as Roberta finished, its occupants awed by what had been said, but Richard had a question.

'But Laura told me to blow the whistle and not give the penalty, but I did. How did I learn the lesson when I went against what she'd said?' he asked.

Roberta gave Laura a look which prompted her to explain. Laura told how, in the last minutes of the football game, she'd suddenly realised what was happening and why she had been doing what she had. In that moment of clear thought Joe had called out to her with the last of his good to tell her to tell Richard to be fair and award what he saw, to make his last decision his own.

But how could she? Could she really trust what was being said to her? Would it, if she had told him what Joe had told her, have been Richard's own decision? And wouldn't Richard ignore her pleas anyway, she was after all only there to guide? Her final decision hadn't been easy, to say the opposite of what she thought to be the right decision, hoping that Richard would ignore her and follow his own mind.

The light in the orb began to grow stronger. 'It is nearly time for you all to be with your relatives in the Light,' said Roberta, 'but I feel you have yet another question unanswered Richard.'

'I'm sorry,' Richard apologised as he stood, aware of what they were on the verge of, 'but I just can't believe that we're going into the Light just because I awarded a penalty.'

Roberta smiled. 'You are right Richard, last of this particular line. And I think it would be wrong of me not to tell you all the truth.' She scanned the rest of the orb's occupants, face by face, smiling serenely at each of them. 'You were all on trial. All in part a piece of the ending. The fate of all rested not only on Richard and Joe, but the Four as well, representative for all relatives.' Roberta placed a small hairy hand gently onto Laura's shoulder.

'Laura learnt her own lesson when she learnt to overcome her selfishness.' Roberta cast her eyes toward the others. 'Sammy when he found the courage to ask for help. Geoff when he found courage in himself.' Roberta smiled at the Chaplain who was frantically racking his brains for what he may have learned. 'You, dear Chaplain, you found your lesson learned when you found flexibility; when you found you could believe in more than just your faith.'

As Richard listened he began to feel a little put out, awarding a penalty seemed pretty pale against what the others had learnt. And what if anything had he learned from it? Nothing, as far as he could make out.

'Nothing is right,' said Roberta suddenly, her small round face smiling up into Richard's, 'except perhaps fair play. But it of course wasn't your lesson Richard, you found the answer to yours much earlier than that. The football match had nothing to do with it at all.'

'But?'

Small fingers reached out and touched Richard's lips halting further words. The orb grew brighter. 'It was the sacrifice,' she explained. Richard's face went blank. 'The sacrifice you made for your fellow man and relatives when you allowed another to share those most precious of moments, your last ones on Earth. That was when your lesson was learnt Richard.' Richard was dumbstruck.

Roberta gently withdrew her hand. 'Now I think it is time for us to go, but first,' she turned to Geoff, 'I think someone should stop worrying themselves about Joe. Dear sweet Geoff, there is nothing wrong with him that a little exercise won't put right.' Roberta waved her hand and the orb grew brighter still until it became so bright, it simply ceased to exist.

Not on that plane anyway.

CHAPTER 39

The crowd, a little disappointed after almost all had diagnosed the severest of heart attacks, started to disperse from around the fat number seven and went to reform around the dead referee.

Sitting up, fat number seven felt himself all over, all seemed in fairly good order, considering.

Next morning at the breakfast table, having finished his yoghurt and fruit juice breakfast, something that had caused quite a stir with his wife, it coming out of the blue like that after many years of non-effectual nagging about the dangers of too many fat-soaked cooked brekkies, the fat number seven thumbed through the local Sunday newspaper. He was looking for something specific; he found it inside the back page amongst the sports.

Small headline, second column in: a small article on the sudden and strange death of a local football referee. Not that the death was strange, the article would say, more the surrounding events. The fat number seven read on.

*   *   *

MYSTERY AS LOCAL REFEREE DIES IN DYING MOMENTS (OF MATCH)

Mystery surrounded the death of local referee Mr. Richard Ross who died yesterday afternoon in the

*last seconds of the local derby match between Roach
Garage Athletic and Valley Garage Nomads.*

*Paramedics, who scanned Mr. Ross at the scene,
found he had died from a sudden brain haemorrhage
thought to have stemmed from an incident earlier in
the year. No mystery there. But on going to retrieve
Mr. Ross's belongings the paramedics were
surprised and mystified to find laying amongst them
a small menagerie of dead animals.*

*It would seem Mr. Ross for some reason had brought
with him to the match his pet dog, no name on collar,
his goldfish, the cola company should be told about
this one, and, strangest of all, his budgie who he had,
for reasons only known to him, covered in black boot
polish.*

*And to deepen the mystery it seems, and this was
verified by the attending paramedics on scanning the
animals, that they had all dropped dead at exactly
the same time as their owner.*

*The match finished 0-0 after a dramatic last minute
penalty miss.*

*   *   *

The fat number seven smiled to himself as he finished the
article. The world was surely strange, but he was sure he
would enjoy this new life of his. That is, he thought tapping
his ample belly with the newspaper, once he'd joined a gym.

280